# THE
# RANGERS
## OF
# ANDOR

## THE BEGINNING

*Lucy M. Coutinho*

PublishAmerica
Baltimore

Hardcover 978-1-4626-1015-0
Softcover 978-1-4626-1014-3
PUBLISHED BY PUBLISHAMERICA, LLLP
www.publishamerica.com
Baltimore

Printed in the United States of America

I would like to dedicate this book to my loyal fans and friends on Storywrite who's encouragement made this book possible.

# CHAPTER 1

Every young boy dreams of being a squire. It's the first step to becoming a knight in the king's service, and having a life time of adventure, honor, and glory. I was one of those boys once. I spent many hours playing with the other boys, learning to use swords and a bow and arrow. Racing horses to see who the better rider was; jousting against scare crows in the fields, pretending to hunt dragons, and dreaming of the harvest fair.

It is during the harvest fair in late September that squires are chosen. When a boy turns thirteen he gets to participate in the tournaments, and the strongest and most skilled ones are selected from all the youths in the kingdom to live and learn from the knights. I was much smaller than the other boys my age, but I had the skills to make up for it, or so my father told me. In the weeks leading up to the fair I trained harder than ever. My father believed that I really had a good chance of being chosen. I was very skilled at archery, able to get a squirrel at two hundred fifty paces. I was also a skilled horse rider, and could hold my own against any swordsman in the village where we lived. So, while my older brothers were busy in my father's blacksmith shop helping my father build goods to sell at the fair, I pushed myself to the limit, determined to rise above the rest of my friends and be chosen. I desperately wanted to be chosen. I wanted it so badly that I could hardly eat or sleep.

\*\*\*

The night before we left for the fair; my father got a message asking him to come to the Inn. A man who my father did work for every few months or so was back and was requesting his services. I didn't think too much about it when the messenger came. My father often met with people in the Inn who he did long term projects for. But when my father returned home there was a strange look in his eyes, and his face was pale. It might have been my imagination, but it looked to me like he was horribly upset by some news he had been dreading. He saw that my brothers and I were putting the last of the horse shoes in the wagon, and stopped us.

"We won't be attending the fair this year lads. Get these things back to the shop. I have an order to fulfill, we aren't going anywhere."

My brothers and I stopped and stared at him.

"Not going? What are you talking about? How can we not go? What about Peter?" my brother Andrew asked.

"I have to complete this order. It cannot wait. We aren't going." My father turned and put a hand on my shoulder. "I am sorry my son, but this order is too important; there is no way we can get you to the fair this year."

I backed out of his grip, shock and anger fighting for control of my mind. "But Sir Lucas will be looking for a new squire there this year, and he's the king's right hand man. This is my one chance at adventure in my life. Only thirteen year olds can become squires, this is my only chance!" My voice was rising, how could he forget this important fact? How could he do this to me?

"I can take him to the fair. That way Andrew and John will still be here to help you."

I looked at Kevin in gratitude. I knew he wouldn't let me down.

"No Kevin, I need Peter here especially. There will be other fairs, you boys will just have to stay here in the village for this one." my father said in a tone that meant the subject was closed.

At that point I did the most un-knightly thing I had ever done. "You're a horrible man! You're ruining my life!" I screamed, pain and disappointment filling my chest. Before my father could react, I broke into a run and took off down the street, not caring that people were peaking out of doorways and windows watching me. I quickly blended into the shadows, and ran silently. I was very skilled at avoiding people, like the bigger boys in the town who liked to tease me for my small size. Now I used those dodging skills to stop my family from following me. I kept running all the way to the edge of town. Then I sat against the Inn and cried.

I don't know how long I sat there crying, but eventually I noticed that a man was standing in front of me watching silently. I scrambled to my feet and wiped my eyes. I looked at the man, he was like no one I had ever seen before. He was wearing a dark green cloak that covered most of his facial features in shadow and reached all the way down to his boots that were made of soft leather wrapped around his feet in a pattern similar to farmer's boots, and well worn, as if he did a lot of walking. He had a sword and daggers on his belt, almost concealed under his cloak, and a long bow made of a wood I had never seen on his shoulder, the quiver of arrows strapped to his back. He was beardless, but not young. His hair rested at shoulder length, and was unkempt, ragged as if he hadn't paid any attention to it in weeks.

"Why are you crying young one? You seem angry." he said. His voice was kind, and full of unspoken wisdom.

"I'm angry because my father is a selfish pig." I answered back, with much more spite then I had intended. I turned away from the man, the pain of disappointment threatening to make me start crying again.

"What has he done that would make his own son say such things?" the man asked in almost a whisper.

"He said we can't go to the fair. Just because he got some rush order, now we can't go, and now I'll never be able to be a knight."

"Why would you to want to be a knight? Why is that path so tempting to you?"

I stared at him, not sure what to say to that question. Why wouldn't I want to be a knight? What else would I ever want to be?

"The same reason as everyone else I guess." I answered finally.

"Which is?" the man prompted.

I shifted uncomfortably. I felt almost like this man was testing me, but I had no idea why this stranger was so interested in my opinion.

"It is the best job in the country sir."

"Is it indeed? How do you know that? Have you traveled all over the country to find out which job is best?" he asked, his tone amused.

"I...I just know it!" I snapped.

I turned and walked away, heading home. After a few yards I realized that the man was following me. I started to walk faster, and he quickened his own pace to match mine. I broke into a run, and fled home, the man easily keeping pace behind me the whole way despite the fact that I was the fastest person my age in the town. I burst into the house and slammed the door behind me, breathing heavily. It was a few seconds before I noticed the man sitting at the table with my father and brothers. For one wild moment I thought that the stranger had somehow gotten into the house ahead of me. But then I saw that even though the man sitting at the head of the table was dressed the same, he was a different man. He had grey hair and wrinkled skin for one, and piercing grey eyes that seemed like they could see into the very core of my soul.

I could tell this because his hood was off, and he was sitting quite at ease, his sheathed sword resting on his lap. I stood staring at him. What on earth was going on? Who were these people?

"Peter, this is Lord Haldor. He...wants to talk to you." my father said, glancing at the man who seemed to intimidate my father. My father, who was able to stand and look the head of the town guards in the eye, was intimidated by this Lord, whoever he was. I couldn't blame him, as Lord Haldor continued to watch me with those piercing grey eyes I found myself trying hard not to squirm uncomfortably. I hated it when people stared at me.

Someone knocked on the door behind me. Three sharp knocks.

"Enter!" Lord Haldor commanded, not taking his unblinking eyes off me.

The door opened and the stranger from the Inn entered calmly. He moved me out of his way, and went straight to Lord Haldor, dropping to one knee and bowing his head. Lord Haldor took the dark haired man's head in his hands and murmured something to him. The man nodded and stood up, positioning himself one step behind Lord Haldor's chair.

"This is my right hand archer, my second in command. You may call him Joseph." Lord Haldor said gesturing to the man behind him.

The man bowed his head slightly to me in greeting. But he kept his hood up, covering most of his face.

"What do you people want with me?" I asked, still a bit testy.

"Peter! Behave yourself!" my father scolded.

Lord Haldor raised a hand, and my father fell silent.

"It is a fair question. He has the right to know why we are here, why he is unable to join his friends trying to become a squire. We are here Peter, because you have been selected from all the youths in the kingdom, to become a ranger."

There was silence in the room except for the crackling of the fire.

"A what?" I asked.

"A ranger, a guardian of the kingdom, set apart from the rest of the army. We are a secret force that protects the people from those things that work in secret to destroy them. We spend most of our time wandering in the wild, or so people think. You will soon learn otherwise." Lord Haldor explained.

"Well what if I don't want to be a ranger? What if I just want to be a knight?" I asked stubbornly.

"I did not want to have to use this, but I will since you insist." Lord Haldor said, reaching into his cloak. He pulled out a scroll tied shut with a purple ribbon. He unrolled it, and read out loud.

"By order of King Stephen II; Peter, son of the blacksmith Richard, will henceforth be under the care and leadership of the Guild of Rangers. He will be trained and will live as one of them. This is done for the good of all Andor, and permission is hereby given to use force to collect the new apprentice if needed."

Lord Haldor finished reading and regarded me with a slight frown. "This is not a choice. It is your destiny to be a ranger, as it is my destiny to come here to collect you. You cannot turn away from this path, it is a life that you were born to live." Lord Haldor rose to his feet slowly and with great effort. Joseph made a move as if he longed to help the old man, but he stayed where he was.

"I will come by to retrieve you in the morning. You may bring only one personal treasure to remind you of childhood, so choose wisely. We travel lightly and swiftly. Be ready to leave at the third hour past dawn. We have a long journey ahead of us, a chance for Peter son of Richard to show his stamina. Good night."

With that, Lord Haldor and Joseph left the house, leaving me and my family to stare after them as they retreated back down the road towards the Inn, soon vanishing into the growing darkness.

*** 

I need hardly say no one in my house went right to bed that night. My brothers and I stayed up for hours begging my father for whatever information he knew about Rangers. I was irritated when he couldn't give much. All he knew about them was that they were dangerous people who wandered in the wild. In the rare times that they would stop in the Inn for the night they told amazing stories about dark evils, stories my father had said he always laughed off as tall tales that one might hear from a bard. Laughed off until tonight that is. When Andrew asked him what the stories were about, my father couldn't remember too clearly. He just knew that they were full of strange creatures of darkness and usually took place in the great forests of the south or the mountains of the west.

It didn't occur to me until many days later that my father was probably being purposely vague about the stories because he didn't want to worry us, but at the time, it just annoyed me that my father had forgotten these important stories, dismissing them as tales told to frighten children. He did send me to bed soon after the moon had set, saying that I would need rest for my journey. I went into the bedroom that we all shared, and lay down on the bed my father and I used. I wondered to myself when and if I'd ever be home again.

When I woke up and entered the main room, my brothers Andrew and John were still sitting at the table. Andrew was nodding off, and John was asleep with his head resting on his arms, his beard twitching as he snored softly. When Andrew saw that I was awake he became more alert, and rose to greet me.

"Father and Kevin are packing a bag for you. The rangers left specific instructions on what clothes and food you'd need. They gave father money to pay to have your clothes died black for you. They'll be back any minute. Here, let me get you something to eat. Those ranger folk, they don't look like they eat very much. After all, if you're wandering in the woods, you don't have a kitchen full of food, do you?" Andrew said, rushing over to the counter where food was piled up, ready to go to the fair.

I sat down and watched Andrew bustle around. Even though he was three years older than me, he always seemed like he was my age. Always ready and eager to play with me and my friends, ignoring his blacksmith duties to day dream about adventures and excitement. He would have been a good squire, but he had fallen deathly ill that year, and so had missed his chance.

John grunted in his sleep, and turned his head to the other side. John had never wanted to be a squire. His mind was filled with "more practical things", as he called it. John was seventeen, and was perfectly content to work long hours with my father, wielding metal, building tools. His mind was always in the present, always on his work. Kevin always joked that John was just trying to impress the girls, but I wasn't so sure.

Kevin. Kevin had been the only one of our family to compete in the tournaments. He had actually managed to be chosen by one of the knights who had his own castle. But then, a year after he became a squire; our mother gave birth to me and died doing so. Kevin had given up his dream, and returned home to raise my brothers and me. I had grown up feeling guilty that it was my fault Kevin had given up his future. But Kevin had always insisted that his future was here with his family. He was Captain of the soldiers of our town now, and seemed content. The only reason he still lived at home, or so he claimed, was that the barracks were dull. But we all knew that he was here to watch over us, often taking me to work with him, and leaving me with his boss when he was out and about on official business.

Andrew handed me a plate with two thick pieces of bread and fresh butter, several slices of salted meat, and three apples. I laughed when I saw the plate. "How can I eat all this? That's as much food as I eat in a day, never mind a sitting." I said, quoting from an inside joke between my siblings and me that we use to say when we knew times were rough, and food hard to come by. But my heart just wasn't really into the old joke. Somehow I found myself missing the winters we were hungry, and would split the little food we had, pretending to be satisfied even though our stomachs rarely felt full in the winter. I had a feeling that as a ranger, I'd probably not have to worry about having enough food ever again.

Andrew sat down with his own food. I wasn't at all hungry, but just to be polite I ate the bread and butter. I had just finished when my father and Kevin entered the room with a travel bag. Kevin came over to me and put his arm around my shoulder as my father started to talk.

"You have here two days worth of clothes, one day of which you'll wear when you leave today. The shirts are both black, as well as the pants. That is what they said to give you. Also there are several apples, some carrots, and one loaf of bread. I baked it fresh for you this morning. The rangers said they have enough meat to share. You also have two full water skins, and a small bottle of berry jam, which they didn't say to give you, but I know how much you love it. Come here; let's make sure it isn't too heavy for you."

I got up numbly and went over to my father. I didn't recognize the bag, it was dark green and compact, barely six inches wide, and made of a strange fabric. It seemed to be able to store an unnatural amount of contents given its small size. The water skins were strapped to the side of the bag within easy reach. I changed into the black clothes and my father put the bag on my shoulders and turned me around so I was facing him. There were tears in his eyes, and a catch in his throat.

"Your mother would be so proud if she could see you now. She'd be proud of all my boys, her boys. Her grown up sons."

My father pulled me in close and gave me a strong hug that knocked the wind out of me.

As he was hugging me, there were three sharp knocks on the door. John's head jerked up as Kevin went to answer the door. Lord Haldor was there, and behind him were two other rangers whose cloaks were up over their faces even though the day was warm and sunny. I guessed that one of them was Joseph, but I wasn't sure who the other one was.

"It is time to leave Peter. Say good bye now." Lord Haldor said in a gentle tone.

My brothers came up to me one at a time and gave me a hug. Even John hugged me, and he was a man who hated to show emotion. When Andrew was finished hugging me, my father dropped to one knee so he wasn't looking down to me. "Here, this is for you. I was saving it for when you moved away from home, so you should take it now."

My father handed me something wrapped in brown cloth. I unwrapped it to find two daggers in sheaths. They were well made, easily the best daggers I had ever seen, with silver handles. Light to

13

hold, perfectly balanced, very sharp. My name was carved into the blade, right at the handles. The handle was designed for an adult's hand, but I knew I could adjust. I hugged my father around the neck, and felt a lump in my throat. It had occurred to me stronger than ever that I may never see my family again, or at least, not for a very, very long time.

I stood there, not wanting to let go of my father, not wanting to leave. Not like this, not with these strange hooded men from far away who had some mysterious reason to claim me. Eventually, my father pried my arms open and turned me around, so my back was to my home, and I was facing the strange rangers. "Be brave my son. Our love will always be with you." my father whispered in my ears, pushing me forward.

Joseph stepped towards me and held out his hand for me to take. I swallowed hard, and gave him my hand, letting him lead me away from my home, my family, my former life. As we walked down the hill through town I turned my head to look back one last time. But the ranger who I had not been introduced to was blocking the view of my father's house. Instead, I turned and took one last look at the small river village I had grown up in. I was determined to remember every detail, every straw roof, every stone of every building, every leaf on every tree, every barrel full of crops outside the store house. The smells from the baker, the meats on display at the butcher's shop, the faint odor of herbs and roots from the doctor's house. The horses in the stables, the cows and sheep in the fields.

I wondered as I was lead away if I'd ever be back. I wondered what lay ahead, what dangers and adventures I'd have. "Sirs?" I asked timidly.

"What is it?" Lord Haldor asked, not breaking his stride. "Will I ever see them again, my family?" I asked, my voice sounding small, even to my own ears.

Lord Haldor sighed wearily. "Not even the wisest can tell what the future holds my boy. For your sake I hope that you will see them again. But don't dwell on the past, for no one knows what the future may bring. It is best if you commit them into memory and move on. You have a long life ahead of you, and many things to accomplish. Live for the present, leave the past behind you."

# CHAPTER 2

We left town by going over the north bridge. When the town soldiers saw the rangers they bowed and moved aside without asking for any kind of identification. I saw them glance at me and quickly look away, as if they did not dare be caught staring. A wild part of me wanted to call out to the soldiers for help, beg them to not let the rangers take me, but of course I held my tongue. If my father was proud that I was a ranger then I'd be a ranger. I'd make sure he had reasons to be proud of me. Resisting leaving town was not something worthy of pride. So I crossed the bridge, Joseph still holding my hand, and didn't comment when lord Haldor ignored the fork in the road that branched off, heading to the towns of Woodcloak, and Narrowmouth. Instead the rangers kept going, right into the fields, walking directly north.

We walked for hours and hours. My feet felt like lead, my second hand shoes that were stuffed with cloth in the toes so they'd fit me were starting to blister my feet. The rangers were setting a fast pace, and I was trying as hard as I could to keep up with them. At one point Joseph saw I was having trouble and offered me help. But I turned him down. If they wanted to test me, I was not going to let them see me as weak. I could pass their stupid test, and I would do so no matter what it took.

Their legs were much longer than mine, and I wondered if they ever got tired. Surely they stopped to rest once in a while, right? But

16

they kept going, hour after hour. The sun passed mid day, and started to sink into the west, and still we walked. As we walked, Lord Haldor spoke softly, telling me about various things that we passed, and what they meant, down to the slightest blade of grass being bent out of shape from the passage of a field mouse, to the obvious trail left behind by a Sheppard driving his sheep through the fields. I ate three apples as we walked, to keep my strength up. We were going so fast that I couldn't eat much more than that. The full grown men with me didn't stop walking to eat either, eating and drinking as they traveled. They just didn't seem to want to stop walking.

Finally, when I was wondering to myself if I could go much further without my legs giving out, we stopped. Joseph let go of my hand at last, and sat down on a boulder, stretching his legs out, and raising his arms up to relieve their stiffness. Lord Haldor sat down slowly on a fallen log, and closed his eyes. The ranger who hadn't yet spoken now put his hand on my shoulder and murmured in my ear.

"Go and collect as much fallen wood and dry grass as you can carry. We shall rest here for the night."

I left the men and did what I was told. I didn't mention that I was exhausted. I told myself that life as a squire would be no different. It was always the job of the apprentice to get the busy work chores. It was a way of building stamina that we'd need later in life. I came back with my arms as full as they'd get, and was sent out for more, and then for yet another arm full. Finally, I was invited to join the men around the fire. Joseph had me take off my shoes, and he wrapped my feet in a bandage soaked in some potion that he said should help the throbbing blisters heal as well as keep my feet protected until they could get me better shoes to wear. I sat there eating some bread and jam, and staring at the rangers. In the light of the fire they looked more mysterious and frightening than ever. They didn't speak much, except to pass each other food and water skins. I was given some salted meat from Joseph, and offered to share my jam and bread. They accepted graciously.

"I have not had jam and bread since before the battle of Hulim.

That was a good seven months ago." Lord Haldor told me.

I was curious. Hulim was the name of the southernmost mountain in the Western mountain range. That much I knew from my studies of maps. I hadn't heard of any troubles out there, certainly no battles.

"What happened? I didn't know there was trouble out in the western mountains." I commented as Lord Haldor took a big bite of bread and jam.

"There is always trouble in the west, especially the mountains. There are many dark creatures living in this world of ours." Joseph answered.

"You mean the orcs and dragons?" I asked, hoping to appear well informed.

"There are much darker creatures then Orcs living in the shadows little one. There is evil in this world that seeks to take control. Evil that wishes to wipe the human race off the face of the planet. There are creatures that hate all things that are good, from the smallest flower bud to the noblest kings. There are creatures so dark that any lesser men would never be able to close their eyes again for fear of the creatures that linger in the shadows. They would scratch your eyes out, rip out your throat if they could get close enough. Yes, there is always trouble." Lord Haldor said in a chilling voice.

There was silence for a while after that. The rangers ate calmly. They seemed not to be affected by what their leader had said, as if it was common knowledge. I sat there with a half eaten piece of meat in my hands, watching them wordlessly. Lord Haldor looked up and noticed that I had stopped eating. He looked at me kindly.

"You need not be afraid of the dark lad. That is why we came to get you, to train you to be able to protect the world from darkness. You are safer in our company then you ever were in your father's arms, and that was a safe place indeed. There is no reason for you to worry. We would never force you to face something you are not able to handle. No ranger has ever been lost in the forest, nor have we ever lost anyone under our care in the wild. Not since the beginning of the guild seven hundred years ago."

I felt a bit better after hearing that. But all the same, I made sure to sleep close to the others, and stay in the fire light. The two hooded rangers flipped a coin to see who would take the first watch, and Lord Haldor and I settled down to sleep.

I dreamed of mountains. I had never seen anything more than a painting of a mountain, but I found myself on the peak of one. I looked east, and saw the whole country spread out before me. The green fields, the rolling hills, the forests, and rivers. I turned and looked in the other direction. The mountain range spread west for many miles. I looked north and saw the sea. It was blue and clear, and stretched on farther than the eye could possibly see. I looked south east next, towards the great forests. There were many tales about the forests; I'd grown up listening to them. Tales about elves and centaurs. The humans lived in peace with the elves. They usually left each other alone. But the centaurs did not like humans. They found us foolish and ignorant of the ways of the world.

Joseph shook me awake. I opened my eyes to see that it was pre dawn. The sky was a deep shade of dark blue, but there was just enough light to see by. When Joseph saw that I was awake he went and knelt by Lord Haldor.

"My lord, the day has begun." he said, putting his hand gently on Lord Haldor's shoulder.

Lord Haldor opened one eye, and looked around. Then he rubbed his eyes with his hand, and sat up, holding onto Joseph's cloak for support. As I watched Joseph help Lord Haldor up I wondered how old Haldor was. He seemed to be older than even the old widow from our town, and she had seen almost a hundred winters. "Where is Thelmer?" Lord Haldor asked, looking around our camp sight.

"He is filling the water skins in the stream." Joseph said, pointing east into the woods where I had found the fire wood last night.

"Go and retrieve him. We must start off early if we are to make it to Quicklake before they close the shops." Lord Haldor told Joseph.

Joseph bowed, and hurried off.

Lord Haldor went over to the packs and began to examine our remaining food supplies. He took out a pear and some meat and handed them to me. "Eat little one. We have another long day of walking ahead. With luck we will make it to Quicklake before they close the gates and you will be able to sleep in a bed tonight. Goodness knows you won't have many chances to do that in our travels west."

Joseph and Thelmer returned as Lord Haldor and I finished eating, and we set off at once. Apparently Joseph and Thelmer had been awake for a while, because they had already eaten, and were alert. That day's journey was much like the one yesterday, with the rangers setting a swift pace, and me doing all I could to keep up. Joseph didn't hold my hand today, he walked along next to Lord Haldor, leaving Thelmer to look after me. As we went on, no one spoke. With the dark cloaks and me wearing black, we passed through the woods silently and swiftly. I found myself copying their trick of gliding from one shadow to another, making it even harder for us to be noticed by anyone.

As the sun was passing mid day, Joseph suddenly shot an arrow through the trees to our side. The group stopped, and I looked from man to man confused. The rangers stood still as statues, looking into the woods. Apparently I had missed something, because they were all on high alert, waiting. When nothing happened; Joseph strode forwards, another arrow in his hand, but not fitted to the bow. He came back after a minute, and gestured that it was ok to follow. A few hundred paces into the woods lay a dead bear. Joseph's arrow had pierced it in the head. "Here is the answer to the mystery. This is who has been following us the last mile. There is something you should know Peter; if you are being tracked, give the tracker one mile to announce themselves. If they don't speak by then, than they are a foe." Lord Haldor said, nudging the bear with his boot. I felt surprised and embarrassed. How could I have not noticed that we were being tracked for the last ten minutes?

20

"Shall we leave it, or collect more meat for our packs?" Thelmer asked.

"No, we have enough meat between us to last almost a month. Leave him for the scavengers of the forest. They need food far more than we do right now." Lord Haldor replied.

With that we turned and left the dead bear where he lay.

After we started off again I mentally scolded myself. I felt embarrassed that I had been completely oblivious of the bear. So I spent the rest of the day listening hard at the noises of the wild, and looking all around me. We reached Quicklake just before sunset. The town was surrounded by a wooden wall with a heavy door. The guards at the door moved aside with a bow as we entered, looking away quickly when they saw that I had caught them staring. "Why does everyone bow?" I whispered to Thelmer.

"They bow to show respect to Lord Haldor. He is a great man, and a good friend of the royal family. He is the head of our guild, and any soldier or knight who doesn't bow to him is in danger of reprimand. No one has ever been punished for not recognizing him that I know of, but you can lose your rank if you fail to show proper respect to a Lord." Thelmer replied softly.

"Why does everyone stare?" I asked as I noticed everyone in the streets were glancing over at us more than at anything else. Thelmer just laughed softly in reply to that.

Lord Haldor led us to a cloth shop. There was a girl there at a stool spinning thread when we entered. She jumped to her feet when she saw us.

"Mother! They are back with the boy." she called to the back room.

A woman came hurrying into the shop room, her arms full of the green material that the ranger's cloaks and my bag were made of.

"I have your order ready to go. I just need to measure the boy to get the lengths right."

Lord Haldor put a hand on my shoulder and steered me forward.

The woman put a dark green cloak around my shoulders and began to pin it to the right lengths.

"How soon can this be ready?" Lord Haldor asked as the woman pulled another pin from her pin cloth.

"How soon do you need it?" she asked, looking up from where she was crouching.

"As early tomorrow morning as possible." Lord Haldor answered.

"I can have it ready by mid morning at the latest." she offered.

"I can pay whatever you need if you can have it ready at dawn." Lord Haldor said, withdrawing a money sack from inside his cloak.

"I'll do my best my Lord. But with the fair in less than a week away I am very busy." she explained apologetically.

"I will pay you five extra pieces of silver if it is ready at dawn."

I glanced back at Lord Haldor. The cloak couldn't possibly be worth much more than five pieces of silver in the first place?

"My lord, you supplied the cloth, the cloak is only seven pieces of silver, and that was what you insisted I charge, just for shaping a simple child's cloak for you! An additional five,"

"Seven extra it is then. Have it ready at dawn. I or one of my men will come to get it."

We left the woman and her daughter watching after us speechlessly.

Our next stop was the shoe maker. He unwrapped the bandages from my feet muttering that it had been a good idea once he had examined my shoes, and went into the back room. He came back with some materials, and made me a pair of boots that were the same style as the ranger's ones as I sat there on a stool. That way he could make sure they were perfectly made. They were soft and light, and designed for hard walking. My old shoes were destroyed after two days at rapid pace, and they were given to the shoe maker to do whatever he wanted with them. For the first time in my life to that point, I had footwear that fit me perfectly.

At the inn that night, the rangers seemed to be truly at ease for the first time that I had seen. Lord Haldor and Joseph both ordered a mug of ale, and talked and laughed with the other men at the bar. Thelmer sat in the shadows near the fire, sipping his tea, his quick eyes darting constantly all around the room. I was left alone at the table with my food. I ate it and watched everyone. I had never actually been inside an Inn before, my father had never allowed me to. He said since our town had become so poor, the inn was no place for a child. But this Inn seemed lively and safe, all the men concerned with their food and drink and with staring at the cloaked rangers at the bar, completely ignoring me.

After an hour or so, Thelmer came and joined me. "How are you holding up? I remember my first few weeks away from home I was incredibly home sick." he asked, handing me a piece of cinnamon cake.

"Thank you. I'm ok I guess. I mean, I was planning to try to be a squire, so I knew I'd be leaving home soon anyways. I just didn't count on it happening this way." I said glancing at Lord Haldor.

Thelmer smiled slightly, as if understanding what I was too embarrassed to say out loud, that Lord Haldor was a very scary man.

"My mother would never have let me go to the fair. She feared that I'd get bad ideas in my head, and run off to be a knight like my father. He fell in battle when I was seven."

"I lost a parent too. My mom died when I was born. I don't remember her at all."

"I remember my father, sort of. He taught me everything I needed to know to be a knight like him. But when he died my mother didn't want to lose me the same way. She ordered me to never practice the skills my father taught me again, and she had me learning from the town doctor. She figured that way I'd be safe." Thelmer paused and seemed lost in memory.

"She was a wreck when I left. She cried all night as I was packing to leave."

"Have you been able to visit her?" I asked.

Thelmer seemed to notice me again, and shook his head. "She died. A year after I was claimed for the rangers, she was killed by illness. She was always ill, always frail. I often wish..." Thelmer broke off, and drained his cup of tea in one gulp.

"Good night." he said, rising from the table.

When I got to the room that the four of us were sharing; Thelmer stood looking out the window, his hands clasped behind his back. I tried to talk to him, but he pretended not to hear me. I got into the bed I had been given for my very own for the night, and lay watching him. He remained as still as a statue, looking out at the stars. When I fell asleep at last he still hadn't moved.

The next morning I was woken up in the light of pre-dawn again. Thelmer seemed to have resorted back to his quiet self, and just nodded slightly in greeting. The bar room was empty except for the rangers and me. The bar maid served us hot mash and tea for breakfast, trying hard not to stare at us.

Lord Haldor sent Thelmer out to fetch the cloak and other things he had ordered from the shops. Joseph took me out to the back of the Inn and started to test my archery skills. There was a target back there, and Joseph had me try my hand at it, using the bow that was beside the target. I was able to hit the bulls eye on the first try. But that wasn't enough to satisfy Joseph. He wanted me to hit the exact center, and even measured it to see how far off I was. Finally, after I hit the exact center three times in a row he told me that my skills were "adequate". I decided to take that as praise, considering how picky he apparently was.

When we went back inside the Inn, Thelmer had returned.

"The cloth weaver refused to take the extra seven silver so I left them in her money box when her back was turned to greet another customer." he was saying to Lord Haldor.

"That is good. She deserves the money for all the work her son does for our people. But she is not the type to take more then she feels she has worked for." Lord Haldor said, nodding for me to come forward.

Lord Haldor put the cloak on me, and pulled the hood up over my head. I felt a sudden tingling and excitement go through my body, and I shivered. Lord Haldor looked down at me satisfied. "Now he looks more like a ranger. But there are still some things missing. Daggers are nice, but in combat you achieve much more with a sword." he said, handing me a child sized sword in a sheath. I took it wide eyed. My first sword. No squire is ever given a sword at my age, yet here I was with one of my own. "Also, here is a bow for hunting and range fighting." Lord Haldor said, handing me a short bow and quiver full of short arrows, just the right size for me. "Now you look like a proper ranger, a man instead of a boy. Your weapons are your tools. Be responsible for them, as a ranger, they *will* save your life one day." Lord Haldor said as Joseph showed me how to strap everything properly.

# CHAPTER 3

We left town heading west. As before, the rangers ignored the road, and instead cut across country. We traveled swiftly, and as we went, Lord Haldor revealed to me one of the secrets of a ranger's success. Putting the cloak on had caused magic to enter me, that is what had made me shiver. The magic would help me be able to pay attention to everything all at once, which would help me do my job better. Now that I had received the magic, I needed to train myself how to use it to the best of my body's abilities.

I felt important somehow. With my face hidden in the shadow from my cloak's hood, I felt like someone important. I was much smaller than the men I traveled with, but I felt like I was somehow more equal to them now that I had magic. I wondered if this was how squires felt as they rode behind the knights, carrying the luggage. I wondered if they felt such a sense of purpose. As if their life suddenly had an important meaning, as if all of a sudden they had huge amounts of power. I smiled to myself slightly when it occurred to me that they probably didn't feel anything like I did. I wondered suddenly why I had never asked Kevin. He was the only person I know who had ever been a real squire, but all I had ever asked him about was the adventures, the chances for glory. Right now glory meant nothing to me. Just to be standing in the presence of these powerful mysterious men seemed to me to be the greatest honor in the world.

The next few days of travel seemed very much alike. But I did notice some changes in myself as we walked. Although the pace was as swift as ever, I was finding it easier to keep up. The pace seemed quite leisurely to me by the third day out from Quicklake. I was able to walk fourteen hours a day without even feeling the need to rest. In fact, I was too excited to stay still when we did rest for the night. The magic surging through me made me want to do things, but I had no idea what I wanted to do. I felt more energetic then I had ever felt in my life.

On the third day out, about four hours past mid day, we reached the great river. "Here our ways shall part for a time." Lord Haldor said to Joseph and Thelmer. "You two will go to the fair, and find for us the best and brightest of the youths. Do NOT fail me, we need to have enough young ones to replace the elderly. You have let me down the past five years, be sure you don't do so again." Lord Haldor said with a slight edge to his voice. I looked up curiously, in time to see Joseph swallow nervously as he nodded his understanding.

Lord Haldor and I watched Joseph and Thelmer head swiftly south towards the capital city, where the fair was taking place. As we stood watching them, a different hooded ranger appeared from behind a rock. He was leading two horses by the reigns. Other then the reigns, the horses were without saddles. I figured that was just how rangers rode. "Peter, this is Sigal. He has brought us steeds so that we can get back to the mountains faster and with less wear on my old feet." Lord Haldor said putting a hand on my shoulder.

Sigal dropped to one knee before Lord Haldor and bowed his head. Lord Haldor told him to rise, and took the reins of the black horse, leaving Sigal holding the chestnut one. Lord Haldor mounted the black horse with more grace then I had expected from the old man who needed help standing in the morning. While I was still thinking about it, Sigal lifted me onto his horse, and mounted behind me.

"Have you ever ridden a horse before Peter?" Sigal asked me as we set off north towards the road and the bridge crossing, the horses going at a brisk trot.

"I've ridden my father's cart horse before, many times. My brother

Kevin taught me how, but I've never ridden without a saddle." I answered.

"After we've crossed the bridge and are away from prying eyes, you will see why we don't use saddles." Sigal told me cheerfully.

After we were a good four miles past the bridge crossing, Lord Haldor did something unexpected. He spurred his horse onwards with his feet, yet pulled the reigns back at the same time. Sigal did the same, and both horses broke into an unnaturally fast gallop. While I was still trying to get over the speed of the horses, suddenly Lord Haldor's horse opened up wings that had been invisible moments before.

I found myself flying through the air, high above the trees, on the back of a winged horse. It was a breathtaking experience to me who had never been higher up then the thirty foot bell tower of the town guard's barracks. The feeling was amazing. The wind felt clear and cool as it blew in my face, ruffling my hood, almost taking it off me. I felt like I weighed nothing at all, like I could have flown on my own if I had wanted to. I looked down, and spread out below me was the whole kingdom of Andor. We were flying swiftly west towards the mountains. They were too far away to see yet, but I knew we were headed for them.

As the sun was setting in the west we reached the border of the forest of Brewn. The winged horses (which I learned later were called Pegasi) started to circle, getting lower and lower each turn, until they were galloping once more on the solid ground. When they came to a stop and I was helped down, it took me a while to regain steady footing. The pegasi walked over to the stream that we had stopped next to, and drank deeply. Lord Haldor stroked the neck of the black one and looked into the forest, frowning deeply. Sigal went and stood next to him. "What is it?" he whispered. I edged my way over to them, listening to the silence of the woods.

"Where is Lance? He is supposed to be guarding this area, I told him to be here to meet me." Lord Haldor murmured.

I looked at the trees nervously. Was there a ranger missing? Lord Haldor said that they had never lost a member in the forest before...

"He was here last night when I left him my lord. He said he'd be waiting for us."

"Aww, are the wangers having twoubles?"

We turned to see a strange man like creature leaning against a tree mocking us with a baby voice. His skin was red, he was only two feet tall, had black eyes, and no hair. Instead, two small horns were on either side of his head.

"Where is he, vile servant of devils? Don't play games with me." Lord Haldor growled, advancing menacingly.

"Oh, I'm so scared. The old ranger is mad at me." the creature said with a mocking laugh that quickly turned into a choked cough when Lord Haldor grabbed the creature by the neck and slammed him against the tree. Lord Haldor held the creature suspended with one hand, and drew his sword with the other.

"Tell me where he is, or I'll cut your little head right off your shoulders." Lord Haldor warned.

"He's been taken for questioning." the creature gasped, his voice hoarse from Lord Haldor's grip on his throat.

Lord Haldor let go of the creature, who dropped back to the ground, rubbing his neck. "You'd better return him in one piece or we'll take such revenge on you that you won't ever laugh again."

"Yeah sure, shoot the messenger. Shesh, no wonder your families are glad to be rid of you." The creature said, taking a quick glance at me as if curious to see how I'd react to what he had said.

Lord Haldor leapt towards the creature, but it scurried away with a lot more speed than the old man could muster, its pointy tail wagging happily behind it.

"What was that?" I asked, as Lord Haldor put away his sword while muttering curses under his breath.

"An imp. One of the more harmless evil creatures when they are alone, but in hoards, which is how they do raids, they are not creatures you want attacking you." Sigal replied calmly.

"Well, shouldn't we go after them? What if they torture this guy Lance?" I asked.

Lord Haldor shook his head grimly. "It is a brave gesture on your part son, but impractical. The imps aren't a big worry to us in general. As Sigal said, they are rather harmless when they are alone. Their only interest is to cause disturbances in our routines. That is what they do for fun, disrupt us, force us to remember that they are around and that they have the ability to cause trouble if they so chose.

"So then they won't hurt him?" I asked.

"Oh they'll try. He'll likely be sent back exhausted and hungry, and probably annoyed to the moon if I know Lance. But no, they can't cause any real harm." Lord Haldor said with a weary laugh.

# CHAPTER 4

"Now that we are in the forest, we can begin your training." Lord Haldor informed me after we had eaten dinner.

"What kinds of things will I be trained in my lord?" I asked, feeling both excited and nervous.

"All kinds of things. Do you see that tree? Climb it and bring me a leaf from the top branch." Lord Haldor commanded, pointing to a tree on the border of the campfire light.

I walked over to the tree uncertainly. There was no branches low enough for me to reach to help me climb. I looked up to see that the closest branch was a good five feet above my head. I considered jumping, but dismissed the idea, knowing that I couldn't possibly jump that high, and didn't want to look foolish. I glanced back to see Lord Haldor and Sigal watching me calmly. Lord Haldor gestured for me to get a move on. I turned back to the tree uncertainly. How was I supposed to climb it then? 'Think like a ranger' I told myself. I examined the bark and saw that I might be able to use it to pull myself up by my hands. I got a firm grip on the bark and tugged at it to see if it could hold weight. To my dismay it peeled right off the tree when I pulled it. That was when I noticed that the wood was rotten and soft. I looked up at the tree and realized that it was long dead, and had no leaves whatsoever. I closed my eyes in humiliation. How could I have not noticed that the tree was dead?

"Is there a problem?" Lord Haldor asked me.

I opened my eyes and turned to face him, standing at attention. "Sir, this tree is dead, and has no leaves."

"Then why were you attempting to climb the tree to get a leaf if there are none?" Lord Haldor asked gravely, piercing me with those scary eyes of his.

"You..." I stopped. I had failed what had obviously been a test. To blame someone else for my failure would be wrong.

"Yes?" Lord Haldor prompted, raising an eyebrow slightly.

"My lord, I did not notice that the tree was dead. I'm sorry, I should have been paying more attention." I stated, feeling my face burn.

"Yes, you should have. If you don't use the powers that come with the magic, you'll lose them." Lord Haldor agreed, his eyes becoming stern, even cold.

I lowered my eyes to the ground, feeling like a scolded child.

"Lesson number one, a ranger must ALWAYS pay attention to everything around him. Failure to do so will cost you your life. Do not forget that, ever." Lord Haldor told me sternly.

"Yes my lord...I mean no sir, I won't forget it." I stammered.

"Then repeat it to me." Lord Haldor commanded.

I took a deep breath, desperate to remember his words perfectly. "My lord, a ranger must ALWAYS pay attention to everything around him." I recited.

"Why?" Lord Haldor prompted.

"Failure to do so will cost you your life." I replied, relieved that I had remembered the exact wording.

"Say it again in full." Lord Haldor commanded.

"A ranger must ALWAYS pay attention to everything around him. Failure to do so will cost you your life."

"Again." Lord Haldor commanded.

After I had recited lesson one a dozen or so times Lord Haldor moved on to the next test he had for me.

"Pull your hood down over your face so you cannot see." he told me, rising to his feet, and motioning for Sigal to do the same.

I did as I was told, feeling nervous. I couldn't see anything at all. The cloth was apparently thicker then I had realized. I felt hands on my shoulders, and I was turned around and around until I was completely disoriented, and dizzy.

"Follow me, and me alone." Lord Haldor commanded.

"How?" I asked desperately.

"Listen to my movements. Be aware of all else that moves, but focus on me, and my distinct pattern of movement." Lord Haldor said, his voice getting softer and softer.

I followed the sound of where his voice had come from. I could hear the faintest sound of him moving through the trees, and followed, my hands outstretched so I wouldn't bump into anything. After several minutes of following him as he made a wide circle of the camp area I stopped uncertainly. The pattern of movement had changed, and the noises were going in opposite directions. I hesitated, unsure which movement to follow. I listened hard, and followed the pattern that seemed to me to be most like the one I had been following before. The other movement was slightly quicker, not as steady as the one I'd been following the past few minutes. A few minutes after that, a third sound of movement had joined the group, appearing out of nowhere, then a fourth, soon after. It was getting harder and harder to distinguish Lord Haldor's movements from the group, but I did my best.

Finally I was told to stop, and was given permission to pull my hood back more. I looked around and found that I had been right about other people joining the group. Two other rangers had shown up, one with his hood on, another with his hood off. I looked at the newcomers curiously.

"Did you hear them approach Peter?" Lord Haldor asked me.

"No my lord, I didn't." I admitted, bracing myself for another scolding.

"That is good. If you had heard them, then we'd have a major problem on our hands."

I looked up at Lord Haldor questioningly.

"We train you to be able to move with complete silence. Only the elves can hear a ranger who is trying to not be heard, and that is because their ears are so good that they can hear your heart beat. So if you had been able to hear them approach then the many years spent training these two would have been wasted." Lord Haldor explained gently. "You did remarkably well for your first try. Well enough to make up for your lack of attention earlier." Lord Haldor added.

I blushed, still embarrassed at my failure.

"He will make a good night guard." The new ranger with his hood off commented. "We need someone who can distinguish friend from foe in the dark."

"Nay, not him! It is far too early to tell what he'd be good at. There are so many things he might have skill in." Lord Haldor said, shaking his head slightly as he regarded me thoughtfully.

"This is Lord Earl. He is the head of the eastern posts." Lord Haldor commented, waving at the man he had been speaking to.

Lord Earl smiled kindly at me. "It is a long time since a young one has passed such a test flawlessly on their first try little one. You should be pleased with your raw skills. You have taken to the magic far better than most children can at your age."

"Not too pleased. Let's not inflate his head. This is Earl's son, Lyle." Lord Haldor said, introducing the cloaked ranger.

"I didn't know rangers could marry." I said, surprised out of formality. Realizing how dumb I sounded, I blushed again.

"It is rare, but not unheard of. There are a fair number of women in our ranks. Often times it is easier to find girls that the knights are willing to let us take then to find boys." Lyle informed me, looking at me curiously.

"Yes, well if we don't get more young lads we'll quickly go extinct. There aren't nearly enough young to replace the old. Not nearly enough." Lord Haldor snapped somewhat sharply.

The two hooded rangers flipped a coin to see who'd get the first watch, and Lord Haldor and Earl settled down to sleep.

"Stay up with me? It's not often I get someone new to talk to." Lyle requested softly. I nodded and joined him sitting by the fire as Sigal sat against a tree to sleep for a few hours.

"Come, tell me the story of your life, as far as it has gotten." Lyle requested.

Making sure to pay close attention to my surroundings I told Lyle about my life, growing up as a poor blacksmith's son with dreams of adventure and battle. I told Lyle about my brothers, especially Kevin, whom I had spent the most time with. I ended with the story about the night the rangers came to get me.

"You're lucky; you didn't have to leave your family. You get to travel with your Dad." I said, feeling a bit homesick for the first time.

"Lucky? That is what the other apprentices' of my year thought too, until they saw how much stricter he is with me then with anyone else." Lyle answered, laughing softly.

I glanced at Lord Earl doubtfully. "Oh, he's kind enough, and praises people when praise is due, unless you are his son. Then you can never be good enough, no matter how much praise you get from other ranger lords. But he's still a great man, and a good father... just insanely picky." Lyle explained, seeing my uncertain look.

"What about you? Tell me about your life." I requested, eager to learn more about the rangers. Lyle hesitated and glanced at the sleeping lords. "What?" I asked, confused.

"There is little I can tell you. I don't want to scare you, or break your sheltered thoughts too soon." Lyle explained in a very low voice.

I wasn't sure what sheltered thoughts meant, but I did feel put off by him thinking I was a scardy-cat. "I'm a ranger aren't I? I'm not easily scared." I insisted.

Lyle studied me with an amused smile, deciding what to say.

"I will tell you of one adventure I've had. But if you start to feel even a little nervous, you are ORDERED to tell me at once." Lyle finally offered.

I nodded eagerly.

\*\*\*

"Three years ago, in the dark forest of Maltron, I was patrolling one winter. It was deep night, and the moon had set, so it was utterly dark. The dark didn't bother me, but the silence did. It was snowing, and so quiet that my own heart sounded loud in my ears. I went on for another mile, knowing that the base was not too far ahead. If I could get there then I could be amongst the other rangers, and also be warm.

But the darkness and the silence confused my exhausted brain, and I strayed off my assigned road, and into the unsafe area of the forest. I heard a rustling in the trees. Before I could figure out what to do, I was struck in the head. The blow was meant to knock me out, but I just got knocked to the ground. The giant spider who had hit me dropped out of the tree and onto me. I fought to escape its clutches, but it was stronger than me, the blow to my head had weakened me considerably. It bound my arms to my side, and my legs closed with its silk. Then, when I couldn't fight it any more, it bit my shoulder, and dragged me deep into the forest, off to its web. The poison was horrendously painful, and if it had not caused me to go as stiff as wood I would have cried out from the pain of the poison. As it spread through my body, I felt like I had been set on fire from the inside.

The spider hung me upside down from its netted web, and began to poke and prod me, to see how good I'd be for eating. Then another slightly smaller spider joined my captor. They talked together in their own foul language, often gesturing to me. Finally, my captor spoke to me in common tongue.

"You just hang there like a good two legger. Let my poison take full effect. In less than an hour all your insides will have melted into liquid, and you'll be just right for eating. Can you feel my poison, two legger? Can you feel your muscles screaming in agony as they start to dissolve? I hope you enjoy pain, because it will be the last thing you ever feel."

The spiders were laughing and poking me, and I was certain that this was the end for me. I couldn't move, couldn't even blink as I was dying, helpless food to giant spiders, tortured from the poison spreading through me. That was when the elves came. They had heard the spiders laughing, and had come to investigate. Most of them went after the spiders, but one came to me. He had brought a potion designed to heal such injuries. He poured the potion on the wound, and cut me free from the web. But I still could not move, although the pain was going away. The elves took me and brought me to their village, where they nursed me back to health for three days before letting my fellow rangers take me home.

The rangers had come looking for me when I did not report back at the appointed time. But they would have arrived too late. I owe my life to the elves. They have always been our friends in our war against evil. The centaurs would have left me at the mercy of the spiders. They would consider it the natural order of things. But the elves have no patience for the spiders, who often try to capture any elf who ventures the forest alone.

\*\*\*

Lyle looked over at me and smiled. "We have never lost a ranger in the forest. Help always comes, one way or another. You can rest assured that you are far safer in our ranks then you would ever be as a knight."

# CHAPTER 5

For the next four days; Lord Haldor, Sigal, and I were flying once more on the pegasi. The other two rangers were headed to the same location, but they were following on foot. As we flew, Lord Haldor instructed me to memorize the landscape and notice everything going on. He told me that the magic could go so far as to make my eyes twice or even three times as sharp as a normal humans, and that practicing while flying was a good way to strengthen my abilities to use the magic for better sight. When we finally reached the mountains, I was surprised how vast they were. It looked to me like a giant green lake of forest, with waves rising out of it in all directions, reaching for the sky.

A river weaved its way through the mountains like a blue snake. The rangers steered the pegasi along the river until we reached a large fortress, almost as big as the capital city itself. The pegasi flew to what can only be described as a landing platform that was level with the tallest of the fortress towers and landed there. We dismounted and I looked around. From the flat place we had landed on I could see in all directions. The stone walls were the same color as the mountain stone, which made sense to me. There was an orchard garden, and farm land in the center of the fortress, and I guessed that the rangers grew and hunted most of their own food. Most of the fortress indoor area was under my feet, and it seemed huge to me.

"Come Peter, I need to check on the latest news of the land. You shall accompany me until Joseph arrives with your peers." Lord Haldor said, placing a hand on my shoulder.

I followed him through a door, and Sigal remounted the chestnut Pegasus and called the other one to follow as he flew away. The inside was nothing like I had expected a fortress to look. The stone walls were covered by a cheerful looking fabric like you might see in the bedroom of royalty. The fabric changed around every corner, being different colors and designs. Some of the fabrics had pictures on them of hunting parties, or castles, or tournaments.

"Gifts of thanks over the years, from the kingdom." Lord Haldor explained, noticing me looking at them.

The floor was covered in furs, making our footsteps silent as we walked. The only indication that we were in a heavy stone fortress was the ceiling and the windows.

"This is the great fortress of Stoneriver. This is where I am based, and where we make sure to never have less than two hundred soldiers at any given time." Lord Haldor told me softly as we walked through the halls and down several flights of stairs.

"Why so many? There hasn't been outright war in our kingdom for over twenty years...has there?" I asked, feeling like I was forgetting something I should have known.

Sure enough, Lord Haldor pierced me with the look of his that meant he was going to scold me.

"Have you already forgotten the discussion we had over the bread and jam?" he asked frowning.

"No Sir!" I replied hastily, suddenly remembering the battle that Lord Haldor had mentioned as the last time he had had jam.

"Then why did you ask such a foolish question?" Lord Haldor asked me. He stopped walking and looked down at me. I couldn't help but squirm as his piercing grey eyes bore into me.

"I had forgotten... a little I guess. But I remember now." I said, my voice sounding weak.

"Lesson number 2, do not forget or cast aside as unimportant any information you are given. You never know when a discussion from long ago may prove to be vital to survival." Lord Haldor recited.

"Yes sir." I said meekly, certain that I was going to be in for another session of reciting.

Surely enough, Lord Haldor made me recite lesson two a dozen or so times, then recite lesson one a dozen times just to make sure I remembered the lesson correctly. I did remember, I was not likely to forget that embarrassment in a hurry.

Lord Haldor led me to his office, and had me stand behind him two paces as he looked through messages piled high on his desk, left there for him to read on his return. I tried my best to stay still and respectful, like Joseph had done when Lord Haldor was at my father's house. As I stood still I practiced with my magic, finding out what else I could do with it. I was pleased to find that it did indeed allow me to focus on everything all at once. I was able to hear the softest sounds from outside in the hallway as people passed back and fourth. I knew that I shouldn't be able to hear those sounds, or not if I didn't have the magic anyways, because the whole floor was covered in soft furs. But I heard whispered conversations here, and a slight cough there. I listened happily, stretching my ears and eyes further and further, wondering just how well I could tune my abilities.

But as the shadows lengthened with the setting sun I couldn't bear to stand still a moment longer, and I shifted my weight slightly, my feet had fallen asleep being in one position so long. Lord Haldor was immediately aware of me, and he turned his head to regard me gravely.

"Yes?" he asked sharply.

I could feel myself blushing, and was glad that my cloak covered most of my face.

"I'm sorry sir, my feet had fallen asleep." I explained nervously.

"Do you need to sit down so soon? It has only been four hours." Lord Haldor asked me, his lips twitching into a frown.

"No my lord, I am fine. I just shifted so my feet would wake up again." I replied, suddenly realizing that this was some sort of test, though I couldn't imagine the reason for it.

Lord Haldor rose from his chair and offered it to me. "If your feet are asleep, you may sit untill they wake." he suggested, regarding me shrewdly.

"I am fine now my lord. Thank you." I said firmly, determined not to be intimidated by his grey eyes. It was true though, now that I had moved, my feet were losing the prickly sensation.

"As you wish." Lord Haldor said sitting down again and lighting some candles. I was right that that meant he intended to keep me here for quite some time yet. As the long hours of the night progressed I became more and more determined. I wasn't sure what the point of having me stand still so long was, but I was not going to let myself fail in this trial. I stayed still as I could; only moving a small bit every few hours to wake my feet back up. Each time I moved, Lord Haldor asked me if I needed to sit down so soon; to which I replied stubbornly that I was fine.

Finally, as the first light of day was clearing away the blackness outside the window, Lord Haldor put down the last of the messages. He rubbed his eyes with his hand, and stood to face me.

"You are full of stubbornness Peter, most admirable for a ranger's apprentice. I must admit, I had expected to break your willpower hours ago; especially since you are a very energetic young man who must have trouble staying still for any period of time. But the long hours just seemed to make you stronger. You truly do have a good bond with your powers, even though you just received them recently."

I looked up at him, not sure how to answer. It seemed Lord Haldor didn't need an answer, because he turned from me and clapped his hands twice, sharply.

A hooded ranger entered the office after a moment, and dropped to one knee before Lord Haldor. "Take the boy to the first year quarters. Let him rest there undisturbed until his peers arrive tonight. He has earned his break."

"Yes my lord." the ranger said rising to his feet, and gesturing me to follow.

"I am Jason, an apprentice like you, but quite a bit older. I didn't go to the fair because my tests are tomorrow, and they are too important to me to take time off. That's why I'm on duty this morning, because I am here." the ranger introduced himself as we walked through the hallway. He was talking in the same hushed tone that I had heard everyone use since we had arrived.

"I'm," I started to say, bust Jason interrupted me.

"You're Peter, son of a blacksmith, and the jewel of Lord Haldor's eye."

I looked up at him in surprise. How did he know who I was, and what did he mean by jewel of Lord Haldor's eye?

Jason laughed when he saw me look at him.

"Lord Haldor has been talking about you for years now. He keeps telling us older students about your skills and even going so far as to suggest that we should feel ashamed that one so young was better than we are after years of training and magic, and before he left to get you he ordered us to watch after you when you arrived and make sure you would be happy here." Jason explained, stepping out of the main fortress and heading down a dirt path towards a cluster of stone buildings off to the right.

"But... I only met him a couple weeks ago." I stammered.

Jason looked down at me in surprise.

"A couple weeks? He's had custody of you for years!" Jason exclaimed.

I stopped walking and stared at Jason in total confusion. What was going on? Did he have me confused with someone else, some other blacksmith son? I knew that I had never seen a ranger before that night we were packing for the fair. What Jason was saying was impossible, completely impossible.

"I've been living with my father and brothers my whole life." I said slowly.

"Yes, I know. Lord Haldor told Joseph that you were too young to take. He said he had your father encouraging you to be a squire so you'd be ready to leave home easier." Jason replied, obviously confused at my reaction.

I stood, wave upon wave of shock running through me. Suddenly it felt as if my whole history was a big secret known to everyone but me.

Slowly I started to back away from Jason who was still looking at me confused. Finally, I broke into a run and headed back into the fortress. I ran all the way to Lord Haldor's office and banged on the door. Lord Haldor had barely finished saying the word 'enter' when I burst inside.

"Tell me the truth!" I demanded, almost shouting. "Tell me my life hasn't been a lie. Tell me that you haven't been watching me for years and years without me even knowing that you existed. Tell me my father hasn't been lying to me!" I had tears streaming down my face, and I was practically screaming at Lord Haldor, who sat and looked at me calmly.

"I can't tell you that Peter." he answered gently.

I heard movement behind me and turned to see Jason had entered the room, the little I could see of his face was pale, and I could see that he was shaking slightly.

"My lord, I'm sorry. I had no idea! I thought," Jason rushed to explain, but Lord Haldor held up a hand to silence him.

"It's alright Jason, I had intended to tell him, but then forgot that I had not done so. A failure of old age I'm afraid, one of many."

"Tell me the truth!" I demanded again, refusing to be forgotten as the main point in the conversation. Looking back later that day I'm sure if I hadn't been so utterly exhausted from riding through the sky since the first light of day, and then standing at attention all night playing with my new sight and hearing abilities I would have been much calmer about the situation. I might not even have gone to Lord Haldor, but pegged Jason for details instead. But exhaustion and shock had gotten the better of me, and I was nearly hysterical.

"Sit down Peter. Jason, report to Rhop, five hundred pushups and two demerits for failure to think before speaking." Lord Haldor said calmly.

Jason bowed, and left to receive his punishment (he told me later that day that he had deserved it for his foolishness, which I soon found out was a pretty common way of thinking by ranger apprentices).

"Peter, do you recall me mentioning how the rangers are on the verge of extinction?" Lord Haldor began once I had sat down in one of the two comfortable chairs by the fire, Lord Haldor taking the other one.

"Yes sir. You keep saying how there aren't enough young to replace the old." I said, trying to get my tired brain to function better, realizing how important this conversation was to my whole life.

"Correct. Ever since Sir Lucas became one of the head knights eight years ago he has done his best to prevent us from having our fair share of the best youths in the kingdom. He's not a bad man." Lord Haldor added, seeing my expression. "He's just proud, and a bit foolish. Very few people realize how important the rangers are to the country. Many of the older knights and of course the whole royal family understand, but there has not been an open war in the country for many years, and so people have forgotten us. The younger generations see us seldom, and then avoid us if they can, viewing us as dangerous rouges who sneak around in the shadows spying on them. They have forgotten, or never learned that we are there for their protection."

"I don't see what any of this has to do with me." I interrupted rudely, my exhaustion making me far more testy then I would otherwise be.

"I'm getting to it Peter. Settle down and listen." Lord Haldor said firmly, but not unkindly. "Now, because the younger knights have dismissed our importance because of lies told to them by Sir Lucas, they have not let us collect young ones to replace the dwindling gaps in our ranks. You see me, and I look old to you. I am indeed, very old Peter. Far too old. I can't even travel alone anymore, because my body has aged beyond my ability to use magic as the young can. Most of the rangers my age who are still alive, and there are only three of us left, have retired to the country life long ago.

I don't know how long I have to live, but it won't be much longer now." Lord Haldor paused and seemed lost in thoughts. After a moment he looked at me, and continued. "I am friends with King Stephen II, I watched him grow up. I was assigned to the capital when he was a youth, and we bonded. Technically, I am royalty. My older brother is the king's grandfather. Since I had another brother who was younger than me, I was permitted to become a ranger when my skills were discovered. I gave up all rights to the throne, but I have no regrets for doing so. Being a ranger is easily the best choice I ever made.

Anyways, when I told the king of the problems we were having claiming youths that had the talents needed to become rangers; the king told me to go and find any youths who I saw potential in, and he'd make sure I had them, despite what anyone else might say. During one of my searches I stopped in your father's hometown for a while. When I was roaming one night, I noticed a small boy sneaking his way through the village square. Fascinated, I watched as he effortlessly avoided the guards on patrol and picked the lock of one of the stores. I made my way over, wondering if he was going to steal money. But all the boy was after was a small cream cake, and to my amazement, he left money on the counter to pay for his treat. I followed the boy and watched him arrive at home and be punished for leaving the house.

But the boy kept at it, sneaking out every night, sometimes for sweets, but most often, just to prove to himself he could. This went on for a week and a half, until the boy's father started to lock him in the family's workshop at night. When I talked to the head of the town guards, I learned that the boy had been doing this for quite some time now, despite numerous lectures and punishments. I left to return here to my post, but came back often to check on you. You were small, and so were picked on by older children when your brothers weren't there to protect you. Because of a desire to avoid trouble you began to teach yourself how to blend into the background even during the day, as you had already mastered night sneaking. I went to the king and told him of my interest in you, and was granted full custody at once. You were eight at the time.

When I explained the situation to your father he didn't want you to be taken away from him. He had lost his wife, and had nothing to live for but his sons, especially since his town had fallen into poverty, and there was little work for him to do to ensure income. I was touched by his plea that he be allowed to keep you. We came to an agreement that you could stay if your father promised to make sure you learned the skills that I told him to teach you, archery, swordsmanship, reading, and geography. I also told him not to tell you about me, because I am well aware of how young people think of rangers, and I did not want the bigger boys to have another reason to cause you grief. Instead, I had him encourage your desire to be a knight; because it would be a perfectly good excuse for you to learn all that I wanted you to learn.

I tried to give your father money to buy you clothes and other necessities, but he pointed out to me that he had three other sons, and so to give you what he couldn't afford to give the older ones would not be fair. So instead I had him make your daggers for you, to the very strict specifications of the ranger design and style."

I glanced down at my daggers that were hanging on either side of my belt.

"I supplied him with the steel and the silver myself, and had him use the money to care for your family. Around the same time, I made sure your brother secured his first paying job with the town guards, so I rested assured that you would have enough money to have the basic things that a person needs in life.

I think your brother Kevin might have been told of what you were to become, but I do not think the younger two knew. Your life has not been a lie Peter. But it has not been quite what you thought. If I have made an error in my way of handling the situation then I am sorry. I wanted you to grow up as content a child as possible, because I know what it is you will be up against in life. Do not resent your father for not telling you, he was following my orders, orders that he had to follow in order to keep you as long as he did."

# CHAPTER 6

Jason came back after his punishment was over, and Lord Haldor dismissed me, telling me that I needed to rest, a fact that I could not deny any longer. This time as we walked Jason said nothing, which was fine with me. I needed time to think over everything that Lord Haldor had told me. Straining my brain as much as I could, I could not remember ever seeing Lord Haldor in my father's village before. I did remember the night he was referring to with the bakery, but I could not remember having any indication that I had been noticed in my escapade or in any of my nightly adventures since then. I looked up to find that we were standing in front of one of the buildings in the giant courtyard of the fortress.

"This is the first year house. You have it all to yourself for the time being, I hope you enjoy it." Jason said, breaking his guilty silence at last.

I turned to him, feeling ashamed that he had been punished because of me. "I'm sorry about earlier. I didn't mean for you to get in trouble."

Jason shook his head. "My trouble was my own fault. I failed to assess the situation clearly. I should have shut up as soon as I realized that you had no idea what I was talking about. I let my tongue ramble, and for that there is no excuse. Don't worry about me, a few hundred pushups and some dirty dishes are nothing compared to what I had expected to receive for saying something so foolish." Jason said with a slight laugh, waving to me as he left to go about his business.

I opened the door to the first year building and walked through the main room not taking in anything. I found a room with bunk beds, collapsed onto the nearest one, and instantly fell asleep. When I woke up it was late afternoon, almost evening. I looked around the room I was in. There were five double bunk beds, each one neatly made and ready for use, with a thick green blanket and soft sheets. There were no pillows, and I figured it was to make sure we would be able to sleep under harsher conditions without too much trouble adjusting. I went out into the main room to see an oak table with a bowl of fresh fruit in the middle, and chairs around it. There were two trays on the table, and when I examined them it became apparent that the rangers had left meals for me, not sure when I'd wake up.

There were two other rooms, and I went to investigate them now. One was a wash room, and the other seemed to be a study room. There were book shelves lined with leather bound books. I went over to these with interest. There were very few books that I had ever had access to, as the area of the village I grew up in was quite poor even for an area of quite poor people. There were so many towns and villages around us that my father's blacksmith skills were not high in demand except for basic repairs. Most of the money he made was at the harvest fair, where he could make profit selling the knives and daggers he was so skilled at crafting. I read the titles of the books to see that they were books on history, magical creatures, and on battle tactics. Opening one at random I saw that the penmanship was beautiful and flowing. I replaced the book and continued to examine the room. There were maps and diagrams on the walls, intricately made, and beautiful. There were several comfortable reading chairs, and also tables with chairs for more formal studies.

I heard a knock on the outer door and went to investigate. A ranger was standing there with a tray of food. "Ah, you are awake at last are you? You had us a bit worried."

I cocked my head slightly, and the ranger explained.

"You have been asleep for almost five days. Your peers have finally arrived with Joseph, and Lord Haldor sent me to try again to wake you." he explained gently.

"I didn't realize how tired I was." I said, mostly talking to myself.

"You've had a lot of information and magic for your brain to sort through little one. No one is surprised when under such circumstances a first year ranger needs more sleep. Come, eat now and then you'll go meet up with your year mates." he offered, putting the tray on the table, and beginning to gather up the other two trays.

I sat down and ate. It was a wonderful dinner. Roasted goose, a hot potato with butter, and steamed greens. I ate hungrily, barely taking time to savor my food as my stomach realized how long it had been since my last meal. When I had finished, the ranger took my tray and stacked the dishes with the others.

"Lord Haldor is in his office waiting for you. I trust you can find your way?" the ranger asked me as we stepped outside.

I nodded and headed off towards the main building. The ranger who had brought me my food went in another direction, probably to return the trays.

Outside Lord Haldor's office I stopped, feeling embarrassed at the way I had been so rude to him at our last meeting. While I was staring at his office door, trying to get up the courage to knock, Joseph came up behind me leading three rangers of around my age. He reached over my head and knocked crisply, his usual three knocks. When he was told to enter he lead us in, went to Lord Haldor's desk, and dropped to one knee with his head bowed, motioning for us apprentices to follow his lead.

"Rise. Where is Peter, is he still asleep?" Lord Haldor asked.

"I'm here my lord. I came in the same time as the others." I explained, deciding not to mention that I had been standing outside blushing for the past couple minutes.

Lord Haldor motioned me to stand next to him, which I did. I tried to look up at him without letting him know I was doing so, to try to see if he was mad at how I had behaved earlier when he had been nothing but kind to me since he came to get me. Lord Haldor put a hand on my shoulder, and I understood then that he forgave my earlier outburst.

"You children may all take your hoods off for a bit. Find out what your companions look like. You may be spending quite a lot of time together if everything in life goes well."

I removed my hood and looked at my companions. There were two girls and one boy. The boy had sandy colored short cropped hair, much in the style squires wear. One of the girls had blond hair that she had pulled back with a green band. The other girl was shorter then her companions, almost the same height as me. She had dark red hair that was in two neat braids hanging down to the middle of her back. She looked nervous and was hanging a step behind the other two. When she glared at me, I looked away quickly as I realized I had been staring at her.

"Where are the rest?" Lord Haldor asked Joseph. I glanced up at him, recognizing the tone as one of extreme displeasure bordering on fury.

Joseph seemed to recognize the tone too, as he swallowed hard before answering.

"My lord, there are no others. These were all Thelmer and I could get." he said, his voice calm despite the nervousness I could feel from him.

"That is not enough. Did I not tell you that we needed as many as possible?" Lord Haldor said in a dangerously low voice.

"My lord, Sir Lucas,"

"Did I not tell you not to fail me again?" Lord Haldor interrupted.

"Yes sir, you did." Joseph said in a resigned voice, as if accepting his fate, whatever it may be.

"Peter, why don't you show the others where they'll be staying?" Lord Haldor more ordered then suggested.

I jumped forward and lead the others hastily from the room. As

I shut the door behind us, I heard Lord Haldor shouting. When we were half way down the hall there was a loud crash, followed by more shouting. Rangers started running towards the office from all directions.

"What happened?" an un-hooded ranger demanded of me. "Lord Haldor is yelling at Joseph for not bringing enough apprentices' back." I explained as the unknown ranger held my shoulder stopping us from being separated as the others ran past.

"Get in there and get Joseph out! I'll calm Haldor down." the ranger said, releasing me and bounding after the others with surprising speed for one so old.

"Get back to your building little ones, we'll take care of this." a ranger told me and my companions as the other rangers burst into the office to deal with whatever was going on inside.

The night air felt cool and refreshing compared to the tension inside. I smiled weakly at the others, who looked scared and confused. "It's ok. Lord Haldor would never harm a ranger, he's just upset. He keeps saying there aren't enough young to replace the old. I guess he expected more than three. Our building is certainly designed for more." I said lightly.

"It's not his fault you know. If anything its mine." the sandy haired boy explained as I lead the way to our building in the fading light.

"How do you figure?" I asked surprised.

"Well, Sir Lucas had his eye on me. I was the very first person called on to be selected by the knights, and Sir Lucas was about to claim me as his squire when Joseph interrupted him and swiftly claimed me for the rangers. Sir Lucas was really angry. So was my mom, though my Dad was beside himself with pride. They're both nobles, my parents." he explained as I looked at him not understanding. "Anyways, Sir Lucas got really angry, and ordered Joseph off the parade grounds. That night Sir Lucas had him summoned. When Joseph came back he was really hurt, I mean he was walking all tender and his lip was bleeding. He had a lot of trouble getting us back because he hurt so much, but Thelmer helped him along, he even carried Joseph on his back for the last few days of the journey. Then some rangers showed up, Lord Haldor had sent them looking for us. So they carried Joseph today. Joseph told the other ranger, Thelmer, that the king suggested them to leave town at once, or Lucas would kill both rangers. I think Sir Lucas has to stand trial, but he has loads of supporters for what he did to Joseph."

I was surprised by the story. I'd never heard of a knight beating up a ranger like that before. 'But then again', I thought as I opened the door to our building, 'I'd never heard of rangers 'till less than a month ago.'

"Here we are." I said, waving my hand around the room. While we had been gone, someone had lit a fire in the fireplace and left an oil lamp lit on the table for us. Everyone went to explore the building, everyone except the red head and me. "You're not curious?" I asked her.

She blushed and ducked her head, muttering something I couldn't hear.

"It's ok, you don't have to look around, I was just surprised, that's all." I hastily explained as the other two came back into the main room.

"This place is great! So much better then life as a squire. Did you see those books, and the maps? Heck, even the wash room is better then what squires are stuck with. Ha! If only they could see me now. Oh, my name's Gene." the boy said, holding out his hand for me to shake.

"Peter, as you know." I said taking his hand.

"I'm Sara. I use to be a shepherdess. But then Thelmer saw me as I ran after and retrieved a stray lamb. So he started testing me for all sorts of stuff like how fast I can run, and how accurate I can throw." The blond girl introduced herself, curtsying even though she was wearing black pants like the rest of us.

We all turned to look at the red head. Seeing that she was suddenly the center of attention she blushed again and muttered something.

"Speak up. Remember, Joseph said if he caught you mumbling again he's tickle you 'till you were sick." Gene reminded the girl with a smile meaning he knew Joseph had only been joking.

"I'm Robin. My family is all gypsies. But Joseph saw me pretending to sword fight the air behind my parent's wagon and bought me from my group." she said in a slightly louder voice.

"BOUGHT you? You mean like a slave?!" I asked horrified at the thought. Slavery had never been permitted in our country, even though it was a common practice by some of the Southern countries.

"No, like a girl who was to be taken away from her family whether they liked it or not." Robin said glaring at me.

Gene stepped in to explain. "When a person is chosen by the rangers they always try to compensate the family for any losses the family might suffer from not having their son or daughter around any more. Sara's parents were paid too. Mine weren't, because they are wealthy and have other children." he explained.

I nodded, recalling how Lord Haldor had mentioned that he had tried to give my father money. "I'm sorry. I was picked up a week before the fair started. There are a LOT of things I don't understand." I said, mostly talking to Robin.

She studied me for another moment, and nodded her acceptance of my apology.

"What do we do now?" Sara asked me.

The others looked at me, apparently taking me as the leader since I had been here longest. "I guess we should go to bed. Rangers wake up before the sun." I said with a shrug.

We took the lamp and headed into the bedroom, where another fire was burning in the fire place.

"Alright, we boys will take one side of the room, and you ladies can have the other side. It's only fair. Peter, which side have you been using?" Gene asked as he examined the room.

I blushed, realizing that we'd have to share the room with girls. I pointed to the bed I had collapsed on, and Gene put his travel pack on the top bunk, laying his weapons on another bunk bed on "our side" next to mine. He saw my dagger sheathes, and turned to me.

"I thought only rangers who had completed their training got daggers. That's what Joseph said when I asked him about his ones." he said in confusion. I wasn't sure how to explain my situation, or even if I wanted to explain to a guy I hardly knew so I answered, "It's my treasure. The one thing I brought from home."

"Wow, you mean your Dad's a ranger, and he gave you his daggers?" Gene asked wide eyed. "No! My Dad's a blacksmith. He made them for me." I hastily explained.

"Oh." Gene said turning away, apparently losing interest.

That night I lay awake listening to the others sleep. Having woken up at sundown I wasn't tired, but I had a feeling that now that my age group was assembled we were going to be very busy tomorrow training. So I lay down and rested, thinking over what Lord Haldor had told me, (had it really been so long ago?) about my past.

# CHAPTER 7

As I had predicted, we were woken up as soon as there was only just enough light in the sky to see by. It wasn't a gentle awakening either. As I had been up all night anyways, I was sitting in the outer room, reading one of the books on monsters, learning what I could about Orcs and goblins. A ranger entered the house quietly, and put a finger to his lips to signal for me not to talk. He put a pot of food and some bowls on the table, and went over to the window and looked out it, waiting for some signal or another. He slowly withdrew a horn from his cloak and put it to his lips. As a bell rang from the main building he blew three loud blasts that made me clap my hands over my ears. Then he entered the bedroom, me following slightly behind him. My three year mates were scrambling out of bed, rubbing their eyes and looking around in confusion.

"Time to wake up first years. The day has begun. Don't forget your weapons and your manners. You squirts have twenty minutes to get ready for the day and eat breakfast. Be fully assembled outside the building and ready to learn, because you have a LOT of learning to do, believe me." With that, the ranger left us scrambling to get ready. I grabbed my weapons and hastily put them on, and then rushed to eat as much porridge as I could in the short time we were given. We stood outside in the very early morning light, relieved that we had judged our timing correctly. Because Lord Haldor was headed our way as we got into a line with our backs to our building. At the other buildings

I could see that the other apprentices were assembling in the same way, much more use to it then me and my companions were. As Lord Haldor stopped at the head of the path that broke off to the different buildings we saw the older apprentices drop to one knee and bow, so we did the same.

"Rise and greet the morning. Today marks a new year of training for all of you, and the end of training for some. Would the fifth year apprentices follow me to your tests?" he said formally.

Everyone applauded the fifth year apprentices, who went forward tall and proud, ready to become full rangers. I saw Jason among them as they passed us, and he winked at me cheerfully. I was also surprised to see Thelmer, I had thought he was a full ranger already, apparently I was wrong. Those two were the only fifth year ranger apprentices. Looking around at the lines I could see quite harshly what Lord Haldor had been so upset about. There were only two other buildings that had apprentices besides the fifth years and the first, and one of those buildings just had two girls. None of the buildings had anywhere near as many apprentices as the buildings were designed to house.

After the fifth years had left with Lord Haldor, two rangers approached us. "I am Lyle, a ranger from the east. I have come far because we need more members in the dark forest of Maltron. You little ones are too young for such an assignment, but since your teacher is busy at the moment I will cover for him."

"Sir?" Gene interrupted nervously. Lyle nodded for him to continue. "Is Joseph hurt? Did Lord Haldor hurt him?" he asked, his voice wavering.

"What happened last night may have seemed scary, but it looked far worse than it actually was. The crash was Lord Haldor turning over his desk in anger." Lyle hesitated. "I will not pretend that we did not fear for Joseph's life. Lord Haldor is a powerful man even in old age, and you would be wise never to make him angry at you. Joseph is not here right now because he has three cracked ribs and a lot of internal bleeding from what Sir Lucas did to him. It was when Joseph told Lord Haldor of the beating he received from the knight that Lord Haldor got angry. Joseph is the head of the archers; second in command of the rangers, Lord Haldor would never hurt him, he would never hurt any ranger." Lyle assured us. "Now, this is Asia. She will be training you girls while I train you boys. We will meet up after dinner to compare notes and tell you the rules of the game."

"What game?" Sara asked.

"You'll find out after dinner." Lyle said with a slight smile.

Lyle took Gene and me to an archery range. There were targets at varying intervals scattered around an area surrounded by a fence of netting to stop any stray arrows from hurting anyone passing by. Lyle spaced me and Gene at different ends, and told us to aim for the bulls eyes. He ordered us never to aim for the same target twice in a row and to use all the arrows. When our arrows were spent he had us go retrieve them marking down how many bulls eyes we hit. Then he had us shoot from different postures, standing, kneeling, sitting, even lying down. That was much harder to do, even for me who'd been doing Archery for a few years now. Once we had done that, Lyle added another challenge. He had us shoot with no more than five seconds between each shot, still making sure to never hit the same target twice in a row. Every time we missed the bulls eye or took too long, Lyle marked us down a notch. At the end of the archery training he gave us our final grades for the exercise. Gene had gotten a five, and I had gotten little better at twelve... out of one hundred possible points. That didn't make either of us feel very good, but Lyle said that today was just a starting point. This way we'd be able to see how far we were progressing from the beginning of our training to the end.

After Archery, Lyle had us go running arround the fortress. He led the run through the trees, scolding us if we were being too loud. We ran the entire length of the fortress, and then turned around when we got to the corner, and ran back. When we got back to where we started Gene looked ready to drop. Lyle led us to a well and let us rest and have a drink, pacing back and forth sipping his water as we rested, not at all tired despite the six miles he had just run with us.

"How does he do it? How does he have so much energy?" Gene

whispered to me.

Just then a ranger approached Lyle, and I took my chance to tell Gene about the rapid pace that rangers walked in the wild, almost running, for fourteen hours a day. Gene looked at me wide eyed, and so I explained how a change had come over me and I had found myself able to keep up with no problem after a few days.

"You get use to it I guess. The magic of course helps too. Didn't you guys walk fast from the capital?" I asked, knowing that Joseph had walked fast when I was with him.

"No, we went kind of slowly actually. I figured that was just how rangers walked, slowly and gingerly." Gene explained.

I turned away to hide my wince at that news. Joseph must have been hurting a LOT if he had walked back slowly by normal standards.

"All right you two, you've had your water break, ready to go again, quietly this time?" Lyle asked as the other ranger headed off. Gene and I got to our feet and followed Lyle back out to the wall rather reluctantly.

We finished the second run somewhere out in the middle of the fortresses orchard garden. Lyle gave us each a water skin, and drank some water himself as he looked around, deciding what to do to (I mean with) us next. After my humiliation in the forest where I had been told lesson one, I was on high alert. I was not going to let myself be caught off guard or tricked again. Lyle seemed to notice this and so his next challenge was for Gene.

"Gene, climb up this apple tree for me and bring down an apple from the top branch." he said, pointing to a pear tree.

Gene got wearily to his feet and began to climb the tree. When he got to the top he looked around in confusion.

"Just fetch me a nice apple Gene, and come back down." Lyle called up to him.

Hesitantly, Gene selected a pear and made his way down to the ground.

"Where's my apple Gene?" Lyle asked. I took a large gulp of water to hide the smile that wanted to burst onto my face.

Gene held out the pear in embarrassment.

"That is a pear, not an apple Gene. It is true that both words have a P and an A in them, but that does not make it the same fruit, now does it?" Lyle asked cheerfully.

"No sir." Gene said ducking his head deeper into his hood.

"Well then go back up there and get me an apple from this apple tree." Lyle said, laying his hand against a branch.

"Sir, apples and pears don't grow on the same kind of tree." Gene said, his tone showing that he knew very well what game Lyle was playing with him.

"Then why did you climb this tree looking for apples, if you can see it is a pear tree?" Lyle asked.

"Because *you* tricked me into doing so." Gene answered stubbornly.

It happened so fast that I almost missed it. Lyle's hand whipped out, and smacked Gene in the mouth. Gene stumbled back in surprise.

"Never blame your own shortcomings on others Gene. You failed to pay attention, and so were easy to trick. Peter, tell Gene lesson number one." Lyle called, bringing me into the conversation suddenly.

"Sir, a ranger must ALWAYS pay attention to everything around him. Failure to do so will cost you your life." I recited dutifully.

After Lyle had Gene recite lesson one a dozen times he put a hand on Gene's shoulder. "Don't feel bad about it Gene. Every apprentice is tricked if caught with his guard down, and no one has their guard up at all until they've been tricked or seen someone else be tricked. I was tricked, Peter here was tricked a few days ago, even Lord Haldor was probably tricked, back when he was first starting out. It's all part of the long process of becoming a ranger. But Gene, never try to blame others for your mistakes. Because it is the blame that got you punished, not the mistake itself."

Lyle brought Gene and me to a clear area and had us draw our swords. He had us practice our techniques, marking down what we did right and wrong. I was relieved that Gene and I were evenly matched when it came to our sword skills. Fighting against Gene was actually somewhat fun; it had been a long time since I had felt truly challenged in a sword competition. When Gene and I stopped, we grinned at each other, and I knew then that he felt the same way I did.

"Nice to be with people of similar skills, isn't it lads? That's why you craved being knights, because you desired those on the same level as you. Let's head back. I feel it's almost time for some dinner, and I'm sure you two will want to hear the rules of the game." Lyle said kindly when he saw our reaction to the sword fight.

Dinner was served in a large meeting room big enough to hold hundreds of men if the fort ever got breached. Despite the fact that the rangers usually talked in hushed tones, it was noisy and cheerful at dinner, as the soldiers guarding the fortress were eating with us. Gene and I found Sara and Robin and sat down with them. As Sara was telling us about her day, which was very much like the one Gene and I had, except that instead of Archery they had been tested on their hand combat skills, I noticed that Gene was looking all around the room for someone.

"Looking for Joseph?" I asked when Sara had finished talking. Gene nodded. "He could easily be here and I wouldn't know it. Why do rangers keep their hoods up all the time anyways?" Gene grumbled.

"We wear the hoods because it is our trademark. The only exception are the elderly and the ranger lords, they wear their hoods down as a way to distinguish themselves as people who deserve respect. Also, it is a sign to us younger rangers which rangers probably should not go dangerous places alone."

We all turned around to see who had answered the question. Joseph was there, leaning heavily against a walking stick that he was using to remain upright.

"Joseph! Thank goodness, we were so worried about you!" Sara cried, slipping off the bench and giving Joseph a hug that made the man grunt in pain and surprise. Sara let go quickly, realizing that she probably shouldn't hug him right now when he was barely able to stand.

"Gene." Joseph said, putting a hand on the worried boy's shoulder. "What happened at the fair was NOT YOUR FAULT. You have done NOTHING wrong. I had suspected foul play when the summons came for me. Believe me, it was not anyone's fault but the man waiting for me with the intent to grievously injure me. If it had not been over you, it would have been over another boy. Lucas had come ready to fight. He and I never did get along, so when he heard that I was around..."

Joseph trailed off and looked at the entrance in concern. I turned around to see a ranger standing in the doorway, swaying from side to side. As he went down everyone in the hall leapt to their feet as one, and hurried forward to help their companion. There was shouting, and the ranger's name kept being called out as the rangers closest to the door discovered who it was.

"Lance." Joseph gasped, using his stick to whack people out of his way as he rushed forward towards the door.

Panic rose in my throat as I recalled the events that had happened with the imp in the woods. "But..." I said in confusion. "Lord Haldor said the imps were harmless."

"What is it, who's Lance?" Sara asked me, tugging on my cloak as I tried to see through the large number of rangers and soldiers all pressed together blocking the way to the door where Lance was. I glanced down, and decided to try crawling. I was small enough; I might be able to get through the crowd between the adults legs. I had just made up my mind to try it when everyone fell suddenly silent as if struck dumb.

Standing on tiptoe I could just make out that Lord Haldor had raised his hands up for quiet, standing on a chair so everyone could see him. "I want the best night hunters ready to track the imps down. Apprentices will go back to your buildings and will stay there until I and I alone come and tell you, you may leave. The rest of you will stay here until we have more news. Make way, let the children through." Lord Haldor ordered in a surprisingly calm tone given the situation.

As we passed the doorway I glanced over at the fallen ranger. His hood had been taken off him and I could see that his face was heavily bruised in a strange pattern across his forehead and his cheeks. "Not the imps. It was a Kronlord. Why he didn't kill me I do not know." Lance was telling Joseph as we passed.

At the name Kronlord, a sudden burning fury washed over me. I turned my head to look back, but one of the older girls put her hand on my shoulder and marched me out of the building. That night, my year mates and I looked through every book of magical creatures that we had. But nowhere could we find out what a Kronlord was. All we knew was that it made everyone but me feel cold with terror just hearing the name. We had the fire burning hot and sat huddled together around it. "Maybe we're looking in the wrong section?" Gene suggested when I threw the last book aside in frustration. "Where else is there to look?" Robin asked, speaking for the first time that night.

"The name Kron, it sounds so familiar to me. I feel as if I've heard it before somewhere." Gene said, scanning through the shelf of history books. "Ha! There we go, the war of Kron." Gene said pulling a book off the shelf. He came over in triumph and opened the book, only to find that the pages were empty. We all looked at each other; we had no idea what to make of that.

# CHAPTER 8

As the moon was setting and we were debating going to bed, Lord Haldor came to our building. He opened the door and entered, looking grim and tired. "Come, you are all rangers, and so you may attend the meeting." He said.

We followed him as he gathered the other apprentices. We entered the hall where we had eaten dinner. The cheerful feeling of the place was gone. The tables had been removed and the benches were all facing the same direction. The casual chatter was replaced by serious murmuring as the rangers conversed in low voices. Lord Haldor directed me and Gene to sit next to Joseph, and Sara and Robin were sent over to their teacher, who held her arms out to hug the girls who looked small and frightened surrounded by the older rangers.

"My brothers and sisters, sons and daughters, hear me." Lord Haldor said, standing at the front of the room. The murmuring died away at once, and every one focused on Lord Haldor. "Lance has returned with grave news. At least one Kronlord has managed to enter the kingdom with us being none the wiser. If one has made it, we must assume all twelve are here. This is probably the most serious threat we have faced in over twenty years. If Kron has sent one of the twelve then it is an act of war..." Haldor broke off as one of the older apprentices was whispering to her teacher.

"What is it?" He asked her frowning.

The girl turned to see that everyone was now focused on her. She rose to her feet. "Sir, I was just asking my teacher who Kron was." she explained confidently.

"You have been in your building for hours. Did you not bother to look him up?" Lord Haldor asked coldly.

"We tried to my Lord, but the book was empty." the girl explained.

"What do you mean empty?" Lord Haldor asked, his frown deepening more and more.

"The pages were all blank my Lord, begging your pardon." the girl said, adding the last part nervously as she noticed how severely he was frowning at her.

"The same with our book sir." Gene said rising to his feet and raising the book up to show everyone.

Lord Haldor strode forward and seized the book, flipping through a few pages, and then looking at the cover confirming that it was indeed the book on Kron and the war. Haldor went over to the girl who was still standing, having been given no orders to the contrary. "Is this the book that was blank in your dorm?" he asked her, holding it out so she could see the cover.

"Yes my lord. As I said, the book was blank, so we couldn't find out who he was."

Lord Haldor examined the blank book for a moment. "What new devilry has he cooked up, what witchcraft erases all mention of him in our archives?" he murmured. Lord Haldor looked up. "Sit down children. Very well, I will tell you in brief, because time is pressing, and we need to act fast if we are to be ready for war before it is upon us."

Lord Haldor strode back to the front of the room and addressed everyone. "Kron is a devil, a real, living, breathing devil. He is worshiped by most of the evil creatures in the world, and in return, he gives them power. Twenty three years ago this kingdom, along with help from the bordering kingdoms was able to overthrow him and cast him out of these mountains, banishing him to the under-earth. As far as we had known, he has been trapped there ever since. There is no way for us to know for sure, because mortal men do not venture into those places. But as there has been no sign or whisper of him, we had presumed that he was there still.

The Kronlords are his army generals. They stand eight feet tall and look like tall men, or small giants, whichever way you want to look at it. They are not men; they are demons from deep in the realms of the under-earth. There are twelve of them left, and since we know for sure that one is here, we must assume they all are. They are very dangerous, and I remind and warn you all never to look at their eyes. They have black magic and we must be very cautious when dealing with them. One of them convinced the imps to capture a ranger and bring him for questioning, which imps, being as they are, were happy to do. The imps claimed that he was being taken for questioning, but the reality is much worse. Lance was forced to be a living sacrifice, and had almost all of the life drained out of him to feed the kronlord. He is very ill, but is expected to make a full recovery.

But now we must look to the safety of all members of the kingdom. I have already sent messages to the other bases, if Kron decides to attack through one of the other border guards we must be ready to go to their aid. The most likely place he will attack however is right here, at this fortress. That is where he came from last time, over the mountains by the river path. As such we must leave only strong fighters here. I want five hundred men, at least twenty rangers guarding these mountains. The rest are to spread out and help the other posts. There are seven hundred good soldiers in the Eastern mountains; I have sent word that two hundred go to the other posts. That way, both mountain ranges will have equal protection. More men will be sent as they're trained." Lord Haldor took a deep breath.

"The best fighters must go with me to the capital. If the very worst happens, that will be where our country makes our last stand. Apprentices also shall go to the capital, for their own safety. Joseph, you are injured. Who would you name to take your place here as head archer, third in command of the rangers?" he asked turning to Joseph.

"If you are asking who my best archer is who also excels at tactics I would name Thelmer." Joseph answered.

There was much murmuring at his announcement. I glanced over to see that Thelmer was sitting very still with the other ranger who had just graduated. Apparently he was as shocked as the rest of us.

"Thelmer is too young. He has only just graduated yesterday. You can't possibly put him in charge of the archers here. He's barely a man yet. He's only seventeen." A ranger sitting a few rows behind us stated.

"You have asked me who I would pick, and I have told you. Thelmer has skills with the bow that rival even my own. He has also passed every tactics challenge presented to him with flying colors, coming up with battle plans that not even his teachers had considered." Joseph said in a loud voice that drowned out the protesters.

Lord Haldor raised his hands signaling silence. "You need not remind Joseph of the seriousness of the situation, he was there during the last war. If he selects Thelmer as his replacement then Thelmer shall replace him." Lord Haldor said in a voice that left no more room for argument.

The meeting went on past the morning, and well into the afternoon. Battle tactics were discussed, and plans were made ready. Finally, Lord Haldor dismissed everyone to prepare themselves, which in me and my year mates case meant packing our few belongings for the dangerous journey to the capital. When we were packed and ready to leave, we received more distressing news.

"Peter is going to be going with me. He will not be joining you at the capital." Joseph informed us.

"But we thought you were going to take us. You're our guide, our teacher!" Gene protested.

"I am injured Gene. I would be a danger to your safety, for I would only slow you down. Right now, speed is your only hope. You must ride pegasi so that it will only take a few days to get there. I cannot possibly ride, not with my injuries." Joseph explained patiently.

"But... what about Peter?" Robin asked.

"Peter has been selected as one of the people sent to help keep the sick and injured safe. There is a protected base hidden deep in the northern part of the mountains. That is where I and Lance must go, for our own safety."

"And Peter is being sent to make sure you get there safe?" Sara asked.

Joseph nodded gravely.

"Why him? I mean... he's no older than the rest of us. So why was he chosen?" Gene said.

Joseph smiled, knowing that Gene was really asking why he wasn't the one selected instead. "Peter has had some personal training from Lord Haldor himself. Enough that he should be able to handle the journey safely. You are being given a far more dangerous and difficult task, Gene." Joseph said pulling the young ranger closer. As Joseph already had me standing beside him I heard what he murmured.

"I need you to look after Lord Haldor for me. He is far weaker then he looks to the untrained eye. I need you to make sure that you stick with him. If he asks, tell him that you are taking my place as his travel companion. He'll know what that means. Keep him safe for me. Can you do that Gene? I'm counting on you."

Gene nodded, standing straighter as he was given such an important task.

Joseph led me away towards where a small group was waiting for him. I glanced back one last time at my friends of such a short time. I wondered if I'd ever see them again. Right now the future looked so uncertain.

"Here is Haldor's gem. He will serve as our extra protection." Joseph said placing his hand on my shoulder. I looked up at the rangers in the group. Besides Joseph and Lance there was a man with one arm in a sling, and a pregnant woman. I looked at Joseph uncertainly. How could he expect me to protect them? I was just a boy, and they were all disabled. How could we possibly journey through the mountains on foot?

My unspoken question was answered as a large covered wagon drawn by several cattle pulled to a stop in front of us. Sigal was driving it, and he hopped down to help the injured climb in the back. I sighed in relief to find out that I wasn't the only healthy person in the group. Sigal was there, he'd be able to take care of things if there really was an emergency. Sigal gestured me to ride in the wagon with the others, and I had barely entered through the flap in the cover when Sigal started off. The wagon went over a rock and I found myself falling into Lance's lap. He gently helped me sit down next to him and I noticed that the pattern of bruises was also on his hands. I wondered if it was all over his body, and how it had felt to have his life drained. But I did not dare ask.

# CHAPTER 9

After a few hours of tenseness as the wagon traveled north Sigal called me to the front. I ducked under the front flap and joined him sitting on the driver's bench.

"How is everyone holding up?" Sigal murmured. I looked out and found that we were traveling on an actual road through the mountains. Noticing my glance Sigal explained.

"If the kronlords are after rangers they will not expect to find us traveling by an actual road. Rangers are well known for avoiding roads, and so it is the safest place to be when you wish to not be pegged as a ranger. How is everyone holding up?" he asked again.

"Lance fell asleep after we'd been going ten minutes. He's very pale and has a slight fever. I've been waking him up every thirty minutes and making him drink water. Joseph told me that is the best way to treat mild fevers like the one he has. I've also been wiping his forehead with a damp cloth. Joseph is in a lot of pain. Every time we go over a bump he balls his hands into fists and hisses through his teeth. I don't know the other ranger's names, but they seem to be fine. The woman has been holding Joseph's hand and trying to comfort him. The other man is just watching out of a gap in the tent flap while I take care of Lance."

"She's a girl." Sigal said.

"What?" I asked confused.

"The pregnant one, she's just a girl, not a woman. She's only seventeen, an apprentice." Sigal explained softly.

"But then, how..." I asked, stopping myself when it occurred to me that it was none of my business.

"She is Thelmer's wife." Sigal explained.

"But if she's only seventeen...he's only seventeen?" I asked, completely confused.

"Rangers marry young Peter, when they marry at all. When you live your life without knowing what the future may bring you cast aside formalities such as waiting 'till the standard age of marriage to become man and wife, or to have children."

"How can she be an apprentice if she has children though?" I asked, lowering my voice even more.

"She can't. Not until the baby is old enough that it can look after itself. Then she can continue her training. But she is still a ranger. She has skills in sword fighting as well as caring for the sick. That is why we are lucky to have her with us, because she has been training as a healer, something she can do when bearing a child. Our group desperately needs a healer, but none can be spared. She offered to come along, not just for her child's protection, but to help you care for Lance and Joseph."

"Help ME? What about you?" I asked, and dreading the answer that I now knew was coming.

"I will only be with you for a short while. In two day's time we will have reached the point in the road that is closest to our secret healing house. From there you must all proceed on foot. I will be continuing on the road so that if anyone tries to follow the wagon they will come after me, giving you time to get the hurt to safety."

"But Sigal, I'm not ready for that! I've had what, one day of training in my life? How can I be expected to protect anyone?" I asked weakly.

Sigal looked over at me in confusion. "Lord Haldor had your father make sure you have been getting trained for years. You are already an expert at avoiding being seen, and even better at sword fighting than I am, and didn't Joseph tell you that he found your archery skills adequate?" Sigal asked.

"Well yeah he said that, but yesterday I did no better than Gene on the archery range, and he's a first year too." I protested.

"Lyle said that you were holding back. He could see it in your expression. He said that it seemed to him like you felt embarrassed about your skills and didn't want to outshine your friend. Were you not aware that you were holding back?"

I shook my head numbly. Now that I was thinking about it, I really did feel embarrassed about being better then Gene at anything since Gene had been raised by nobility, and I was just a blacksmith's son. "I guess I just wanted Gene to like me, and not feel incompetent at archery." I realized. Then, as we went over a large bump, and I heard Joseph actually cry out in pain the present came rushing back.

"But even so, I can't do this. I can't protect everyone! I'm not ready for this." I pleaded.

Sigal put his arm around my shoulder, holding the reigns with one hand. "Peter, Lord Haldor is the one who hand chose you from all the children throughout the whole kingdom. He's been watching you and monitoring your progress. The training that your peers would have, and hopefully will receive in the next few years, you already know. We weren't planning on training you with your year mates for more than one year, and that was just to make sure you had enough stamina built up for prodigy training, which is much more rigorous. You traveled with Thelmer for a time, he too is a prodigy, the first one we've found in many years. You saw how he was traveling with Joseph instead of staying in the fortress with Jason and Ebony, his year mates? That was to be your future, and may still be... if all goes well."

"But what if we're attacked? What if Ebony starts to have her baby out in the middle of the forest? What if Lance gets worse? What if,"

Sigal held his hand up to cut off my stream of fears. "Joseph is capable of helping you to a great extent. Yes he has trouble walking, and he'd be no good in a defense against a siege on the fort, but he is still quite capable. Also, Fletch's arm may be broken, but he is still deadly with his good arm. They can both help you if there is an attack, which is somewhat unlikely as we are taking every precaution to avoid danger. As for Lance, I don't know what will happen to him, but I think he'll make it, one way or another. No one's ever survived a kronlord attack, so the fact that he made it back is a VERY good sign."

We made camp that night on the side of the road. Sigal fed the cattle from a barrel of oats and grains, and then tied them in a makeshift fence he made out of wrapping a few ropes around several trees with the cows in the middle. Sigal had me take the first watch, giving me very strict instructions on what to do.

"Keep your eyes and ears wide open and alert. Stay hidden in the brush here, and stay as still as stone. If you must move be sure that you do not disturb the plants, for any noise would alert a stalker of your position. Keep an arrow on your bow at all times, but do not draw it back until you need to use it. Remind yourself of lesson number one, for it is not just your own life you are guarding, but that of injured companions as well. Do not let yourself panic. If there is any danger, you will sense it before you see or hear it. If you feel a deep and cold terror shout out, for it will mean a kronlord is near. If that happens, STAY WHERE YOU ARE. Do NOT try to help us. Keep yourself safe, no matter what happens."

I nodded, feeling more nervous then I'd ever felt in my life, including the first time I had ever tried sneaking through town after dark. Sigal got down to one knee and held my hands. "I have to give you those instructions, but you shouldn't worry. The Kronlords will almost definitely NOT be coming after us of all people. They would go after the rangers heading to the capital, a very different direction then we are headed in. It is those rangers who are going to the king to assemble the army that are a threat to the kronlords."

I heard a sound behind me and turned quickly. The others were also aware of the sound, heavy hoof beats as of a great war horse.

Joseph got to his feet using his walking stick as a crutch. He drew an arrow and strode over to where Sigal and I were standing watching the shadows. "Who goes there? I warn you, we are heavily armed. Be you friend or foe, show yourself or I shoot." he challenged the unknown figure.

Out of the shadows into the firelight came a centaur. I had never seen one before, and looked up at it in awe. The bottom half was that of a tall red haired horse, and the top half was that of a man with no shirt and a very hairy chest. He had a red beard, and stood tall and proud.

"Why do you wish to shoot me, little ranger?" he asked. His voice was rich and majestic like I imagined the king's voice would probably be.

Joseph put the arrow back in the quiver. "I don't. But we are out in the wild with little protection other than our own weapons." he explained bowing his head in greeting.

"What need have you of protection? What are you worried will attack such powerful humans as you are?" the centaur asked sadly.

"Kron has sent his demons into our country; they have already captured and feasted on a member of our guild. We don't know where on when they will strike next."

"Or why." the centaur added, looking up at the trees.

"Yes, or why." Joseph agreed.

The centaur looked down at us gravely. "You are wise to fear them. They are hungry from going so long without humans to feed off of. Their hunger makes them all the more bitter, and their hearts all the more black. But they are not here. Where they are the trees can't tell us, but they are far away from your small group." the centaur assured us. Then he looked up at the trees again.

"Yes, you have nothing to fear from those servants of night in your first watch little one." he said looking down at me, as if he had read my mind.

I smiled at him weakly.

"Your rangers seem to be getting younger and younger. Why do you rely so heavily on a baby for protection? Can you not see he is young and scared?" the centaur asked Joseph.

"We have little choice. Open war is upon us. Everyone, no matter how young or old, must do what he can to help." Joseph answered firmly.

"Humans are strange creatures. They would shield their young even to their own death one day, and then the next they treat them as miniature adults and rely on the smallest ones to do all the work caring for the grown ones. Why are humans so unpredictable?" the centaur asked the trees. I glanced up at them, wondering if they had an answer.

"I shall leave you strange people now. I recommend that you be on guard even though your biggest fear is not here. Kron has many servants these days. His army is almost ready, soon he will launch a trial attack against the elves, because he thinks that to destroy them is the only way to ensure his victory." the centaur said, turning and walking away, his tail swaying as he talked. "Why would the elves defeat ensure victory for him? Where will he strike? Where is he hiding his army?" Joseph asked, taking a step towards the retreating centaur.

The centaur looked over his shoulder at Joseph. "Ask the magic." he answered.

Joseph watched the centaur disappear into the shadows and sighed wearily. "Well, that was far more information than they've given in my life time. Now we know who Kron plans to attack first." he said going to the wagon and retrieving something wrapped in a silver cloth that he had kept on his lap during the ride. He unwrapped it and I saw that it was a silver bowl that was wide and shallow. Joseph sat down with the bowl in his lap, took a sip of water from his water skin, and poured the rest of it into the bowl. The water seemed to glow with a dark green light that lit up Joseph's face as he bent over the water.

"Lord Haldor, I have news." he said to the water. I found myself edging closer for a better look, my curiosity at its peak.

For a while nothing happened, the water continued to glow, but there was no change. Joseph waited patiently. The green light suddenly got brighter, and Lord Haldor's face slowly took shape, as if he was made out of the green water.

"What is it Joseph?" he asked. His voice sounded distant, and muffled as if he was talking from under water.

"We have been fortunate enough to be visited by a centaur. He knows far more then he has said, but that is their style. What he was willing to share was that the kronlords are bitter because they are hungry from having no humans to feed on. He also said that Kron is building an army somewhere, and that he will soon attack the elves." Joseph said.

"Why the elves?" Lord Haldor asked with his usual frown.

"I don't know my lord. He just said that Kron needs to get rid of them to ensure his victory. Other than that he told me to ask the magic, whatever that means." Joseph answered.

"Very well, thank you for the update. Be careful all of you. I will be in contact soon." Lord Haldor said in a resigned tone.

The water sank back into the bowl and the light died away.

Joseph smiled when he saw that I had come right up to him. "This is a message basin. The elves taught us how to make and use them when our guild was first established. It is the easiest way to get messages across the country with speed. The elves predict that someday all humans will have a sort of message system where the words are sent through the air to places all over the world. But for now, only the elves and the rangers have the ability to communicate with each other like we just did. Come, you should go on watch now, and the rest of us should get some sleep." Joseph said, addressing the last part to everyone.

I sat in the shelter of the tall grass off to the side of the road and began my watch. It was a long night, where every gust of wind and every animal made me jumpy. Half way through my shift I was sure I could hear something huge and menacing walking towards me. I turned my head slowly and carefully so as not to be seen moving and tried to see through the trees. The sound continued, getting louder. As I started to get really nervous about the invisible stalker the pace seemed to quicken to a run. I pulled back the string of my bow slightly, and forced myself to remain calm and still. As I took several deep breaths the pace slowed down again. It was then that I realized with some embarrassment that I had been afraid of the sound of my own heartbeat. My heightened senses had made me able to hear everything that moved, which apparently included my own heart.

When the moon was half way set I carefully made my way over to Sigal to wake him for his turn. Then I went and felt Lance's face to see if the fever had died down. To my dismay, he seemed to have gotten more feverish when no one was there to ensure that he drank water. "Sigal, Lance is getting worse." I whispered as Sigal made his way over to me.

Sigal touched Lance's cheek and then felt his neck to check the speed of his pulse.

"Go wake up Ebony." he whispered, shaking Lance to try to wake him.

I made my way over to where Ebony was sleeping next to Joseph. She was curled up under her cloak, making it look like there was just a boulder if you didn't know she was there. I shook her uncertainly. I had very little experience with girls, and felt aquard touching her. But at the same time I didn't want to wake Joseph when I knew that he would have another painful ride in the wagon to endure in a few hours. Ebony lifted her head and looked at me questioningly. I put a finger to my lips and gestured for her to follow.

Sigal was sitting with Lance's head and shoulders in his lap. Lance was awake now, but seemed to not know where he was or what was going on. He was mumbling something about imps and orcs, his head moving from side to side, his face covered in sweat. Ebony pulled a sack of powder out of her bag and ordered me to get one of the wood bowls from our supplies and fill it with water. I did so, and handed it to her. She took a handful of the powder and sprinkled it into the water, making sure it was evenly dispersed throughout. Then she stirred it with her hand and brought it over to Lance.

"Make him drink this down." she told Sigal. Sigal took the bowl in one hand and propped Lance's head up with the other. Lance drank some, and then turned his head away.

"No, you can't make me. I won't do it, you can't make me drink your poison kronlord." he protested feverishly.

"Shhh, its ok Lance, just drink. You're going to be ok." Sigal whispered, trying to calm the man down. Sigal brought the bowl to Lance's lips again, but on tasting it Lance thrashed and shoved the bowl away, almost spilling it.

"No! I won't! You can't make me, I won't!" he shouted wildly.

Joseph and Fletch were awake at once, hearing Lance cry out. In the end; Sigal and Fletch held Lance's arms down, and Joseph forced his mouth open as Ebony poured the medicine down his throat. Lance was struggling and shouting, wildly trying to escape, refusing to swallow until Joseph tilted his head back, forcing him to swallow in order to get any air. I stood back and watched quietly. My heart went out to Lance, who apparently thought he was still being tortured by the kronlord. When Lance had finally finished the medicine the rangers let him go. Lance immediately curled up into a ball and shielded his head as if he expected us to beat him. Joseph signaled us to back off, and we sat a couple yards away from him, waiting for the medicine to break his fever. We rebuilt the fire which had died down to embers, and heated some water for tea. After the incident that had just happened no one felt like sleeping. Joseph's eyes were grim and distant, and he seemed lost in memory. Sigal went to hide in the bushes in case we did go back to sleep. Fletch was poking the fire with a stick until it broke. Then he just stared into the flames silently. Ebony sat rubbing her very round belly. When she saw me watching her she smiled at me, making me blush and quickly look away.

"It's not a crime to look at a girl you know." she teased softly.

I blushed harder and ducked further into my hood to hide my red cheeks.

Ebony took my hand gently and placed my palm against her stomach. "Can you feel him kicking?" she asked me with a smile.

My eyes widened as I could feel the baby moving inside her.

"It won't be long now. Just a couple weeks and he'll be born." she said gently, letting go of my hand.

"How do you know it's a he?" I asked quietly, pulling my hand away.

Ebony smiled. An elf told me; even before I knew I was pregnant she told me that I'd give birth to a son before the winter's first snow fall. My Thelmer, he was so happy that he was almost crying when I told him the news, he's such an emotional sap. He was relieved when I offered to come as the healer for this group, because he feared for me and the baby if the fortress should be breached, and our people cut down. He worries too much, my Thelmer does." she explained, becoming lost in her own thoughts.

There was silence for several minutes as everyone was absorbed in their own thoughts. Finally, Lance made his way towards us unsteadily. I jumped to my feet, and got him a cup of hot tea. He thanked me and held the cup with both hands to try to keep it still as his whole body was shaking. Some of the tea splashed onto his hands, but he didn't seem to notice despite the fact that steam was rising from the spilled beverage. Joseph gently took the cup from Lance and held it for him. Lance sipped at the tea and nodded that he'd had enough for the moment.

"When you were feverish you thought that we were a kronlord trying to poison you. Do you know why you might have thought that?" Joseph asked, getting right to the point.

Lance frowned thoughtfully. "I remember very little of what happened to me Joseph. It was early morning and I was on patrol. A swarm of imps came at me from all directions throwing ropes and nets at me as they came. They dragged me to the ground, bound and gagged me, and carried me off into the heart of the forest. There was an alter there, and they tied me to it, leaving me there alone all day. Try as hard as I could, I wasn't able to break the ropes.

After sunset they came back and lit torches, putting them all around me, and leaving again. I saw the Kronlord come, and he examined me, turning my head from side to side as if I was a calf in the marketplace. Seeming pleased with the imps offering, he started to laugh. I felt a cold terror wash over me as he looked at me with his eyes full of cruelty, and hunger. The next thing I remember I was alone in the forest, a few miles away from Stoneriver, free of the ropes, and in more pain then I had thought possible. I got to my feet and came straight to the fortress. I've told you all this already. That is all I remember." Lance said.

"If the kronlord poisoned you it's important that we know." Joseph insisted gently.

"If I knew what had happened I'd tell you. Now stop asking." Lance snapped furiously.

# CHAPTER 10

That night I had a nightmare. I found myself lying on a stone table at the foot of a statue. The statue was made of black stone and was that of a man with a cruel face and no hair. He was sitting on a throne that was made of actual skulls and bones from all sorts of different creatures. There were torches lit all around me, causing scary shadows to dance on the ground. I heard heavy footsteps, and I saw a really tall man approach me and the statue. He was huge, as tall as the statue I was laying at the foot of. He had thick black hair and a thick black beard that reached half way down his chest. His eyes were red, and glowed in the firelight. He came over to me looking smug. I tried to get up, and realized that I was tied to the table. Then I realized that I was dreaming about what Lance had been through, what he had told us about a little while ago.

The Kronlord grabbed my head and turned it from side to side, examining me with an expression on his face of mild boredom, as if I was nothing more than a fish on display at the butcher shop. He chuckled and I found myself looking into his glowing red eyes. They were full of hunger, and greed. The Kronlord took a flask out of his robe removed the gag from my mouth, and shoved the flask between my jaws. The liquid burned as it went down my throat. Even though I knew that the liquid was poison, I found myself unable to resist swallowing it. After the flask was empty, the Kronlord laughed again. He pulled a small potion bottle from his pocket and opened it with his teeth, spitting the cork out onto the ground. "Here comes another one ranger. Open wide." He mocked me as he forced the potion down my throat, holding my head still with his free hand.

When he was done poisoning me he laughed, his eyes growing more hungry, and more blood red in color. "Look over here, human." He ordered, pointing to his eyes. I stared at them, transfixed and powerless to look away. He took a deep breath as if he was about to take a giant dip under water. I found myself screaming as it felt like every nerve in my body was being ripped right through my skin. But the scream wasn't mine, it was deeper, stronger, it was Lance. He was the one who had gone through this.

I woke up to see Sigal was just coming over to wake me, so we could get going. I got to my feet and wondered if I should tell everyone about my dream. But I dismissed the idea, deciding that no one needed to know that I was having nightmares. I remembered Lyle talking about how he didn't want to scare me with his stories, and decided that I wasn't going to let people think I couldn't even handle Lance talking about what had happened. "It was just a dream." I told myself as I was handed some dried meat to eat for breakfast.

The next night I didn't sleep at all. I lay awake watching everyone sleep. Somehow I knew that if I were to fall asleep, I'd have that nightmare again, so I lay there awake, thinking over what I had dreamed about. I was lying next to Lance, and I found myself slipping my hand into his, wanting to comfort him, wanting him to know that I knew what he had gone through. Lance sighed in his sleep, and closed his hand around mine, the tense look on his face relaxing into peaceful sleep, without pain.

We reached the point in the road I'd been dreading, the area that was closest to the healing house, where Sigal was going to leave us to continue on down the road in case the wagon was being followed. The part of the woods looked no different than any other section we'd passed while traveling on the road through the mountain forests. I looked hard for the hidden signal that told Sigal that we were at the right place. As we had been riding, Joseph had been teaching me about rangers and their carefully disguised ways of communicating. I knew he was talking mostly so he could distract himself from the pain, but I soaked in the information eagerly. So as Sigal helped the injured out of the wagon I looked around for anything that seemed like it didn't belong.

Finally, as Sigal was helping Joseph who was the last one to leave the wagon, I noticed two fallen branches laying next to a rock that were a little too perfectly placed pointing in the same direction to have happened by accident. Looking up I saw that there were no trees near enough for them to have fallen off of that would land them exactly there.

"You have good eyes little one. I've never seen someone with so little training be able to spot ranger coded messages in the wild."

I looked up at Lance who was also looking at the branches. "Two medium size branches next to a rock mean that there is shelter at a forty five degree angle to the right of where the branches are pointing, two days away." Lance murmured to me.

Sigal jumped back onto the wagon seat and rode off, continuing north. Joseph led the way into the trees following the directions the branches were pointing in. He reminded us to step only where he stepped, exactly where he stepped, and to make no sound. The pace we went was about right by normal standards, but was slow for rangers. We went in single file, with Lance taking up the rear, carefully making sure to step exactly where the person in front stepped. Unlike when we had been traveling with Lord Haldor, we went in a straight line, not dodging from shadow to shadow.

When we went through a muddy area I understood the wisdom behind this method of walking. By all stepping in the same footprint it made it harder for anyone who might be following to know how many people there were. It also made sense now why Lance was last. He was taller and more muscular then the rest of us, and his feet bigger. When he stepped onto the footprints his big feet and weight erased any indication that there were multiple people, leaving the trail looking like there was just one man traveling at a normal speed through the forest covered mountains.

The sky above us was heavy with clouds, and around sunset it opened up as if it couldn't hold back one more second. I pulled my hood forward more so my face was better covered, and found to my surprise that the water soaked into the cloak, but didn't make me wet. As I was wondering what the cloak was made of that caused it to absorb water, but not make the wearer any colder or more damp, Joseph beckoned us to him to talk.

"My strength is waning, I am nearly spent. But the heavy rain offers us an opportunity to go faster with less chance of being hunted, as any tracks we leave will be washed away. We have so far been going deliberately in an off course angle, but if we use the rain to our advantage we can shake off any pursuit and make straight for the healing house. How is everyone holding up?" Joseph asked, looking from one injured companion to another.

Everyone looked tired but determined as they understood the rare opportunity to shake off pursuit. With the ground being as soft and muddy as it had been all day, it would not take an incredibly skilled hunter to follow our carefully disguised tracks.

Joseph lit an oil lamp and led the way through the driving rain. The pace was now the almost running pace that I had gotten use to from rangers who were traveling on foot. For a time, I was able to keep up with the group. But I had not slept the night before, since my mind had been so busy wondering what Lance had been put through, and the lack of sleep was conquering me. It just wasn't possible for me to keep up with the rapid pace without any sleep. I tried to force myself to keep going, determined not to give up. I tapped into the magic, as was becoming habit, and pressed on. But eventually my legs gave out, and I fell face first into the mud, too tired to move, or even cry out to the lit lamp light that was still going at the rapid pace, getting further and further away.

Suddenly I felt strong arms lift me, and I found myself being carried like a small child. I wrapped my arms around Lance's neck, and tried to stay awake. But my body won the struggle, and I fell asleep, my head resting against Lance's shoulder as if I was five years old again, being carried home by my father after a long day of excitement. Almost immediately the nightmare from the other night took hold, and I found myself reliving it again, unable to stop the chain of events that I knew were coming.

\*\*\*

When I woke up I was surprised to find that we had arrived at the healing house. Everyone was taking off their soaked cloaks and throwing them into a pile.

"We have made good time. Now that our guard dog pup is awake perhaps he wouldn't mind doing a few chores so the rest of us can rest at last?" Joseph said smiling at me. My face flushed with embarrassment and I rushed forward to light a fire in the fireplace Joseph was pointing to. Why was I sleeping so much?

I puzzled over this question as I bustled around the small kitchen making hot stew using the dried meats and vegetables and powdered spices that were stored for use in the event that someone decided to stay here for a time. There were barrels of food in the store room off the kitchen, enough to last for months. In the main room, the older rangers had sagged exhausted into the comfortable chairs around the fire. They had walked all night, and the sun was setting on yet another day when we arrived. Somehow I had slept through all of it, and they had somehow managed to keep on going without rest.

When the stew was ready, the others joined me in the kitchen; sitting on the stools around the table. I served the food and poured tea for everyone. They all appreciated the hot food after the long cold rain, even if the cloaks did keep us from getting wet.

"You're an impressive cook for a boy." Ebony complimented me as she helped herself to the last of the stew (the men had all had multiple helpings already, and I was fine with just one serving since I had been sleeping, not walking).

I smiled at the praise. My father had taught me how to cook. Cooking was one of the only things I had in common with him since he had always been busy in the workshop, or doing errands, leaving Kevin to teach me the skills Lord Haldor had insisted I learn. I could remember many afternoons spent with my father as he taught me the secrets to making even the most common meals taste wonderful.

I studied the faces of the rangers while I had the opportunity. Our cloaks were hanging up near the fire in the main room to dry, so I had a rare chance to see the faces of my companions fully. Ebony's hair was black and full of curls that bounced and swayed in their ponytail when she moved her head. Her nose and cheeks had a few light freckles, and she seemed to have a never ending smile in her brown eyes. Lance had brown, shoulder length hair and reminded me of my brother John, but Lance had no beard. I could see that the bruises really were all over, even on his ears. They continued down his neck, to be hidden from view under his shirt. They had gone from dark purple to a lighter shade, healing as some of his strength returned to him. Joseph had black hair, but it was even shaggier then I had thought that night I first met him. Where the others looked like they at least occasionally brushed their hair when they had the chance, Joseph let his hair do whatever it wanted. Fletch had graying hair and several scars on his beardless face. His expression was grim, and he looked as if he had never smiled in his life. His lips were thin, and his skin pale. He narrowed his eyes at me when he noticed me looking at him, and I hastily looked back at my food, intimidated by his serious mannerisms.

Most of the rangers went right to bed after supper, leaving me to clean up the dishes. But Joseph stayed up and helped me clean. Afterwards Joseph invited me to join him and we sat in the main room near the fire with our tea.

"As much as I regret not being able to do my rightful duties to my people, I can't help but feel peaceful here." Joseph told me. "This place is protected by magic, no one but an elf or a ranger can come at us here. We are completely invisible to any unfriendly eyes." Joseph explained, looking out at the darkness outside.

When I didn't say anything Joseph looked at me with concern.

"What's on your mind Peter?" he asked me, taking a sip of his tea.

"It's just that, well...I let everyone down sir." I explained, my shame causing a lump to rise in my throat.

"Did you indeed? Have you asked everyone had had them tell you so?" Joseph asked, his tone amused.

"No, but I fell asleep on the job! You brought me along to help and I fell asleep, making it so Lance had to carry me." I said, slightly distressed that Joseph wasn't taking me seriously.

"That was my fault Peter." Joseph explained, his amused tone fading as he saw how upset I was.

"Your..." I started to ask, completely confused.

"I pushed you far too hard. No first year ranger apprentice could possibly be expected to keep up with the pace I set. But I knew that the rain offered us a chance to get here much faster and safer then we could have gone if we had stopped to rest. In my eagerness to get to safety I forgot that there was a child in our ranks who would need to be accommodated."

I was about to protest to being considered a child, but Joseph held up his hand, and I closed my mouth again.

"The reason Lord Haldor was planning on having you stay with your other year mates instead of throwing you right into prodigy training was because your body isn't able to keep up with full rangers yet. Yes, you have a special connection with your powers, but they are still new to your body. You need time to adapt. If Lord Haldor had brought you to us as soon as he had gained custody of you then perhaps things would be different, you might have been able to keep up far better. But Haldor learned that it is best not to tear a child away from their parents too young when he took Thelmer. Thelmer cried himself to sleep for a month after he went away from home, and when he got word that his mother died, he didn't talk to anyone, not even to me, for over half a year. Yes, he had built up stamina very early, but at great personal cost. We didn't want to do that to you, and I should have remembered that you were nowhere near ready to stay awake for days and days without sleep. I became so use to Thelmer that I forgot that you only just joined us." Joseph explained.

I sat processing that information. I remembered Thelmer telling me about his mom, and about how homesick he had been. At the time, I had just assumed that he had been my age. "How old was he?" I asked softly.

"Eight. Haldor saw Thelmer fighting against some bully squires of Sir Lucas' and defeating them without being hurt himself, even though they were twice his age. His majesty had already given Lord Haldor permission to choose any youths he saw potential in, so he took out a claim on Thelmer almost at once. I wasn't there at the time; I was in the forest of Brune doing an archery exercise with a host of other rangers. Lord Haldor trained Thelmer himself for a few months, and then he brought the boy to me, knowing that I have a talent at connecting with apprentices. He felt that Thelmer needed a parental figure, so asked me to train him. We've been traveling together ever since, and now that Thelmer is a ranger, Haldor asked me to train you, since I myself went through prodigy training and so am most qualified to train others."

"So is that why you brought me here, because Lord Haldor gave me to you?" I asked, feeling a bit like a piece of luggage.

"No. I brought you here because we needed someone here who can help us, someone who is healthy and uninjured. Lord Haldor recommended you since he didn't want your training to be put on hold, and as Sigal pointed out, you already know everything your year mates are being taught at the capital. If you don't keep your magic exercised it will die." Joseph answered firmly.

"So how come Lord Haldor sent you to go get the new apprentices?" I asked.

"Because, as I said, I have a special bond with children. Take your own experience for example. You were clinging to your father, yet you took my hand and let me lead you away from everything you knew. If I hadn't been there, it might have been much harder on you. Lord Haldor, as much as I love him dearly, is quite intimidating until you get to know him. He realized this when he took Thelmer, and so made sure to bring someone who wouldn't scare you as much. I was going to train both you and Gene for the first year, and then have Gene work with the girls when you had built up enough stamina to be able to travel with me. We figured the transition would be easier for you that way. But open war changes everything, as you can see."

Joseph and I went to bed soon after our talk. I felt tired again, having received so much information to think about. Joseph led me into one of the rooms in back. There were two bunk beds there. Lance and Fletch were asleep on one of them, and Joseph and I took the other one. Ebony had been given the "Doctor's room" as it was called. It was a room where there was just one bed. It was reserved for the doctor, since it was the doctor who would have the most work to do healing anyone who came here sick or injured. As she was the only girl, it made sense to let her have that room. Before Joseph went to sleep he checked on Lance, and cursed under his breath when he found out that Lance's fever was coming back. But it was far less serious than it had been the other night, so Joseph gave him some water to drink, and decided that would be enough until morning.

I had the nightmare yet again, and woke up frustrated at myself. I couldn't believe that I was being such a child, scared from just being told about what had happened. But I didn't feel scared, if anything, I felt angry, as if I wanted to give the Kronlord a piece of my mind. A large part of me had the strange urge to go and sit next to Lance, but I dismissed the idea. I was way too old to be feeling like this. I turned over, and made myself go back to sleep, telling myself to grow up.

# CHAPTER 11

When I woke up I groaned and scrambled out of bed. Everyone else seemed to already be up, and their beds were neatly made. I hurriedly got ready, and went into the main room. Then I realized that it was just now dawn, and calmed down a bit. At least I hadn't overslept by too much. Joseph, Lance, and Fletch were sitting in the far corner of the main room, huddled around the message basin, listening to someone talk. Before I could decide what I should be doing, Ebony came out of the kitchen and came over to me. "Come help me in the kitchen, the rangers will tell us what apprentices' need to know when they've finished." she told me in a low voice.

Before I could decide whether or not to protest, Joseph looked up at us, and beckoned me over. "It's ok Ebony, Peter is like Thelmer, he may join us if he wants." he said with a kind smile.

Ebony nodded, and returned to the kitchen without further comment.

Feeling suddenly special, I went and sat next to Joseph.

"Shall I continue, or start over?" the disapproving face of Lord Haldor asked from the green water.

"Sorry Sir, but Peter should be able to hear this from you himself." Joseph explained, apparently unaffected by the disapproving frown on Lord Haldor's face.

"As I was telling those who actually woke up ON TIME today, I have arranged for Kevin to go to the healing house so you and Joseph can make your way to the capital. Something has come up that needs to be taken care of, and I need Joseph here. You will go with him to continue your training." Lord Haldor told me. Then he addressed Joseph. "Take the mountain road and head east to the capital. Stop in each town, village, and city and tell them the recruitment message. This way it saves someone else from having to do that route, and will ensure you time to heal less painfully, as you'll be staying in the inn for a few days a piece while you enable the town's reserves for battle."

"My Lord, the city of Askia is on that route." Joseph pointed out, unable to hide the tension in his voice.

I glanced at Joseph. Askia was where Sir Lucas' castle was.

Lord Haldor's frown deepened, and there was a fierce anger in his eyes that was evident despite the fact that his face was shaped out of the green water. "I have spoken to the king about the incident in September. From now on, anyone who attacks a ranger, regardless of rank or reason will be executed as traitors to the country, and rangers have been given permission to fight back to the death. Lucas is NOT going to attack you again, he wouldn't dare. If he does, he faces execution, either by Peter's hands, or the kings'." Lord Haldor informed Joseph.

"ME?!" I exclaimed, surprised.

"You are to look after Joseph while he is hurt. If anyone gives him trouble, you be there to back him up. Now that Thelmer is a ranger, you are Joseph's apprentice, so act like it. Stick with him, and help him do his job." Lord Haldor informed me.

I sat there, distressed at the thought of being expected to kill someone if they attacked Joseph. Joseph bowed his head in acceptance, swallowing hard at the news of the new law.

"Kevin should arrive within a week; he'll be bringing money for you. If you need more for whatever reason, send word. Kevin is bringing a message basin with him, so you take this one, and I'll see you in a month or so."

Lord Haldor's face started to sink back into the water, but Joseph quickly interrupted. "My Lord, we think Lance has been poisoned by the Kronlord."

The water took form as Haldor's face again, and he frowned deeply.

"Why do you think that?" he asked, glancing at Lance. "Oh, I see." Haldor said softly, as he saw Lance's face.

I glanced over at Lance, who was sitting next to me. He looked even worse than he had looked when I had first seen him in the dining room of the fortress. His face was pale, making the bruises seem even darker on his skin, and he was sweating like rain, leaning against Fletch's good arm, barely aware of what was going on around him. Lord Haldor sighed in an exhausted way. "I'll make sure Kevin brings the antidotes to all of Kron's known poisons. Meanwhile, Lance, get yourself back to bed at once! The more you fight Kron's poisons, the stronger they get. Lie down, and stay down before you kill yourself." Lord Haldor told Lance firmly.

Lance didn't seem to hear Lord Haldor; he just stared numbly at the message basin, his eyes glassy.

Joseph started to rise to his feet. "Not you, you have three cracked ribs, you can't support him!" Lord Haldor snapped.

Fletch got to his feet, and with a grunt, dragged Lance up with him. I hurriedly got up and held the door to the back room open as Fletch made his way over, half carrying Lance with him.

As Fletch lay Lance down on the bottom bunk where he had slept last night, Lance started mumbling in protest. "I need to see what Lord Haldor's message is." He told Fletch feverishly.

"Lord Haldor already gave us the message. His message was that you need to stay in bed." Fletch answered, putting the covers on Lance.

"No, I need to patrol. I'm late for patrol; I was supposed to start before dawn. Joseph will be mad at me if I don't patrol." Lance said, throwing back the covers, and trying to get out of bed.

"It's your day off Lance, just rest." Fletch insisted, pushing Lance back down again with so much force that the straw mattress shook.

"Lord Haldor's coming with his new prodigy today. I need to be there to tell him. I need to tell Haldor." Lance insisted, feverishly shoving Fletch back a step.

"I'll tell Lord Haldor. What is the message?" Fletch insisted, his calm tone growing strained as Lance continued to resist him.

"Tell Lord Haldor...tell him." Lance murmured, too weak to keep fighting. He was fading into unconsciousness, but was desperately trying to continue speaking.

"Sure, Lance, what should I tell him?" Fletch asked.

"Tell him the imps are acting strange. I think they're planning another village raid soon. They've been watching me, trying to learn my patrol route. Tell Lord Haldor, the imps..." Lance fell silent as he lost consciousness.

"How is he?" Lord Haldor asked when Fletch and I rejoined Joseph at the message basin.

"He's delusional my Lord. He thinks it's still September and that you are going to meet him during his patrol today. He said to tell you the imps are acting strange."

"Delusions, loss of memory, fever... that can only be Kaltya poisoning. I'll make sure you get the antidote." Lord Haldor promised, as the water sank back into flatness, and the green light died away.

\*\*\*

"Kaltya, of course." Joseph breathed to himself.

"What is Kaltya?" I asked, following Joseph as he went outside to dump out the extra water from the basin.

"Joseph looked down at me, frowning thoughtfully. "Nothing that you should be worrying about at your age, you have bigger things to do right now." he said.

"Like what?" I asked, wondering if I had exceeded my limit of receiving information.

"You see that water barrel?" Joseph asked me, pointing out the large barrel that held the days water for the cottage. "Fill it. The well is behind the back. You see that fire wood? Cut it, and bring it into the main room. You see the main room? Sweep and dust it, mop the floor. Ebony will give you your lunch later. You already missed breakfast."

I suppressed the urge to sigh as Joseph went back into the cottage. I realized that I had a busy day ahead of me. After all, Joseph HAD told me that I had been brought along because they needed someone healthy to take care of things. Apparently what he had meant was house chores.

After supper, Joseph helped me feed Lance. Feeding Lance was a two person job. Whenever Lance was awake, he tried to get out of bed to go patrolling. So I held the bowl of mash and chicken, and Joseph sat on Lance's legs and spoon fed him. After Lance had eaten, Fletch came in to go to bed, so Joseph and I went out to the main room and sat by the fire. Ebony had gone to bed as well, so it was just Joseph and me again, like the night before.

"Sorry I was short with you today, making you do jobs that didn't need doing. It's just that Kaltya is a very nasty poison, and my mind was worried." Joseph told me once he had the fire blazing warm.

I shrugged in response. It was irritating to be doing house chores all day, with Joseph coming up with more and more of them to keep me busy with, until the cottage was cleaned to within an inch of its life. But at the same time, I knew that Joseph couldn't possibly make me do it again tomorrow, since I had done such a good job.

"So what IS Kaltya?" I asked, wondering if I was pushing my luck asking a question I had already been rejected an answer to.

"A cursed plant." Joseph answered shortly.

Glancing at him I noticed that he was sitting stiffly, and frowning slightly at me. I searched my mind for a different topic, knowing that if I pressed Joseph any further I'd be in trouble. "So what will happen when we get to the towns on the way to the capital?"

Joseph's tense posture relaxed, and he sat back in his chair. "The king has been sending rangers to the entire kingdom to assemble the army. In each town, all the young to middle aged men who are strong enough to fight will be summoned to join the army. Unless they have a specific specialty such as archery, they will make their way to training camps where they will learn the skills needed for battle. Once they are trained they will be sent to wherever they are most needed. Those who are already trained, the knights, the town guards, and the reserves, will train those who need training. The border guard part of the army is of course already active, and they will likely be getting more members soon, once the men are trained. Craftsmen will be working overtime to build weapons and other supplies used in battle, and each farm will have to turn in forty five percent of their harvest instead of the usual twenty percent."

"You said young men... will that include my brothers?" I asked quietly.

Joseph looked at me with understanding and sympathy. "Up to two men from each household may be chosen. Usually they try to pick people whose families can still manage to support themselves in the man's absence, which unfortunately, would be your family. Your brother Kevin of course will be one of them, as he is a captain of the town guards. I don't know which other brother the ranger who lives in your town will choose." he said kindly.

I sat in silence for a while, staring into the fire. Kevin would never be willing to be left behind, even if he wasn't required to fight as a town guard. But what about the others? John was stronger, more muscular, but Andrew was more lively and energetic. So which one would have to go to war?

"I wish none of them had to go." I admitted softly, a lump rising in my throat.

Joseph reached out, and put a hand on my knee, wincing slightly from the pain it caused to his ribs from bending over. "Your family lives on the east side of the great river. They might not have to go to battle right away. The longer they get to wait to go to war, the better trained they'll be, and the better chance they have of surviving." he told me. I nodded, but all I could picture was a battle field after the battle was over, with bodies everywhere. Three of those bodies had the faces of my brothers in my imagined scene, and they lay there, with arrows sticking out of them, dead. I shuddered at the thought, and buried my face in my hands, trying to get rid of the image.

"It's not fair! Why should they have to go to war? What does Kron want anyways?! Why does he want to kill people?" I moaned.

Kron is a devil. He wants to kill people because people are good, and refuse to worship him. I know war is horrible. Believe me, I have seen people be cut down in front of and beside me, I know how bad war can be. But we beat Kron back before, and we can do it again. If he really does attack the elves first, that will give our army more time to prepare, and the rangers will be sent to help the elves, because elves won't accept help from other humans. Kron won't be able to defeat us." Joseph told me firmly.

Suddenly, something stirred in my head. "Waite, what do you mean the ranger who lives in my town? We don't have a ranger in my town." I said confused.

"Yes you do. You've met him many times before; he's been keeping an eye on you for Lord Haldor." Joseph said, looking at me confused.

I shook my head firmly. "I've never seen a ranger before the night you guys came to get me." I insisted.

Joseph looked surprised. Carl taught you how to read, but never told you he was a ranger?!" he asked.

Now it was my turn to be surprised. Carl was Kevin's boss, one of the overseers of the town guards. He had taught me my letters, and how to use maps. He had also let me watch the town guards do their drills, giving me tips and tricks for sword fighting in close combat.

But I had never had any idea that he was a ranger, I hadn't even known there was any such thing as a ranger. I had always assumed Carl was a knight, especially after he took Kevin under his wings. "Why didn't he wear a cloak?" I asked, feeling numb with shock.

"Because he's retired. People do retire when they get old you know. But as a ranger, you never really stop working. There is a ranger in almost every big town, and usually more than one per city. We're the elite force of the army, it's our job to uphold law and order for the king. Carl never told you? Well, that explains why you asked Haldor what a ranger was. I had wondered about that." Joseph said, still looking incredulous.

I shook my head, at a loss for words.

# CHAPTER 12

Joseph woke me up from the nightmare that had been plaguing me whenever I slept by putting a hand over my mouth. He put a finger to his lips to warn me to keep quiet so I wouldn't wake Lance who was tossing and turning in his feverish sleep, and motioned for me to follow him. Joseph led me outside into the cold night air. The moon had set and it was utterly dark. My eyes could still see, thanks to the light coming out the window from the main room fireplace.

"What's going on?" I asked, shivering slightly in the cold as Joseph softly shut the door behind us.

"I'm going to teach you about night life. Most of the dark creatures prefer to roam at night, so it's important for you to learn how to track them through the dark."

"There are evil creatures out here, near the healing house?" I asked nervously.

"No, so I've had to improvise. I've spent the last few hours creating tracks that look like the most common dark beings, imps and orcs. So let's go learn, shall we?"

Joseph lit a small torch, and led the way along the "orc trail" first, since it was the most easy to follow. The ground was trampled and stomped down with many heavy footed tracks. Joseph showed me how to hunt with complete silence, stepping carefully so that I wouldn't even rustle the leaves on the ground. He had me keep an arrow ready to hand, but cautioned me not to shoot unless there was certain danger. Joseph told me that if a ranger is hunting a dark creature, chances were strong that if I was in the forest or the mountains, the elves would also be hunting. If they saw a ranger, they'd likely stop to compare notes. As we walked, Joseph also taught me about nocturnal animals, and how to recognize their tracks as well.

The imp trail was not nearly as obvious. The prints were small, and much harder to see in the dark. The imps didn't wear shoes, and were most distinguishable in the wild by their three pointy toes, and dragging tail. Joseph reminded me that imps tracks wouldn't be half as deep as the makeshift ones he had made by shaping wood models and tying them to the bottom of his boots. At first I followed the wide zigzag pattern the tracks were going in until Joseph pointed out to me that I'd save time and energy if I followed the ultimate direction the trail was headed.

"Why do they zigzag like that then?" I asked, accepting the correction to my tracking technique.

"Because, they are like… Will-o-wisps. They like… to get people lost." Joseph explained, his breathing shallow as the long night of work he had put in despite his injuries caught up to him suddenly.

Joseph signaled that he needed to rest, and sat down carefully. He put a hand to his ribs and closed his eyes, waiting until he was able to breathe normally again. He took slow careful breaths, trying not to cause more pain to his chest. I stood watching him apprehensively. After several minutes I wondered if I should go for help. But just as I was going to ask, Joseph opened his eyes and got carefully back to his feet, using his walking stick as a crutch.

"I'm alright." He assured me. "I just need to remember that I am hurt and so need to pace myself better. If I don't start taking more care of myself, I'll be as bad off as a first year apprentice."

"What do you mean by that?" I asked as we set off slowly for the healing house, Joseph leaning heavily on me and his walking stick.

"Magic is very willing to work with you, but it refuses to let you push it too far. The magic has free reign of a ranger's body. It has to, so it can help us in all areas possible. If we push the magic, demand that it do too much, it pushes back. The result is that you end up sleeping for several days, or until the magic feels that it has made its point. Magic is very nice, but we are still humans, and humans don't have unlimited stamina. Not even with magic helping us." Joseph explained.

"How come Lord Haldor didn't warn me of that?" I asked, finally understanding why I'd been sleeping so much.

Joseph shrugged. "Lord Haldor is of the opinion that the burned hand teaches best." He explained with a slight smile, his eyes going distant as if recalling a fond memory.

"I don't understand sir." I admitted as we reached the healing house. The sky was slightly less dark, the pre-dawn color I had gotten used to as the time of day rangers woke up.

"You can tell a small child as many times as you want, to not touch the fire, pretty as it may look. But a child won't really understand why not, until they try it despite your warnings. Once the child feels how much fire hurts, then the lesson sinks in, and they are careful from then on. On the same note, Lord Haldor believes that if you let the apprentices' find out on their own that magic doesn't make them Gods and that they need to rest, they will learn the lesson far better than if they are just told to slow down." Joseph told me as he took his usual chair by the embers that were still glowing in the fireplace.

"But you told me." I said, mostly thinking out loud as I rebuilt the fire.

"It takes most apprentices' several months before they learn their body's limits, and how to pace themselves properly. Prodigies like you and I take even longer since we have so much more potential uses to develop through the magic. The excitement often blinds people to what otherwise should be obvious, at least it did for me when I first started. I don't have several months to wait for you to learn on your own. As soon as Kevin arrives we must be off, and I can't afford you time to pass out on me for days at a time." Joseph explained as he watched me rebuild the fire.

I was glad my hood hid my red face. I knew Joseph hadn't meant what he said to be mean or embarrassing to me. He was just stating facts in his usual way. But all the same, I felt humiliated at the fact that Joseph seemed to expect me to keep sleeping for days at a time. As Ebony entered the main room and greeted us cheerfully, it dawned on me that if Joseph hadn't told me, I probably would have kept pushing myself too far. But now I knew better, and I'd make sure to pay more attention to the magic, and to my body's signals for rest.

After Lord Haldor gave Joseph the daily update, Joseph went to go sleep for a few hours. As I sat eating breakfast with Ebony and Fletch I wondered what I was supposed to do now. Joseph hadn't really left any instructions for me. So I cleaned up after the meal, and made sure there was plenty of water and firewood. I helped Ebony fill the tub with cold water and helped Fletch get Lance into it, to try to keep Lance from dying of fever. Then I ran out of things to do. Ebony was watching over Lance, and Fletch sat down to stare into the fire, ignoring me.

Having been given nothing to do, I wandered outside and sat down next to the well. At home in my father's town I had always had loads of things to keep me busy. There were other boys to play with, and training to do. If worse came to worse, there were always lots of blacksmith chores that needed doing. But out here, there was nothing. Ebony was busy taking care of Lance, and I didn't really play with girls anyways. In my father's town, it was inappropriate for girls and boys to play together at my age. Lance was sick, Joseph was sleeping, and Fletch obviously wanted to be left alone. Besides, I had heard Fletch grumbling the other day to Joseph that he hated kids anyways, so I wasn't in any hurry to look to him for company. So for the first time in my life, I had nothing to do. I had never been left to my own devices, so I had never really learned how to keep myself entertained.

I got the cover to the water barrel and propped it against a tree. I decided that since everyone said I needed to keep the magic exercised, it would be good to get some practice in. I lay down on the ground, and took out my bow. I had lost the most points in the archery practice I had done with Gene when it came to shooting while lying down. So I decided to start there. In my mind, I asked the magic to help. I was amazed to find that the magic responded almost instantly. My eyes sharpened, my hands became more balanced, and my arms stronger almost at once. I found myself able to shoot as easily as if I had been standing up. I shot a few arrows at the center of the barrel cover, and then I decided to see just how good I could get. So I started to use the arrows to create a picture. I left the three arrows in the center, and added eyes and a bunch of arrows in a curved line for a smile. I got to my feet, excited and pleased with the magic's willingness to help me excel.

I stood for a moment wondering if I could keep testing myself. After all, I had been using the magic already today, when I was learning from Joseph a few hours ago. I wondered how I would know if I was pushing the magic too far. I remembered that I had been completely exhausted right before I slept for several days, and wondered if that was the magic's way of telling me to stop. I decided that it might be, and also knew that I felt full of energy right now. So I took out my sword from its sheath and examined it. It was sized so that it was equivalent to a long sword in regards to my own height. I smiled to myself. I was really good at sword fighting even against Carl, who was apparently a retired ranger. I had often wondered if he was holding back when dueling with me, but he had always promised that he wasn't. I gripped my sword in the way Kevin had taught me, and began to practice with it. The magic helped me go faster and faster. I was careful to not get carried away and start swinging wildly. My movements were controlled, and I used the fighting techniques I had been taught, seeing how fast I could go, and adding extra moves into the standard patterns, moves that would be deadly to my opponent.

I was really excited at how awesome the magic was. But after an hour I forced myself to stop and take a break. I drew some water to drink, and sat down with my back against the well. The autumn was evident in the golden and red colored leaves. The air was a crisp cold, pleasant to feel, unlike the often painful cold of winter. The morning sun reflected off the leaves, making the area look beautiful. I sat for several minutes admiring the simple beauty of the area. I watched the leaves fall and get carried away south by the cold wind. As boredom and restlessness started to set in I heard the cabin door open and shut. I got up to find Fletch waiting for me.

"Lord Haldor wants you to learn how to fight to defend yourself, since you're going to Askia. We don't THINK anyone would attack you with the new law, but you never know." He informed me. "How much do you know about self defense? You're small; chances are you've had to defend yourself before. How well did you do?"

I bit my lip and didn't answer. I had taught myself how to hide from people and make hasty escapes because I was afraid of fighting. I always made sure to stay with my brothers when possible, and when I had to go through town alone, I made sure to stay away from the bigger boys.

Fletch made a noise of disgust, apparently realizing what my silence meant.

"So you know nothing then?" He snapped at me, exasperated.

Instead of waiting for an answer, Fletch turned and led me to a clear area where there was a large gap in the trees.

"Well, I guess I won't have to un-teach your bad techniques then." He said looking down at me in disapproval. "I suppose that MIGHT make things easier."

Fletch held up the little finger of his good hand. "If you know what you're doing, you can drop a man to the ground with one finger. Have you ever heard of pressure points boy?"

I shook my head, still trying to imagine how you could accomplish such a thing with just a single finger. Fletch advanced on me, and I found myself backing away nervously.

"I'm not going to harm you lad." Fletch promised, making an obvious attempt to soften his gruff tone.

I stood still, and waited apprehensively to see what he was going to do. Fletch pressed his finger into a specific spot between my shoulder and neck. It was only a little painful, and I felt my knees bend. Sure enough, I was brought to the ground by one finger. I jumped to my feet, eager to learn that trick. Fletch had me take off my cloak, and spent the next hour or so showing me how to use pressure points to give me an advantage.

We stopped for a food break, and sat outside with dried fruit and some dried meats. As we ate, Fletch's tone became more serious again. "Pressure points work well if you can reach them, and if there is only one opponent armed with just his own body strength. But that is rare. If you are ambushed, there is little time to try to find the exact location that will disarm your foe. Fortunately, the human body offers other weak spots. The eyes, the throat, the back of the head, the back of the knees, and the groin. If you strike those, and strike hard, you may not have to strike more than once."

Fletch got up and started to show me how to hit those areas to the best defense. I learned that if you hit a man in the right spot of the throat you could paralyze him. Different blows to the different parts of the head would cause different reactions. Fletch also taught me how to knock the wind out of a person, and the best spots on the leg to strike to stop your opponent from being able to chase you. I listened and learned silently, nodding to show I understood. I hated the idea of fighting, of hurting other people. I knew that it was important, but I didn't think I'd be able to do it. Fletch ended the lesson by saying "Of course, we provide you with weapons from the very beginning. So if you have any skill with them, which you proved that you did this morning, then no one will be able to get in close enough to attack you. Whatever happens, keep yourself safe. Don't worry about the state you leave your opponent in, if they are foolish enough to attack a ranger, then they deserve whatever state you leave them in, even if it's death."

# CHAPTER 13

Ebony's baby came. She had spent the day in the wash room with Lance, pouring the cold water on him despite his protests that the water felt like liquid fire. Joseph insisted that we needed to keep Lance as cool as possible until the antidote arrived. Lance seemed to be aware of what was going on, and didn't fight Ebony, understanding that she was trying to help. When I peeked into the wash room after supper, Lance had a look on his face of utter agony. It was as if he really was being tortured by the cold water, but he seemed to understand the need for it, so he endured the pain it caused.

I heard someone approaching me quickly, and before I could turn around, I was yanked away from the wash room door by the scruff of the neck.

"That is NOT a sight you should be seeing at your age. You are far too young for such things." Joseph told me harshly, dragging me to the other side of the main room by my cloak. He pulled me around so I was facing him, and he grabbed my shoulders, looking down at me, firm and angry. "Stay away from Lance. We'll take care of him. There is no need for your sheltered thoughts to be broken at thirteen years of age. You sit down, and do as you're told."

I sat down in my usual chair by the fire meekly. I'd never had Joseph this upset at me before. I couldn't for the life of me understand why he was so determined to keep me from knowing what Lance was going through. But I didn't dare ask now. As Joseph continued to glare at me, I lowered my eyes, and stared at my hands that were resting on my lap.

"I thought I made it clear to you that I don't want you to worry about Kaltya. You are far too young to worry about such dark things!" Joseph scolded.

"Yes sir." I said quietly, still staring at my hands.

"Then why are you so eager to find out about it?" Joseph insisted.

I twisted my hands in my lap, trying to come up with an answer.

"Joseph!" Fletch called from the wash room.

Joseph made his way over as Fletch lead Ebony out of the room. She was breathing rapidly, and protesting. "It's too soon! It hasn't been nine months yet! This can't be happening, he'll be too small."

"Nine months is an estimate Ebony, not a time frame set in stone. It's been over eight months, so it isn't unexpected that the baby is ready." Joseph explained in the soft calm tone of voice that he usually used. "Fletch, see if you can use the message basin to get Thelmer. He can't be here physically, but he should be part of this, it's his child. Peter, have you ever helped with a birth before?" Joseph asked me.

"NO!" I exclaimed, shocked at the thought. Birth was a private family matter. There were no girls at all in my family, and my brothers were unmarried. Besides, birth was a private thing between the mother and the midwife, Joseph didn't really expect ME to…"

"Well, then it's about time you did. Go get the spare clean towels from the storage room, also the sheets and pillow from the doctor's room. Then get a bucket of water."

I hurried away, my mind racing with surprise and confusion. When I came back, Joseph and Fletch spread the sheets out in the middle of the room, and had Ebony lay down. "Shouldn't we have a midwife?" I asked hesitantly as Joseph and Fletch helped Ebony get undressed. Fletch looked up at me annoyed. "Do you see any other woman here boy? Or maybe you'd like to tell the kid to wait and not be born for a few weeks until we can find one?"

"Fletch!" Joseph snapped, frowning and shaking his head. "He's just a child; let him grow up before you decide if he's foolish. It's different with rangers Peter. Believe me; if we were at the fortress she'd have a midwife."

"Oh! It hurts, I can feel it, oww!" Ebony cried breathing rapidly.

"It's ok, Ebony. Just breathe. Slow deliberate breathes, just like you were taught." Thelmer's voice said from the message basin.

"Thelmer, Thelmer, I wish you were here!" Ebony said, tears in her eyes.

"It's ok Ebony. I'm as close to you as I can get, I promise. Breathe, you're going to be ok." Thelmer assured her.

"Peter, hold her hand." Joseph told me quietly.

Ebony forced herself to calm down, and after a few minutes the pain died away. "What about Lance?" Ebony asked then.

"Don't worry about Lance; he's perfectly capable of pouring water on his own heavily poisoned head. Just focus on what you're doing!" Lance shouted from the wash room, where the door had been left open.

"It's starting again, it's… oww, oww!" Ebony cried, crushing my hand in hers. I gritted my teeth and tried not to let her know that she was hurting me.

It went on for hours. Ebony would be crying in pain, then the pain died away, and she'd lay there exhausted. Thelmer kept up a steady stream of encouraging words and reassurances, as Joseph and Fletch sat and waited for something to change. I did my best to not watch them. I felt uncomfortable enough being present for an event that was usually considered private and even sacred. I focused my eyes on Ebony's face, dabbing her forehead with a wet cloth when she needed it, and keeping my hand in hers, no matter how many times she crushed my fingers.

"Ok Ebony, I think it's time to start pushing now, I can see the head." Joseph said some time during the late morning. Ebony had been grunting and crying a lot more frequently, and for a lot longer the last hour or so.

Ebony shook her head fearfully. "I can't! It hurts too much, I can't do it! I'm not strong enough for this. The magic isn't willing to help at all, I can't do it!" She sobbed.

"Ebony listen to me! You're strong. You don't need the magic to do this; you have the strength without it. You're my warrior, remember? You can do this, I know you can!" Thelmer insisted firmly.

"I can't Thelmer! We made a mistake. I'm not able to be a mother, I can't do it!" Ebony pleaded.

"Mistake or not, it's happening. You can do this, you MUST. The sooner you do this, the better it will be, I promise. Come on my Ebony, you are strong, you know you are." Thelmer insisted kindly.

I closed my eyes for the last part. Joseph and Fletch gave Ebony directions like "Push, ok, rest now. Big push, get the shoulders out. It's going to be ok. He's coming…"

Finally, I heard the baby cry. I opened my eyes, and watched Joseph wash the baby with the bucket of water and a cloth. Joseph wrapped the baby in the biggest of the cloths, which was part of an old rangers' cloak, and carried the baby over to Ebony.

"Oh, he's so beautiful! Thelmer I wish you could see him, he looks just like you." Ebony sobbed, taking the baby into her arms. "Have you ever seen anything so wonderful?" she asked me tearfully.

I grinned and didn't answer. In all honesty, I had never seen anyone less beautiful. The baby looked all wrinkled and red and had a fat belly and legs. He had only a few wisps of hair, and looked nothing at all like what I had thought I remembered babies looked like. He hardly looked human. But I wasn't about to tell that to Ebony, especially since she looked so exhausted, and happy.

"Thank God she had such an easy birth." Joseph commented to Fletch as the two cleaned Ebony up. "I don't think I have the skills if she had run into any problems."

"That was an EASY birth?!" I asked shocked. Joseph just laughed lightly, and suggested I get some sleep.

When I woke up later that day and went into the main room Ebony was curled up in a chair singing softly to the baby, who was breast feeding. Before I could slip away into the kitchen Ebony called me over. "I wanted to thank you for helping earlier. You holding my hand really helped me a lot." She said softly.

"You're welcome." I replied, determined not to look at her, not wanting to be disrespectful.

"Here, you hold him for a bit." Ebony said, standing up carefully, and transferring the baby into my arms. Ebony showed me how to hold it, so I would be supporting the head. Then Ebony left to go to the washroom.

I looked down at the little creature in my arms. I had never held a baby before. He looked at me with his grey eyes, so much like Thelmer's. In fact, it was the only resemblance to Thelmer I could see. When the baby and I looked into each other's eyes, I knew we'd become good friends. The baby kicked his legs inside the cloak rag he was wrapped in, and yawned widely. It was then that I noticed that he had no teeth in his mouth. I stood puzzling over that until Ebony came back. "Isn't Colin amazing? Look at his little hand!" Ebony said, holding out her baby's arm for me to look at. Colin's hand really was amazing. It was so tiny, with such small fingernails that they were barely specks.

"I've never seen a brand new baby before." I admitted in little more than a whisper as Ebony took Colin back, and began to tap his back gently, pacing back and forth.

"Oh, you mean the redness? That will go away. I'm still amazed that my Thelmer and I created this little angel. He's so beautiful." Ebony replied.

I smiled again without commenting. I knew that I'd never tell her or Thelmer what I really thought about their son's looks. If they thought he was beautiful, then that was what mattered.

# CHAPTER 14

Once the excitement of Colin's birth died down again, Joseph returned to the lecture he had started to give me about Kaltya. Joseph had me sit with him at the kitchen table, and he spoke in a soft, firm voice.

"Peter, Kron specializes in painful deaths. His poisons are designed to torture the victim before they kill him. When I tell you that I don't want you to be involved in something it isn't just because you are a child. There is a reason grown-ups don't want children to know about certain things. Believe me when I say we don't keep you in the dark just to annoy you. Kevin should be here any day, and then Lance will be fine, if we can keep him alive until then. You just stay out of it. Do what I tell you to do, and stay out of things that are too big for you, understand?"

"Yes sir." I said, staring at the rough wooden table.

"If we can just get the antidote for the Kaltya, he'll be fine." Joseph assured me, rising to his feet.

"I don't think Kaltya is the only problem, I think there was another poison." I started to say. But Joseph didn't hear me, he was busy talking to Fletch.

I spent the next two days almost entirely outside. Joseph didn't want me anywhere near the washroom. Lance was dying, I knew he was. I could tell in the way everyone was whispering and acting, but even more, I could feel it in my heart. The little bit of life he had left from the Kronlord's attack was almost spent. I wanted to go to him, to hold his hand. I wasn't sure why, but I desperately wanted to touch him, to be at his side. But Joseph would never let me, every time I so much as glanced at the washroom Joseph shot me a warning look, and I quickly found something else to do. Lance was no longer in pain from the water. Or if he was, he didn't even have enough strength left in him to show it. He just lay in the water, too weak to do anything, even talk. I sat outside with my back against the well sadly. I knew somehow that if Lance didn't get cured soon, he wouldn't survive through this night.

In the back of my mind came the faintest sound of rapid hoof beats. They got steadily louder, and I stood up to see what was happening. I saw a ranger approaching on horseback, riding as fast as the horse could gallop. He slowed to a stop and jumped off the horse once he reached the healing house.

"Here boy, tend to the horse." He said, throwing the reins at me, and entering the house rapidly.

I led the exhausted horse to the well and drew a bucket of water for him to drink. I loosened the saddle and tied the horse to a tree, entering the healing house.

Everyone but Ebony and Colin were in the wash room. Ebony and Colin were in the doctors room napping. I hesitated about entering the washroom, but decided that Joseph wouldn't care so much, now that the antidote to the Kaltya was here.

"This should work almost instantly. We should see massive improvements soon." Kevin was saying, as everyone watched Lance apprehensively.

But the massive improvements didn't come. Lance only got a small bit better. His fever died, but he was still limp and unconscious, his life still fading away.

"I don't get it. This should work. I know it should." Joseph insisted softly, checking Lance's pulse.

"The Kaltya wasn't the only poison. The Kronlord had something else as well." I insisted.

Everyone turned to stare at me. I blushed slightly at the attention, but I stood firm, positive that I was right.

"Why do you say that, Peter?" Joseph asked softly.

"I… I dreamed it." I admitted, suddenly realizing that dreams weren't exactly solid evidence. Sure enough, Kevin's response showed the reaction that I had expected to receive.

"You dreamed it." He repeated, rolling his eyes. "A first year apprentice has a dream, and suddenly everyone acts like he knows better than someone who has studied Kron's poisons since before the kid was born?"

"*I'm* not acting that way." Fletch insisted, turning away from me in a dismissive fashion.

"He just needs more time for the poison to be neutralized." Kevin informed me, turning away as well.

"He doesn't have time! We have to find out what the other poison was, and fast. In my dreams there were two bottles, a flask, and a little potion bottle. What kinds of poisons would be stored in such containers?" I insisted.

"There you see, he's just trying to get information after you told him to stay out of it." Fletch informed Joseph.

I clenched my hands into fists trying to keep my anger in check. "I would never do that! I'm telling you, there was another poison. You just hate kids, that's why you're taking Kevin's side against me." I accused, pointing at Fletch angrily. I couldn't believe that he was so biased about young people that he'd risk Lance's life like this.

"That's enough Peter. Go play outside." Joseph told me firmly.

"But Sir," I started to protest.

"Do as you're told, boy!" Kevin snapped.

I looked from one ranger to another. No one looked like they were willing to listen to me. I glanced at Lance's limp unconscious body, and stormed out of the building. I couldn't believe this was happening. Why were they just dismissing me like some ignorant child? Why couldn't they even attempt to hear me out? Even Joseph wasn't listening to me, and he knew me better than the other men. Or at least, I had thought he did. Now they all seemed like arrogant fools to me. I sat next to the well sulking. I was so angry that I felt like I wanted to break something, like the one good arm of a certain ranger who sided with a guy who'd never even met me. As soon as the violent thought entered my head I regretted it, feeling ashamed at myself. Fletch didn't understand me, but that didn't make him a bad person. I drew my knees to my chest and rested my chin on them with a sigh. "I need someone here who will believe me." I told the horse who opened one sleepy eye to glance at me before going back to its nap.

"You have someone." An unfamiliar deep voice said from behind me.

I stood up and turned around, and almost choked in my effort to suppress my surprise. Standing next to the well was the most majestic creature I had ever seen or even imagined. It seemed to be a huge lion with eagle's wings, and some human-like facial features. He was golden in color, and his eyes were a rich cat yellow, and filled with more wisdom and knowledge then anything or anyone I had ever known. He was standing and watching me calmly.

"Did…did you just… speak to me?" I stammered.

The lion creature nodded calmly.

"O…Oh." I answered.

Before I could feel too foolish, the creature spoke again.

"You are worried about the death of your companion. You are feeling angry and hurt because no one will listen to you, is that correct?" he said, sitting down and keeping his eyes fixed on me.

"How… who are you? How did you know that Lance was dying?" I asked, still too amazed to be able to talk easily.

"I did not know that 'Lance' is dying. I knew that someone you love is dying, and that you know why. I also know how to save your friend."

I took a step forward eagerly. "You do?! Please, tell me how. Tell me what I need to do to save him. The grownups, they won't listen to me." I said softly, forgetting my fear in my eagerness to save Lance.

"There is a fruit tree that grows only at the very top of mountains. Those trees are protected by good magic, evil has never touched them. Only those who are not evil or selfish or even conceited in any way whatsoever CAN touch them. The juice of that fruit will cure any poison or injury caused by the touch of evil." The creature said.

"How can I get some of that juice then?" I asked, realizing that there wasn't enough time for me to climb a mountain and come back to save Lance. Lance didn't have enough time.

"You miss-understand me child. There is no way for you to get to one of those trees alone. Besides, once there, you would not know how to get back." The strange creature explained gently.

"So then, there is no hope." I said, the excitement dying out of me.

"I said, you can't get to one of those trees ALONE." The creature told me firmly.

"Then what do I need to do?" I asked, feeling desperate.

"I must take you, and bring you back. But you can't delay, if you are to go, we must leave now. There is no time to waste. We must get to the tree as soon as possible in order to return in time for you to save your Lance person."

I hesitated for a moment, glancing at the healing house. I knew that I could get into a lot of trouble by going off like this. But my eyes hardened as I realized that I mustn't let the threat of being punished stop me from saving Lance's life. "Let's go." I agreed.

The winged lion crouched down, and I jumped onto his back. He took off into the air, flying three times as fast as any Pegasus could fly. We raced through the trees, breaking free of the canopy into the bright sunlight. The wind rushed past us, taking my hood off me in seconds.

We were going so fast that I didn't dare let go to put it back on, I was holding onto the mane as tightly as I could, crouching almost flat against the golden fur, my eyes shut tight against the wind blowing in my face. We flew right towards the tallest mountain, which already had snow on its peak.

When we landed in the snow, I tumbled to the ground, breathless from the shocking flight. "Hurry small human, there is no time to waste." The lion creature said, pointing to five trees that had silver colored bark, white leaves, and silver apple-shaped fruits. The trees were built close together, with the four smaller ones surrounding the much taller one in the middle. The taller tree stretched hundreds of feet high. I went over to the trees softly. I felt suddenly as if I was in a sacred location, one where humans usually weren't welcome. Without really knowing I was doing it, I removed my weapons, and my boots, approaching the trees unarmed and barefoot. The snow wasn't painful to my feet though, it felt soft, like walking on lambs' wool.

"Please, may I have some?" I asked, touching the bark of the tallest tree, not having any idea why I was asking permission, but knowing that it was the right thing to do.

I stepped back as the tree began to move as if in a strong wind, swaying from side to side. Several of the fruits fell off all around me, landing in the snow with soft thumps. I looked over at the creature who had brought me here.

"Look in the snow at the base of the tree." He suggested.

I started to run my hands through the snow until my hand closed around something solid. I pulled it out to find that it was an empty bottle made of something that might have been glass. Silently I started to picked up the fruits and used my fingernails to cut up the soft fruits and squeeze the thick silver colored juice into the bottle. When the bottle was full, I put the cap on securely, and put the bottle into my bag. I stood up and turned to look at the winged lion, ready to leave.

"You must not waste the fruit." He told me, nodding to my feet. I looked down to see that there was one silver fruit left. Hardly aware that I was doing it, I took my dagger out, and used it to dig a hole in the ground, planting the fruit and the left over pulp from the other ones half way between two of the smaller trees.

We flew back a bit slower, and I used the time to ask questions.

"What was that place?" I asked, curling up my toes under my boots. They were finally feeling the effects of the cold, and were taking a long time to warm back up.

"That was the home of a dear friend of mine, a very powerful being of goodness and healing. He and I have had a long talk about you, and have agreed that you are worthy of our help."

"Thank you very much!" I said, surprised and honored to be considered worthy by this stranger.

"You're welcome." My new friend replied simply.

"May I ask you a question?" I requested.

"You just did. However, you may ask another one if you wish."

"Right…" I said, pausing to process why he sounded amused. "Can I ask what you are?"

"It is not an impossible question to ask by any means that I can see." He answered.

I smiled, understanding what he meant that time. "Ok, what are you then?"

"My name is Abiyram, or at least, that is my entire name as far as it is pronounceable by your people." He replied, landing softly next to the healing house.

I turned to him. "Thank you Abiyram. I really mean it, thank you." I said earnestly.

"I will see you again soon little human. You take good care of your people, and make sure not to lose that juice."

"I will, and I won't." I promised seriously.

Abiyram nodded once, and took off into the air again.

I went into the healing house to see the men had left the washroom and were crowded around the message basin. I overheard the word poison as I entered the washroom unobserved. Lance had been taken out of the tub and was lying on a towel fully clothed, and pale as death, his hands crossed on his chest. I couldn't help but feel as if they had put him that way so he'd be able to die with some dignity. His breathing was shallow and his heart more sluggish than ever. I propped his head and shoulders up, and wondered how I was going to get the juice to him if he was unconscious. But Lance opened his eyes and looked at me weakly. "I brought something that will cure you Lance." I whispered, holding the bottle to his lips. Lance drank a few sips trustingly, as if he was the child, and I the adult. After he had drank an ounce or two, Lance closed his eyes again, and rested his head against my shoulder. I put the cap back on the bottle, and put it back into my bag, making sure it was well protected by my change of clothes so it wouldn't break. I looked at Lance, and was relieved to see that some color had already come back to his face, and his bruises were fading away as I watched.

"There is another problem my Lord, Peter has gone missing; Fletch thinks he might have run away." I heard Joseph's voice say.

I hastily lay Lance back down on the ground and rushed into the main room. "No I haven't, I'm right here!" I told Joseph.

Everyone around the message basin turned to me in shock. Apparently no one had heard me come back inside. "Peter, where have you been? WHY did you leave the area?" Joseph demanded, rising to his feet and hurrying towards me.

"Why is your hood off?"

"Your hands are covered in dirt, what have you been doing?"

"WHAT were you thinking, running off like that?!"

I stood still and let the questions continue unanswered. The message basin was abandoned as everyone came over to me. Through the questions I heard Lord Haldor's voice say, "let ME know what happened!"

Finally, everyone seemed to realize that I couldn't answer all the questions at once, even if I wanted to. So they settled down a bit, and stared at me instead, waiting for me to explain myself. I told them what had happened since I had been sent outside. When I finished, there was a dead silence in the room.

"Let me see if I got this straight, a strange creature that looked like a lion with wings brought you to some sacred garden with magical fruit trees?" Fletch asked, breaking the silence.

"Yes, that is another way to put it I suppose." I answered calmly.

The adults glanced at each other with raised eyebrows. "Peter, do you know what a winged lion is called?" Joseph asked me.

"He said his name was Abiyram." I replied.

"They are called Lammasu. They are a legendary creature that is the symbol on the back of our country's coins." Joseph informed me.

"Ok." I said, storing the information into my head for next time I saw Abiyram.

"They aren't real. There's no such thing." Kevin informed me matter-of-factly.

"But they are real, or at least HE is real. I didn't ask if there were any others like him." I insisted.

The adults glanced at each other again. I looked at them feeling slightly impatient. "Peter, are you positive that is what you saw?" Joseph asked cautiously.

"Yes, it was just as I said. He was a huge winged lion with a man's face, and a deep voice." I insisted firmly.

"I suppose it is possible that something could have bewitched him, tricked his mind into thinking that he saw a Lammasu." Kevin suggested hesitantly.

"But nothing can approach the healing house, nothing that would trick him like that. Only elves and rangers can come here." Fletch protested.

"Elves, rangers, and Lammasu." I corrected him.

Everyone turned to stare at me again. "Your Lammasu came here, to the healing house?" Joseph asked.

I nodded. "Yes, I met him by the well." I agreed.

Everyone looked worried now, and I couldn't blame them. The thought of the magic protections that kept people here safe being breached must be an alarming notion.

"Show us." Joseph said, gesturing for me to lead the way. I brought everyone outside and over to where Abiyram and I had met. "He was sitting right there when we talked." I said pointing.

Joseph and Kevin went and examined the area. Then, without a word, Joseph lead the way back inside. "Lord Haldor, SOMETHING was there, something big, with paws." Joseph said, going back over to the message basin.

"It was the Lammasu!" I insisted, following him over to the basin.

Lord Haldor studied me for a moment. "If he says he saw a Lammasu, then that is what he saw." Lord Haldor declared.

Any protest that Kevin or Fletch might have had died in their throats. Because at that moment, Lance came out of the wash room, looking as healthy as he could ever be.

# CHAPTER 15

I stood at attention talking to Lord Haldor, telling him every detail that I could remember about the strange garden on the snow covered mountain. The rangers sat in a semi-circle around me, listening silently to my account, and to Lord Haldor's interruptions and questions.

"You're sure there were four trees around the big one?" Lord Haldor asked.

"Yes sir. They were standing like a square, with the big tree in the center of the square."

"Very well, continue." Lord Haldor said, nodding to himself, as if confirming something in his mind.

The bottle of juice was on the floor next to the message basin. At first, I had offered it to Joseph to examine, but he and Lord Haldor told me in unison to let no man other then the one it was given to handle it. I had at first, assumed the bottle to be made of clear glass, but Lord Haldor had seen such a bottle before (though he hadn't said where) and informed me that it was made out of magically treated diamond, and would never break. I asked then if he had ever heard of the garden since he had seen one of the bottles before, but Lord Haldor shifted the discussion abruptly, and had me tell him again what the Lammasu and I talked about on the way back to the healing house.

Finally, after what seemed like a year of being questioned about every detail imaginable, Lord Haldor said he had to leave. That

120

seemed to be the signal for all the rangers to find something else to do. Fletch and Kevin went into the kitchen to start making dinner, Joseph went to check on Ebony who had retreated back into her room when she had seen the serious looks on everyone's faces, and Lance stayed sitting where he was, still staring at me as I put the bottle back into my bag.

"Tell me what the Kronlord did to me." He requested softly when I had turned around to see him still sitting there.

"But not here." He added as I was about to speak. "Let's take a walk."

"I have no memory of any of this. I didn't even know I had been poisoned until Joseph told me." Lance said softly watching the leaves blow past us being carried by the wind. "But your dreams didn't tell you how I came to be free, or why the kronlord didn't kill me like they do to the rest of their victims?"

I shook my head. "I always wake up while you're in pain. It's like every nerve inside you is being ripped through your skin." I said, shuddering at the memory of the dreams.

Lance nodded thoughtfully. That would be the Kronlord feeding off me. It's what causes the bruises, having your energy ripped out of you like that."

I shuddered again, and Lance looked down at me in concern. "Perhaps we shouldn't talk about this. It is obviously distressing to you, and I know Joseph will be angry if I traumatize you just because I want to know what happened." Lance suggested softly."No, please... it helps to talk about it. I NEED to talk about it. I can't get more traumatized then I am, after all, I've had to live the event multiple times now." I pleaded desperately.

"That is true..." Lance murmured, considering me thoughtfully.

"How come I can relive something you can't even remember?" I asked curiously.

Lance walked for a while, thinking over that question. We were walking in circles around the healing house, staying well within the protected area, but far enough away from the building to offer some privacy to our conversation. We made two full circles before Lance answered my question. "Rangers can do that sometimes. It's a rare but useful function of the magic. The magic will, on occasion, show a ranger what they need to know in order to get something done. Also the magic will sometimes show rangers events that are currently happening, but that is much more rare, and usually takes many years of having a relationship with magic in order for it to happen. Dream magic is a strange thing. It only happens to one or two people out of thousands, and many rangers doubt that it is even real."

"Like the existence of Lammasu?" I asked.

"Actually, a Lammasu is easier for some people to believe in than dream magic. People have all sorts of dreams all the time. It is when you are aware that you are dreaming that we know that it is real." Lance stopped walking, looking down at me curiously. "Why didn't you tell us you were having nightmares?" he asked.

I lowered my eyes, and stared at my boots. "Because everyone keeps talking about how they don't want to scare me and stuff. I thought if I told anyone, they would become even more protective and try to keep me from knowing about anything at all." I admitted.

Lance smiled slightly in understanding, and put an arm around my shoulders.

"Well from now on, you need to be completely honest with Joseph at least. Lord Haldor wants Joseph and you to work together, and you need to be open with each other in order to do so."

"How can I be open with him if he thinks I am too young to be trusted?" I asked, kicking a stone with my boot.

"I have a feeling that is going to change as you grow older Peter. I know you may feel like you aren't very young, but believe me; you have a lot of growing up to do yet. Don't try to rush into maturity. You should enjoy childhood while you have it."

"Yeah, that's what my father use to say all the time when my brothers got to do fun things without me." I muttered under my breath.

\*\*\*

After dinner that night, Joseph and I packed to leave. Lord Haldor had told Joseph that he was injured and so shouldn't carry much. This left the burden of most of our food and supplies to me. Since Joseph was planning to take the horse to the first city, I wouldn't have to walk with a heavy pack yet. But all the same, I was going to be responsible for all of Joseph's things other than his weapons and the clothes on his back. Joseph told me what to pack for food, and how to pack it. He also had me fill our water skins and wash our cloaks and change of clothes, so we'd be ready to leave in the morning. Now that Kevin was here, Joseph wasn't wasting any time. I slept in the main room near the fireplace. Kevin had taken my bed. As I lay staring into the fire, I wondered what it was going to be like to be an official messenger for the rangers. I knew that Joseph was really the one everyone would be focusing on, but all the same; I looked forward to the prospect of people thinking of me as a ranger and not just a boy, for once in my life.

"What I find most surprising was that he seemed to not be concerned with the fact that he had to be practically flawless in order to get to the garden." Lance's voice said from the back room. I stayed very still and tapped into the magic to make the voices a little louder, curious to know what was going on.

"I don't think the thought even crossed his mind. He seemed to be more focused on being able to get to the tree; I don't think he even considered the implications behind the requirements to enter the garden." Joseph said in reply.

"Well, shouldn't he be told then? I mean, if he had any idea how incredible,"

"If he had any idea, he might cease to be so. Think about it, if he was told, think what it might do to his ego. If his ego becomes inflated, then he'll never be able to return there, and the Lammasu might reject him and never come back."

I quickly clamped my hands over my ears. I didn't want to hear any more. I wasn't sure exactly what they were debating about telling me, but I knew enough to know that I didn't want anything to happen to break my relationship with my new friend. I stared into the fire, and filled my head with a children's song my friends and I use to sing as part of a dueling game we played.

*"A knight on his steed,*
*is mighty indeed*
*as he hunts dragons for gold.*
*A drunk on his stool,*
*is considered a fool*
*if he stays there from young to old."*

I filled my mind with the children's song and game, trying to erase the conversation from my memory. I mentally asked the magic to help me keep whatever I needed in order to stay friends with Abiyram. I calmed down as I felt a sense of reassurance from the magic that everything was going to be fine. I lay there gazing at the flames. That had been a close call. I would need to be careful what conversations I tapped into in the future.

# CHAPTER 16

Joseph and I set off for the road at dawn. We had taken the time to say goodbye to everyone, and Kevin had wanted to talk to me in private and apologies.

"I've been a fool. I should have known that anyone who had been given the title of 'the gem of Haldor's eye' would be someone who knew what he was talking about, even at such a young age. I really am not usually this blind when it comes to being rational, but Lord Haldor had told me that speed was of the essence because Lance was dying. Lance and I... well, we grew up together. He's like a brother to me, and I let my concern for him blind me to the reality behind who I was dealing with."

"It's ok. Maybe it was even better, because if I hadn't been sent outside, I never would have met Abiyram and been able to get the cure in time." I said with an uncomfortable shrug. Kevin had gotten to one knee before me and was holding my right hand, making the apology formal in a way I had never been addressed before.

Joseph and I rode at a soft pace, one where there wouldn't be too many harsh movements to hurt Joseph's ribs. I sat behind him on the horse, my hands wrapped around his waste, so I wouldn't fall off. Really, we weren't going fast enough that my doing so was necessary, but for some reason, I just wanted to be touching Joseph. A tiny part of me felt like if I touched him, it would somehow make him all better, but I knew that was silly of me. I felt like a girl, wanting to have personal contact with people, but I didn't say anything. He didn't seem to mind, and we didn't speak as we went on, paying attention as always, to everything going on around us.

When we stopped for the night, Joseph began to teach me about battle tactics. He cleared a space of the ground of leaves and grass, and using a stick, he drew in the dirt. I listened and asked questions, absorbing the information eagerly. I loved to learn, and the more I learned, the more I found myself wanting to know. Joseph explained the basics about combat positions, and what each row of fighters would do in a battle. When it got too dark to see any more, Joseph suggested that I get some sleep, and took the first watch. I slept well for the first night in a while, not haunted any more by the scene with the Kronlord. Instead, I slept a deep, dreamless sleep. Joseph woke me up for my watch, reminding me to be careful, and to wake him at any signs of trouble or feelings of fear. But the night passed without incident, the only movement being an owl who landed on a branch to rest, staring at us with its huge eyes.

When we had been traveling on the road for about two days with battle tactic lessons each night, we reached the first sign of humanity I had seen since we had left the healing house. There was a sign on the side of the road, announcing that the city of Woodward was five miles away. Joseph stopped at the sign and turned to look over his shoulder at me. "Do you know any rules of conduct when addressing nobles and other members of court?" he asked.

"Um..." I stammered nervously.

"I'll take that as a 'no'." Joseph said, dismounting. "Get down here, there are some things you will need to know if you're going to be a ranger in a city that has a castle.

Joseph spent the next twenty minutes or so teaching me how to bow to men, with one fist on my chest, the other behind my back, and how to bow to woman, taking their hand and pressing my lips briefly against their knuckles as I bent forward. He also lectured me on the proper ways to address people of such high rank and class. When we were riding again, he also told me a bunch of things about how to act at social functions with them, such as how to eat each dish during feasts, and what to say and to not say when spoken to.

My head was spinning with information by the time we got to the city gates. There were so many rules of conduct, I wasn't sure I'd be able to keep track of them all. I had grown up poor, and I had the feeling that I would stick out like an iron glove on a princess's hand.

"Joseph?" I asked softly, once we had paid the city's travelers tax and were walking through the crowded streets, leading the horse since it was impossible to ride with so many people around.

"What's wrong?" Joseph asked, noticing my soft voice.

"I don't think I'm ready for any of that. I mean how to act and stuff. What if I make a mistake?"

Joseph smiled. "Don't worry about it Peter. If you mess up no one will look down on you. You're a ranger, not a prince. People understand this. But Barron Rice likes to give visiting rangers the red carpet treatment. It's his way of saying to the world that he is behind anything we say and do." Joseph explained.

As we walked, most heads turned to watch us. I found myself ducking my head deep into my hood to hide my face. I could feel that I was blushing, and that alone made me feel embarrassed. I hated it when people stared at me. But since Joseph and I were wearing cloaks with hoods on them, we were rather noticeable in the crowded streets where the most head gear anyone was wearing were the city guards helmets. I found myself longing to blend into the shadows and disappear, but I dutifully walked next to Joseph, telling myself that he was the one people were staring at, not me.

Joseph led me to an area of the city that was mostly family homes. He made his way to one house in particular. The house was well tended to, all except the lawn, which was vastly overgrown. Joseph let the horse graze on the overgrown lawn, and headed towards the house. There was a small dagger pained right below the door knocker, and Joseph explained to me that this was where the rangers stationed in this city lived. While we were walking up to the door, it opened, and a hooded ranger stepped outside.

"We were told you would be coming at some point. The knights already made the lists of the men who are to be drafted, and they are just waiting for you to assess their skill levels." he said, leading us into the house.

"My apprentice and I will do that in the next couple days. In the meantime, I need to pay my respects to the Barron." Joseph said, his tone was that of a person who was talking about a burdensome task.

The ranger laughed softly. "No doubt he will be looking forward to seeing you again my old friend. You know how fond he once was of your father."

"Yes, unfortunately I am reminded all too often what Barron Rice thought about my father." Joseph said, his tone carefully neutral.

"You can have the spare room, and your apprentice can sleep on the couch if he'd like." the ranger offered, opening the door to a small bedroom.

"Peter would prefer to sleep on the floor." Joseph said, his tone lightly joking.

The other ranger laughed again. "I wouldn't blame him for that! That old couch has certainly seen better days." he agreed. "My name is Mark." The ranger said, cheerfully offering his hand to me in greeting.

"I...my name is Peter, son of Richard." I replied, stumbling suddenly over how to speak.

"Ahhh, so you're Haldor's gem huh? Well rumors of your raw talents have reached us here, even at this remote outpost. Welcome!" Mark said, his eyes growing wide as he found out who I was.

"Thank you." I said in surprise. I found myself wondering if there was a ranger out there who Lord Haldor hadn't told about me. Then I wondered what people had been told. But Before I could ask, Joseph spoke.

"Well, I suppose there's no point delaying the chore. After all, we don't want to insult the lord of the city. Come Peter."

Joseph and I walked through the crowded streets, me holding onto his cloak to stop us from being separated. I had never seen so many people wandering the streets before, with the exception of the harvest fair. But the busy streets were made far more uncomfortable for me because everyone turned to stare at us.

"Sir?" I asked, hurrying forward so I was walking next to Joseph instead of behind him. "WHY does everyone stare at us?"

Joseph glanced around at the crowd as if he had only just noticed their interest in our business. "Oh, pay no mind to them. These people are simple city folk, and more often than not, they believe whatever rumors they are told. By now everyone has at least heard a rumor about the draft, and they know that we are here to carry out the king's order. They're just nervous that their sons and brothers, or even they themselves will be drafted." Joseph said lightly.

I thought about the explanation for a while. It certainly made sense, but then it occurred to me that long before Lance came back injured people had still stared at us. I remembered Thelmer laughing softly when I had asked him about it. Obviously, Joseph's explanation couldn't be the only reason. I was about to mention that they had been staring since the beginning, but Joseph said to me in a low voice, "Ask me when we're alone. You don't want to offend anyone, do you?" He asked, looking over at some of the bigger and more suspicious looking men to drive his point home. I glanced over at them, and nodded my understanding. I certainly wouldn't want to offend those guys.

The crowds were much thinner as we reached the more classy part of the city, near the castle. The houses were bigger, and the only people who were walking around seemed to be servants and messengers running errands for their masters. They hurried past us, too wrapped up in what they were doing to give us more than a quick curious look. Joseph steered me out of the way as a carriage was driven past us, heading for the castle we were going to. Two boys were riding on the back of the carriage, standing on a rail above the wheels. They were dressed in fine clothing, the kind I would expect to see if they were heading to a wedding ceremony in my father's town. But I knew that this was some sort of uniform, because the coachman was also dressed the same. The horses were riding at a brisk trot, rushing to wherever the coachman was leading them. I watched it pass in fascination. I had never seen a carriage before, just carts that went through town pulled by sleepy horses, offering rides to anyone who had enough money to pay for such transportation. I vaguely wondered to myself how expensive it would be to ride in a carriage like the one rushing up the hill to the castle.

At the castle gate, Joseph told a guard to inform Lord Rice that the king's messengers had come to pay their respects to the lord of the city. One of the guards left to deliver the message, and another guard led Joseph and me to a bench in the courtyard to wait. Joseph sat down carefully, the walk through the city had been hard on him, but he didn't slow down his pace, not wanting to let anyone wonder if he was up to no good. Joseph now explained to me that when a ranger has lived in a town or city for a while, people tended to forget that they were there. This made it easy for the rangers to make sure the laws were being upheld, because no one noticed if they were around, and so they would be able to collect facts without suspicion. But a visiting ranger wouldn't blend in so easily. They were something that people were unaccustomed to seeing, and so they were watched carefully, in case they were really a thief or rouge pretending to be a ranger.

The guard came back, and led the way into the castle and over to where the Barron was waiting. I looked around in awe at the stained glass windows, and the tapestries on the walls. The castle was made of grey stone, but the decorations made the place look lively and cheerful. Joseph touched my arm lightly, and I tore my eyes away from the coat of arms hanging from the ceiling and looked at the Barron. Barron Rice was a large round man with a grey beard that still had a few streaks of red in it, rosy cheeks, and laughter in his eyes. He had the largest belly I had ever seen on a man, and the buttons on his coat looked like they were having a hard time keeping the coat closed.

When we had bowed to the Barron he gave out a roar of delighted laughter. "You never cease to surprise me lad! Always popping in when you please, never giving me time to prepare a proper reception! If I didn't know better, I'd almost think you didn't like my parties. Sometime in the future, when there is peace once more, you simply must come for a proper visit, and we'll have a grand old time, with the wine and beer flowing like waterfalls!" He said, clapping Joseph on the back so hard that Joseph lurched forward, instinctively putting a hand to his cracked ribs and gasping in pain. But the Barron didn't seem to notice this, he was still talking. "Yes sir, I never get nearly enough warning of your coming. Besides, I am tired of you only coming to visit me on official business! I've known you all your life, certainly even Lord Haldor allows you vacation time? No matter, I will make do with what I have. You and your little partner here shall dine with me tonight, and than tomorrow, you can do whatever unpleasant business you were sent to do. But for now, we shall have some fun, yes?"

The Barron didn't wait for an answer. He took a small bell out of his pocket and rang it wildly. Several servants rushed forward bowing. "Take my guests and find them some proper clothes to wear. Then tell the kitchens to prepare a feast fit for a king!"

I looked at Joseph uncertainly, and he nodded that it was ok for me to follow the servant who was assigned to me. I left nervously. I hadn't expected to be separated from Joseph, especially in such a foreign situation to anything I had ever done.

The young man led me to a room with mirrors on the walls. I was rather hesitant about taking off my cloak. It had become such a part of me that I felt almost vulnerable without it. The servant measured me and left the room. He returned with several different outfits the likes of which I had never held before. They were made with the finest materials, so that they were as nice to wear as they were to look at. The servant had me try the clothes on, until he was satisfied that he had found the outfit that looked best on me. I stood staring into the mirror feeling like I was looking at a stranger. My hair had grown somewhat shaggy as I had spent so little time bothering with it, knowing that no one would notice it under my cloak. There was an unfamiliar gleam in my eyes, and a wisdom that hadn't been there before. But more than that, the clothes made me look like a completely different person.

Now the servant had me take off the clothes again, and he proceeded to wash me where I stood. I was completely uncomfortable with that. I had never had someone wash me before, not since before I could remember. I stood and let him wash me, feeling horribly vulnerable. I realized suddenly that the rumors that my friends and I heard in our village may have more truth to them than we had thought. It was a common joke amongst the poor that some of the rich were so rich that they had become lazy to the point where they barely chewed their own food. We had heard stories from passing bards about how princes stood like statues, their servants tending to them as if they were dolls, dressing them, bathing them, picking up everything that the prince let drop.

The stories had seemed so ridiculous to me and my brothers that we often laughed until we had cried at the thought of a prince who had never once dressed himself. But I had never believed the stories could possibly be true, until I was being treated like this. I squirmed uncomfortably, and was politely asked to stay still. I did, more out of surprise at the request than because I wanted to. It really had been a request. I had gotten so use to people telling me what to do, and what not to do that being asked by an adult as if it was up to me, was a completely new feeling.

Once I was washed, dressed, and smelled faintly of some scented oil that the servant dabbed onto my neck and wrists, I was led out into the main castle again. I touched my belt, as if confirming to myself that I was still me. I had been allowed to keep wearing my weapons belt, since apparently young nobles also had swords that they carried everywhere. I felt completely uncomfortable. The clothes were fancy, more fancy and expensive than anything I had ever seen, much less worn. The outfit was emerald green colored with shiny black shoes, and made me look completely different than I had ever looked. The clothes felt to me like some creature who was clinging to me, completely separate from who I really was. As I was led through the castle, I found myself longing for this whole thing to be over, so I could retreat into the safe familiarity of my own clothes once more.

Joseph was dressed in a similar fashion, and for the first time I had ever seen, his hair was neatly brushed, and sat softly on his shoulders. He was wearing his clothes as if much more accustomed to the treatment than I was. He smiled slightly when he noticed how uncomfortable I was. "You look fine Peter. I know you're not use to this kind of treatment, but don't worry about it too much. This is the only place where it is likely to happen between here and the capital. I doubt that Sir Lucas will be as happy to see us in Askia, so just grit your teeth, and get through the night." he murmured to me.

I felt overwhelmed at the feast. I was sitting at the grand table with the Barron, Joseph, and some other rich men from the town. The table was set up so we were facing the rest of the room where the remainder of the guests were seated at several round tables. There were a good thirty people all together, but the room looked like it was designed to sit over a hundred. During the dinner, I tried hard to remember what Joseph had said about which fork and spoon to use. But my discomfort put the whole lesson out of my head. So I glanced around me, and copied what everyone else was doing, hoping that I wasn't making a fool of myself.

I quickly came to discover why the Barron was so round in the belly as plate after plate after plate of food was brought out to the guests. First, there was a hot damp hand cloth so we could wash our hands before eating. Then a creamy soup was served. After the soup was a plate of fruit slices "to cleanse the palate between courses" as the man sitting next to me explained. After the fruit came a vegetable salad with sliced chicken on top, fish, followed by more fruit, followed by beef and vegetables, fruit, pork, fruit, chicken and potatoes, more fruit, and finally, after dinner tea and sugar biscuits. I was full half way through the beef dish, but Joseph whispered to me that I needed to eat at least one bite of each thing served, so as not to be rude. The

Barron ate all his food, plus several of the slices of bread from the baskets scattered around the table.

He was a very loud man, his voice booming over the chatter of the people as they talked and ate. Most of the time, he talked to Joseph, telling him about little things that seemed to have no significance to a ranger. He was going on and on about the city's harvest, and the amount of taxes that he expected to receive from this and that person by the end of the month. Joseph listened politely, and I couldn't help but wonder how he could possibly stand to listen to the Barron ramble on and on about such minor affairs as whether or not the Barron was going to give out a pay raise to his stable boys. I found myself losing interest after five minutes, my mind wandering as I looked out at the grandly dressed people who were present.

After the meal was finally over, everyone moved into another room where there were musicians waiting. When everyone had entered, they began to play music, and several men went up to the woman and girls bowing and asking if the girl wanted to dance. Most of them said yes, obviously well accustomed to being asked by their partners. But one young lady turned down everyone who asked, in a politely bored manner. She stood against the wall, a few yards away from me and watched the dancers with a strange look in her eye. I followed her gaze, and saw that she was watching one couple in particular. A young man of around her age was dancing with a girl who looked just like the one standing against the wall, only her dress was pink, where the girl near me had a yellow dress. The girl stood in that position all night, watching her double dance with the young man.

I wandered around from time to time, mostly to keep myself from being bored. People would dance for a while, and then stop for a break, flagging down the servants who wandered the large room with trays of cakes and fruit and drinks. I couldn't imagine that anyone could be hungry after such a huge feast, but I just stood and watched silently, taking everything in as a silent observer to how the rich lived. Near the end of the night, a boy of around my age approached me. "I don't believe I recall seeing you here before." he stated.

I turned to look at him, quickly sizing him up. He was a blond boy who was about a head taller than I was. He was wearing a navy blue outfit, and had a very aristocratic mannerism about him, his hand resting casually on his sword hilt, and a somewhat pompous look in his eye. "My name is Peter. I am a ranger sent by the king as a messenger." I said, repeating what Joseph had suggested I say if asked who I was.

The boy raised an eyebrow in suspicion. "That is all fine, but who is your father? What city are you from?" he pressed.

"I'm not from any city. I grew up in a small village near," I started to explain, but the boy turned away from me abruptly.

"Ah, Lady Pricilla, how lovely to see you." He said, striding away from me to talk to a girl on the other side of the room.

I stood there surprised and a little annoyed, wondering if I should feel offended or not. The boy hadn't even let me say who I was. As soon as he had heard that I was from a small village he dismissed me, as if I wasn't worthy of talking to for some reason. I watched him for the rest of the night, but he determinedly looked everywhere but in my direction. I stood wondering what I had said wrong. I kept running the brief conversation over and over in my head, trying to figure out what I could have possibly said that would make him hurry away from me so quickly. The only conclusion that my mind kept coming back to was that he dismissed me because I had grown up poor. But I kept rejecting the thought, because it was an idea that I considered unfair to the young man. To accuse him even in my mind, as being prejudiced against poor people was a nasty way to think. Instead, I tried to come up with other explanations. Perhaps he was easily distractible. Perhaps the girl he had gone to talk too had been ill and he had simply gotten excited that she was well, and forgotten about me. But none of those explanations seemed to be believable for some reason, and I felt secretly ashamed that I couldn't help but think the worst about the boy.

# CHAPTER 17

Joseph and I changed back into our own clothes as the guests were leaving the castle. I felt a wave of relief run through me as I pulled my cloak on once more. Finally, I could stop pretending to be someone I wasn't. Finally, I looked like myself again. I paused and thought about the feeling for a moment. I realized that I was happy as a ranger. I still thought of myself as a blacksmith's son, but I was a ranger as well, and proud to be so. It occurred to me now that the reason I was reluctant to wear rich people's clothes wasn't just because I was poor, but because I wanted to be seen as a ranger.

"What's on your mind Peter?" Joseph asked me as we headed through the courtyard to the gates where the last of the Baron's guests were still saying goodbye.

"Tonight was a strange night sir." I replied, and then went on to explain what had happened between me and the blond boy.

We had stopped walking, and were standing a few yards away from the other people; as Joseph listened to me tell him about how I felt angry with myself for assuming the worst. When I finished talking, Joseph and I continued to the gate, and said our thanks to the Barron for the nice night.

"You come back for a real visit soon, you hear?" Barron Rice said to Joseph, hiccupping slightly as the vast amounts of wine he had drunk slurred his speech.

Joseph said he would see what he could do, and the Barron signaled for a coach to pull up to bring us back to the ranger's house. Joseph had me climb in first, and sat across from me on the other leather cushioned bench. There was a lamp that was swinging slightly as the carriage set off.

"Isn't this... kind of expensive?" I asked delicately. I was sitting gingerly, uncomfortable to be traveling in such luxury.

Joseph smiled slightly. "The Barron always pays for it. He has a habit of throwing quite a lot of parties, and he always pays for transportation home for his guests. It's kind of a fancy parting gift to be sure, but for a man as rich as he is, it doesn't seem so extravagant. Certainly the more wealthy guests, like the boy you were telling me about, wouldn't think much about the cost of transportation." he explained.

I nodded, taking in the information thoughtfully. "About the guy I was telling you about..." I said, unsure of what to say next.

Joseph sighed softly. "I'm afraid Peter that your conclusion about him is likely enough to be true." he said gently.

"But... how could it be true? I mean, he doesn't even know me. So how could he possibly not like me, just because I am poor, if he never had so much as a conversation with me? I don't judge him because he is rich, so why would he judge me just because I'm poor?" I asked.

"Because money makes some people blind." Joseph explained calmly.

I stared at him, not understanding. Joseph sighed and explained further. "For some people, like many of the guests who attend those sort of parties, money has made them unable to see things clearly. When money is the central focus in your life, you lose perspective of the things that should be important. It doesn't happen to everyone, but it happens to enough people that it is considered common knowledge that rich people are snobby. There are some people who become so obsessed with taking advantage of every little luxury that money can buy that they become weakened by their wealth, and put their children at distinct disadvantages. Many people who have grown up rich have never learned to even care for themselves. These people grow up as spoiled brats, who know that they will never have to work hard for anything. The dancing you saw tonight is probably the most exercise that some of the children will get all week."

"They don't run and play games, or climb trees, or dig for grubs, or anything?" I asked, surprised at the concept.

Joseph shook his head. "Most of the children aren't even allowed to do things like that, for fear they might smudge their clothes, or scrape their hands. Heaven forbid a child run the risk of being dirty or sweaty. No, the play that they do is mostly in the form of table games, story book reading, and light sports that don't involve much talent or effort. At least the boys are usually good with a sword, and they get a fine education in the areas of reading and such, but that is about all they can do."

"But what if there was an attack on the city?! How could they defend themselves if they never learned how?"

"Fighting is for the 'lesser' folk. Those with money don't want to fight to defend themselves. After all, what good is money if you can't have other people do the hard work for you?" Joseph explained gently.

We rode in silence after that. At first I had been annoyed at the young man, but now I felt sorry for him. I couldn't imagine what it must be like to grow up without being allowed to run through town racing against other boys, or never climbing trees or playing in the mud puddles, looking for worms to tease the girls with. I couldn't imagine even worrying about getting my clothes dirty or torn. Clothes could be washed and patched back together any time.

\*\*\*

The next day was very busy. The rangers and I went to the city barracks to assess the new troops to see what their fighting skill was.

Joseph was going to test everyone at Archery, and he gave me a long scroll with a list of names of people to test for sword fighting. I felt nervous about being given the task, but Joseph said that I didn't need to worry.

"Just call their name, and watch them fight against Mark. Give each person a ranking from one to five, five being an expert, and one being next to no skill. Don't worry, you'll do fine." Joseph promised me, heading off towards the archery practice area.

"But what do you consider an expert sir?" I called after him.

Joseph turned around so he was walking backwards so he could look at me when he answered.

"You're the judge of that, not me." he replied, waving and disappearing into the large crowd of nervous men.

"Great, thanks a lot." I muttered, staring at the group of people who were looking down at me. I glanced over at Mark, hoping that he would take command. But he just raised an eyebrow. "The men are assembled." he told me, gesturing to the group."Ok, I can do this. I can pass this test." I muttered to myself, opening the scroll and glancing at the names. "Alright, when I call your name, it's your turn. You have four minutes to show us your sword skills. Remember, the better you do, the better we can figure out where to send you all next." I glanced at the men, they were watching me silently. So far so good. "Aaron, son of Aaron, you're first."

I stood to one side with a small sand timer, watching the men fight. Each man got two turns of the sand timer, and I studied them carefully. All in all, the scores were twos or threes. Sometimes there was a fighter who I gave a four, but for the most part, people were only average. I reminded myself that there was a reason these men were not overly skilled. After all, they had never been trained in the town guards barracks like I had been in my childhood. The most skill any of them probably received was basic lessons, and children's games. Half way through the morning, one of the city knights came to replace Mark so he wouldn't be fighting nonstop all day. I did give out one rank of five at one point. It was to one of the rich people I had seen at the castle the night before, the one who had been dancing with the girl whose twin had watched them all night. He seemed to have quite a lot of skill, although he was of course nowhere near a ranger's skills. But his skills were definitely more advanced than the men around him.

At an hour past noon I finished the list. I closed the scroll with a tired sigh, hunger gnawing at my stomach, as I hadn't eaten since before the sun rose that morning. The other ranger from the city named Jack approached me and murmured in my ear. "Dismiss the men to go get lunch." he suggested.

"You all did a good job. The Barron is providing food for you all out back where the jousting range is." I told everyone, pointing to the area where Joseph has told me the men would go to eat for the next couple days.

Jack and I followed the men, keeping a few yards behind them. "That went ok right? I mean, I did what I was supposed to do, right?" I asked Jack.

Jack looked down at me curiously. "How old are you again?" he asked me.

"Thirteen." I answered.

"Wow, you're young. I figured you were just short, but I guess you're young too. Yes Peter, you did fine." Jack assured me. I lowered my eyes, not wanting to show my annoyance at being considered so young. 'Why is thirteen so young to these people? By my age, some people have jobs.' I thought to myself.

Jack went over to join Mark in the food line, and I looked around for Joseph. I found him talking to a group of city guards, making gestures with his hands to mimic what he was saying about archery. When he saw me approaching, Joseph dismissed the guards, and walked over so we met half way. "So how did it go?" he asked me, sounding as worn out as I felt.

"You sound even more tired than I am, sir." I commented, handing him the list.

"Have you ever had to teach two hundred men how to hold a bow and arrow properly?" Joseph asked in reply.

Joseph frowned as he skimmed through the list. "Why did you give three people scores of negative two?" he asked me. I glanced at the names he was referring to. "Oh, because they were REALLY incompetent. I mean, they were so bad that I worry that they won't survive for half a minute if they are in a real battle. I don't think they should be anywhere near something as sharp as a real sword, much less be expected to survive by their skill with one! They were stumbling all over themselves, and dropping the sword, not to mention holding it all wrong. Mark knocked the sword out of their grip each time his sword touched them. It was ridiculous! If they had been from the same family I would have concluded that they had some sort of birth disorder, but they were on different parts of the list." I explained.

"Is that so?" Joseph murmured distractedly.

Joseph made his way over to where the knight commander of the city was watching the men who were in line receiving sandwiches and carrot sticks from one of the guards who had been put on serving duty. When the knight saw us coming, he gave an order to one of his underlings, and came over to us. "What can I do for you sir?" He asked Joseph, using formality since the situation of the day called for protocol.

"My apprentice seems to think you made a mistake in drafting a few people." Joseph explained calmly.

"I didn't say that!" I gasped.

"'They were REALLY incompetent. I mean, they were so bad that I worry that they won't survive for half a minute if they are in a real battle.' Is that not what you just told me?" Joseph asked, raising an eyebrow slightly.

"Well yes but, I didn't mean it like that!" I stammered nervously, my heart racing, sure that was in trouble for suggesting that a fully trained knight commander couldn't do his job, which hadn't been my intent at all. "I just meant that the guys had no skill, honest, I didn't mean…"

"Calm down Peter, no one's in trouble. This is your first draft, of course you don't understand what this means." Joseph said with a slight laugh, putting his hand on my shoulder.

I'll go get the men." Mark offered from where he had been listening a few yards away.

"No, wait until after lunch, Peter needs me to explain the situation to him." Joseph said, leading me over to the serving line.

"So what is going on then?" I asked, once Joseph and I had sat down against a tree with our food.

"I don't suppose you are familiar with the term draft-dodgers, are you?" Joseph asked, opening his turkey sandwich and eating it part by part.

I shook my head as I took a bite of my own sandwich.

"Well, many people don't want to go to war. No one blames them for that, war is a messy business with an almost certain guarantee that people are going to die. But when a draft happens, you are legally obligated to report for duty. For anyone who doesn't show up when the summons come for them, the penalty is very harsh. Two years of hard labor is a light sentence for such a crime. So, to try to con their way out of their troubles, some people try to trick the knights and rangers into thinking that there was a mistake in them being one of the people chosen to go to war. They will pretend to have no skill, or to be too foolish in the head to understand orders. There are some people who are so desperate to avoid battle that they will injure themselves. The men you described to me sound like they are trying to trick you. Anyone can tell by your size that you are inexperienced, and so they probably figured you'd be easy to trick... which you were." Joseph said, his voice kind despite the fact that I had failed to realize that I was being fooled.

"So what do we do with draft-dodgers?" I asked, as I saw the three men making their way over to us with Mark and the knight commander.

"I'll show you what we do." Joseph said, pressing down hard on my shoulder as he used me to help him get to his feet.

"Hello gentlemen. My assistant here seems to think that there is something lacking in your skills with a sword." Joseph said in a pleasant and friendly tone.

"Well sir, we are just city boys. We haven't really been trained in fighting you know." One of the three answered, mistaking Joseph's pleasant tone to mean that he had been fooled too.

Joseph nodded his head in understanding. "Yes, I am sure that being in a city makes it hard for you to have any chance at learning how to use a sword." Joseph agreed in a sympathetic tone.

"Very hard sir. Being raised in a big city like this, we don't get much chance to develop any battle skills at all really." the man said, encouraged in his lie by the understanding he seemed to be getting from Joseph.

Joseph sighed in a sad way. "It's such a shame that you don't have any skills at all. That forces us to put you right on the front lines you know." he said.

"The...front lines sir?" One of the other men asked, his face paling slightly.

Joseph nodded sadly. "Yes indeed. We can't afford to let the people with skills be cut down at the very beginning, so you people with no skills will have to shield them against the first wave of assault." Joseph explained. I glanced over at him; that was certainly a different description of the front line men than he had given me during our tactics lessons.

"Well, I have skills at archery!" The second man hastily offered.

"I think I can learn how to use a sword... if someone will teach me." the man who hadn't spoken yet added.

The first man who spoke looked at his companions in disgust.

"Splendid! That makes things much easier." Joseph said, resuming his cheerful tone.

"Peter, make sure to retest these two and send them straight to the commander this afternoon, ok?" Joseph said, dismissing the two who had spoken up in their own defense to return to their food.

"Yes sir, of course sir!" I said crisply.

When they had gone, Joseph dropped his abnormally cheerful tone and regarded the man who had been lying to him. The man stood there defiantly, refusing to back down on his lie.

"Rangers are brought up to be brutally honest, and so we know when we are being lied to. I will give you ONE last chance to be honest with me. If you don't start telling me the truth, you will find yourself working in a mine until you die from old age, or lack of sunlight, whichever happens first." Joseph said in a no-nonsense tone.

The man hesitated, glancing around as if looking for a way to get out of the situation. Finally, he turned back to Joseph and admitted, "I have training in both Sword fighting and horseback riding. I don't want to be sent off to die in battle, but I don't want to be worked to death either." he admitted in a low voice, his eyes full of bitterness.

"I went to battle at twelve years of age. The boy with me has done more brave things in his thirteen years than you have ever done in your simple city life. Are you trying to tell me that you aren't half as brave as young boys? How much training do you think I had received before my first battle? Yet I threw myself at my foe, holding my head high; determined to avenge my friends. Fear is not a foreign concept to me. But to let the fear of death drive us away from trying to protect our families, our species, that is lunacy. What do you think will happen when Kron makes his move? He will do everything in his power to kill off the army so that his demons can harvest our woman and children as food. If we give in to fear, we are handing him our wives and daughters and young sons on a silver platter. Do you really want the blood of innocents to be on your hands because you were too cowardly to fight for their lives?" Joseph explained firmly, with none of his usual kindness in his tone.

Joseph's face softened a bit, and he spoke in a quiet voice. "If you stick to your training and actually learn how to fight, your chances of surviving this war will be much better. That is the best I can offer you, or anyone in this country right now."

The man nodded, and gave me his name so I could re-test him with the other two.

# CHAPTER 18

That night; Joseph went to the area pub with the other two rangers, leaving me a tactics scenario to consider. I sat trying to think of the best way to defend a town with no wall against three hundred orcs. Joseph had given me all sorts of information about the town, such as weakest spots, retreat paths, and skills of the town guards. I sat staring at the map and information he had given me, trying to think through the best defense tactics. But I couldn't focus. What Joseph had said about the front line men to the draft dodgers was still running through my head.

When Joseph had been giving me lessons about tactics while we had been on the road, he had made the job of the front line sound almost glorified. He had told me that the front line were the shield holders, who carried big wooden shields and long spears. He had said that they waited for the mad rush of the orcs, and let them hack at the big shields in vain, as the arrows and spears took them down easily. He had told me that the front line was a place of high honor to have, and those who did fall were given all the respects and honors of any of the other positions in battle; more usually, as they were considered the bravest men. But now all of a sudden, he told a very different story. Now the front line men were cowards? People who were sent to die so that the rest of the army would have more time to be safe? The thought of sending people off to battle just to die bothered me. How could they do that to anyone, force them to march to their deaths, just because they were afraid? This caused me to have a very hard time deciding which men in the tactics scenario should be put in danger.

By the time the rangers came back, I hadn't managed to get much done with my task. All I had managed to accomplish was to have the guards in prime locations to intercept the orcs while the woman and children used the retreat paths to flee to the nearest city available. I hadn't managed to plan beyond that. Joseph and Mark were laughing softly as they entered the house, apparently sharing some joke. I stood up from the table, and waited for Joseph to address me, hoping to talk to him and find out why he had been dishonest. Mark must have seen something in my expression, because he and Jack made a hasty retreat to their room as Joseph came to see what I had gotten done.

"I told you to plan out the whole battle, thinking up as many possible plans you could for the different tactics the orcs might use. Why didn't you do so?" Joseph asked, frowning slightly as he looked at the small amount of planning I had done.

"I couldn't focus." I said calmly.

Joseph's frown deepened, and I was reminded suddenly of Lord Haldor's reaction when I would say something that wasn't acceptable. "What were you doing the past two hours then?" Joseph asked, glancing up from the parchment to look at me.

"I kept thinking about what you had said to the draft-dodgers at lunch." I replied, trying to think up the best way to ask for an explanation.

"What I said about bravery?" Joseph asked, genuinely confused.

"No, what you said about the front line men." I hesitated, but my next question burst out before I could stop myself. "Why did you lie? You said rangers are trained to not lie, yet you lied... either to me or to them." I accused.

I blushed in shame at my accusation and a flash of understanding went across Joseph's face, quickly replaced by the kind look he usually wore when he explained sensitive things to me. 'Peter, I didn't lie. I exaggerated a bit yes, but I didn't lie." Joseph held up his hand to stop me as I was about to interrupt. "If you remember my lessons to you, which I hope you do, the front line, or more correctly, the front five lines; are the shield men. They hold shields that are almost six feet tall, made of the firmest wood in the kingdom. They are trained to have the shields work as a moving wall. Orcs are what we call chaotic attackers. They attack without any thoughts to their own safety, rushing straight at the shield men. The men will repel the attack with the shield, and move the shields to the side just enough to use their long spears to stab their opponents. Do you not remember me explaining this to you?"

"Yes sir. But today you told the men that the front line was made up of cowards who had no skill whatsoever. You made it sound like they were just sent to die first, so the rest of the army would live longer." I said, trying hard to not show how upset I was.

"Yes I did. I said it to see how easily the men could be encouraged to do what they were told. As you saw, two of them were quite willing to do whatever they had to. Their fear was simple fear of death, which is a basic human instinct. You don't have that fear because you weren't handed a paper that seemed to you like a death sentence. But the way those two men were thinking, they had been sentenced to death, and it is just a matter of what they can do to delay the inevitable. Will they die? I have no idea. But what I did was show them that the whole point of training was to prevent their deaths, and so they were willing to be trained. So what I said was true, from a certain perspective. The front line often is the first to be wiped out, but they do far more damage to the opposing army then any coward who turns and fleas from his civic duty will ever do."

I frowned. "You are talking about PEOPLE! It is MEN who you are talking about having die. How can you talk about people's deaths so calmly? They have the right to live!" I said angrily.

"You don't think I know that? I've had my people, including my dearest friend, cut down in front of and beside me the last time Kron attacked us!" Joseph snapped, a sudden flash of anger on his usually kind face. He took a deep breath to calm down and continued. "I'm sorry Peter. I know how you feel, I use to think the same way. I suppose I have seen so much death that I have become more immune to it or something. With age, those who have been in battle come to realize that there is a time and a place for thinking about the people, and a time and place where you have no choice but to look at just the numbers, not at the souls lost.

I will never deny that battle is horrible. But we have no choice. The first lesson of war Lord Haldor taught me is that young men will die. After that, it becomes a matter of how few people will do so. If you look at tactics and think about the people, you will never be able to protect them. The only way to win is to stand our ground, but if we try to look at battles as how many souls will be lost, then the whole fight is lost, and we all die. Perhaps you are too young to understand, but in order to win, lives will be lost sometimes. That is why the men felt like they had received a death sentence, because the fact of the matter is that people die. But Peter, would you rather have a few people die so the rest of the world will be safe, or would you rather back away and let the Kronlords harvest us like they did Lance?"

I looked Joseph in the eye, understanding what he was saying. "I would rather have a few die than everyone." I agreed firmly.

I lay on the couch late that night staring into the fire thoughtfully. Today had been the first day Joseph had openly talked to me about Kron like he would talk to an adult. For once he hadn't decided I was too young to worry about such things. But what had changed? Why was he suddenly treating me like an adult? Less than a week ago he had scolded me for trying to find out about Lance, now all of a sudden he was expecting me to accept the evil facts of war.

I sneezed and rubbed my nose with the palm of my hand. The lumpy couch I had been given to use as a bed had a definite musty smell. I shifted so I was lying on my back instead of my side, but that didn't help much. Last night I had been so tired that I had fallen to sleep easily, but tonight I couldn't get comfortable. Finally, I got to my feet and walked around a bit. My cloak was on the floor folded up under my weapons. I put the cloak on, and stepped outside for some air. I shivered in the cold. The temperature had dropped quite a lot the past couple days as winter approached rapidly. I blew on my hands to warm them up, and considered going back inside. But a slight movement caught my eye. There was something slithering through the overgrown lawn towards the house. I squinted, trying to see through the darkness. "Who's there?" I challenged. There was no answer except for a raspy breathing. I touched the door handle, ready to go back inside, but my curiosity was still roused. "Show yourself!" I demanded.

A dark shadow rose up six feet tall from the grass. I saw glowing red eyes, and multiple rows of sharp teeth. The shadow sprang at me, and I cried out in alarm, flinging my arms up to protect myself. The weight of the creature threw me flat on my back on the ground. It was all I could do to keep that face and those rows of snapping teeth away from me. I could feel its hot breath, and I recognized the distinct odor of blood. I felt scaly hands wrap around my throat, and tighten. As I was gasping in vain for air, the door behind me flew open and the rangers rushed at my attacker, who let go of me with a strange hiss. The creature backed away, and tried to escape back into the shadows, but Joseph had four arrows in the dark shape before it had gotten more than a few feet. The creature hissed once more, and lay still in death.

"Did it bite you? Did its teeth scratch you at all?" Jack asked me, looking me over in concern bordering on fear. I shook my head, watching Joseph and Mark look around for more of the creatures. "Wh...what is that thing?" I asked, unable to stop shaking.

Joseph looked over sharply. "Jack, take Peter inside, right now. Get him to safety!" he ordered.

Jack had me sit down at the table, and he made me a cup of tea made with dried mint leaves in it (a common ingredient that people in Andor use to relax). I calmed down a bit as I sipped at the soothing beverage. "What was that thing?" I asked again once my hands had stopped shaking.

Jack shook his head instead of answering. He wouldn't stay still, sitting for a few seconds, jumping to his feet to look outside, and then pacing around, his hands constantly touching his weapons as if to reassure himself that they were still there.

It was almost an hour before Joseph and Mark returned, looking grim and tired. "Did you find them?" Jack asked, approaching the two rangers.

"We did, but we were too late. Unfortunately; Peter was their second victim of the night, not the first." Joseph answered, moving the kettle back into the fire to heat the water inside.

There was a bang and the sound of splintering wood near the door, and I turned quickly. Mark was wringing his hand which he had used to punch a hole in the wall in his anger. His knuckles were bleeding, and he stared at his injured hand as if the pain he had inflicted on himself wasn't nearly enough to make up for whatever had happened.

"Who was it?" Jack asked, his voice strained, his face screwed up like men's faces get when they are trying hard to not let people know how upset they really are.

"Alex's youngest girl, two years old next week, just two years old." Mark answered, sagging onto the couch and burying his face into his hands.

There was a silence in the room, and everyone's eyes were downcast. I stared into the soggy tea leaves in my cup. If one of those creatures that had attacked me had gone after the girl Mark was talking about, no wonder he was upset he had gotten there too late to save her.

"Well, they will never kill again, that is a victory in the end I suppose." Mark said finally, going over to remove the steaming kettle from the flames.

"Will someone *please* tell me what that creature was?" I asked quietly, bracing myself to be dismissed as too young, as usual.

"It was a Grimold, a child snatcher." Joseph explained quietly.

I sat and stared into the fire. Child snatchers were a thing of ghost stories. They came to villages and stole babies out of their cradles, taking them into the forest to eat them. In the smaller villages, people would put heavy locked shutters onto the windows of rooms where small children slept and hung sacks of paprika above the windowpane to repel the demons. "My father said they were just a myth, a superstition passed down from the old days." I said weakly.

"If only! No Peter, you will find that most evil creatures that people try to claim aren't real turn out to be all too real. It is dangerous to assume anything evil isn't real. That is why you need to learn lesson number two, which you will now recite for us." Joseph said calmly as he poured himself a cup of mint tea.

"Do not forget or cast aside as unimportant any information you are given. You never know when a discussion from long ago may prove to be vital to survival." I recited obediently.

"But didn't the parents lock the windows? I mean, in my father's town everyone has heavy shutters and paprika, even if they don't believe in monsters." I said weakly.

"Yes of course they did. But they live in the poorest part of the city, and the street is plagued with rats. Some of the rats had gnawed right through the Paprika bag, and eaten most of its contents." Mark explained.

"Did Kron send them?" I asked nervously.

"The Grimold? Probably not. Those creatures travel in groups of three, going from place to place hunting for their next meal. They may feel Kron is getting stronger, but I doubt they went hunting here tonight on his orders." Joseph reassured me.

There was silence as everyone drank their tea. Mark rose after a while, and rummaged in one of the cupboards. He returned with a bottle of brown alcohol and several shot glasses. He poured drinks for everyone including me, and put the cap back on the bottle. We all stood up with one fist behind our backs in formality, and Joseph raised his glass. "To Stephanie, daughter of Alex and Ruth, may her soul find its way to paradise without falter or fear. I'm sorry we couldn't get to you in time."

We all drained our glasses as one, and sat back down, me coughing violently due to the strength of the drink.

I was dying to ask why the Grimold had gone after me, but I had a feeling that the time was inappropriate for me to be focusing on myself. Fortunately, Jack asked the question. "Why did they go after Peter though sir? I mean, he's quite a bit older than their usual victim preference." He said to Mark.

Mark shrugged and turned to Joseph for an explanation. Joseph sat examining the shot glass thoughtfully. "Possibly the Grimold saw in Peter the same qualities that Abiyram saw." He replied.

"Who?" Mark and Jack asked in unison.

"Joseph blinked, coming out of his thoughts and back to the rangers looking for answers. "Peter is very much like a small child in his virtues. He probably felt like an ideal victim to the Grimold, who go after small children specifically because of their purity of soul." Joseph translated for the men who had not been there at the healing house.

"Peter, go sleep in my bed. I need to tell Lord Haldor what happened, and you need to put this behind you." Joseph told me. "Oh and Peter," Joseph prompted gently as I started to get to my feet, "next time the mood strikes you to go outside alone at night, take your weapons. We give them to you for a reason you know."

I got to my feet slowly, and entered Joseph's room. It was a small room with the only furniture being the bed, and a small table with a vase of dried flowers on it. The covers were thrown at the foot of the bed as Joseph had gotten up so fast. I untangled them, and lay down.

I could hear the rangers murmuring from the main room, and I tapped into the magic, curious to know what they were saying now. "I'd never say this to the boy of course, but thank goodness he DID go outside. If the Grimold had come after him while he was asleep, he would have died, and we probably wouldn't even know he'd been grabbed until morning. It's not like we bought any paprika, who the heck expects a Grimold to go after a boy his age?!" Mark was saying.

"Shut up! For all we know, Peter is listening in. Haven't you ever heard Haldor talk about his gem? Peter listens in on conversations constantly." Joseph replied harshly.

There was immediate silence from the main room. After a moment, everyone went into the back room so they could talk with less chance of me hearing them. I stopped listening, remembering harshly why I had resolved to be more careful about which conversations I listened in on.

I lay staring at the closed door. I was horrified at what I had heard. Had I really come so close to death? I silently resolved not to go back to sleep, despite the exhaustion I felt as my body recovered from the shock. What if there were more Grimolds out there looking for people like me? What if there was something even worse? I lay clutching the blanket protectively until the soothing tea and alcohol pulled me down into sleep. After a couple hours, I woke up slightly to the sound of movement. Joseph had come back into the room. He sat down on the floor near my bed, took my hand into his, and closed his eyes to sleep. I squeezed his hand sleepily to reassure him that I was ok, and he squeezed back gently. I went back to sleep feeling much safer now that Joseph was with me. I knew nothing would try to attack me with Joseph there.

\*\*\*

The next morning, Joseph told me to stay at the house. "How come? I mean, you let me help yesterday, so why not today?" I asked, disappointed at being left behind.

"Because you never did finish your assigned tactics practice, and I have three more for you to work on. You have your lessons, and we have our work. That is what being an apprentice involves, learning." Joseph answered, fastening his cloak and leading the way out of the house. I sat down at the table and looked over the scenarios. I closed my eyes as I thought them over, calling to mind everything Joseph had taught me, as well as the little bits about battle I had learned from hanging out in the town guards barracks with Kevin, and the meeting Lord Haldor had had with us in Stoneriver. The time went by fast, and before I knew it, Joseph had come back to have lunch with me. He looked over my work as he ate, and I sat trying not to squirm as he considered my plans. "Very well thought out Peter; with these plans, the towns would indeed have the advantage. How did you know so much about orcs?" he asked, handing the plans back to me.

"I read about them, back when I was at the fortress." I explained.

"Good for you! I'm glad to hear you took initiative to do that on your own." Joseph said; sitting back, pleased with me.

After we had eaten, Joseph told me that he had a new challenge for me. "There is a bag in a heavily guarded office that Lord Haldor wants you to retrieve for us. You have until midnight to get the bag out of the office and bring it back here. You will have to avoid the guards, and make sure you are not heard or seen by any of them. They will be looking for you, so you need to be careful. If you are caught, you have failed the challenge. If you succeed, you will get rewarded.

I grinned as Joseph told me the rules for the challenge. It seemed like it would be a pleasant afternoon after all, certainly better than sitting inside all day.

I set off through town dressed just in my black shirt and pants, no cloak. No one stared at me as I made my way through town, as I wasn't wearing a cloak or carrying weapons other than one dagger I had slipped into my pocket, just in case. I was just another face in the crowded streets of the big city. When I got close to the castle, I walked more carefully, looking in all directions to see if there were any guards around. I watched the actions of the guards and the castle workers for a while, studying their routines. When a carriage rode past, I swung myself onto the back with the boy riding above the wheel. He looked at me curiously, and I grinned at him and winked. I got off the carriage as soon as I was through the drawbridge, and slipped into the stables.

"Hey! Who are you?" One of the stable hands asked in surprise. I put a finger to my lips and hurried over, glancing over my shoulder to see if one of the guards had heard him. "My name's Peter. I'm a messenger sent by the king to the city." I said in a hushed voice.

"Well what are you doing in the stables?" The young man asked, his own tone automatically hushed to match mine.

"I need to know where the Barron's office is. I was told to get something there." I explained.

"Oh, alright then. But why not ask the guards?" The young man asked, frowning suspiciously.

I shrugged casually. "Because I decided to ask you instead of course." I said in a tone as if it was the most obvious answer in the world.

The stable boy blinked in surprise, and looked like he felt silly for asking such an obvious question. He led me through the stables and out the door nearest to the main building. "It's right up there, at the top of the tower." He said pointing it out to me.

"Right, thanks then." I said cheerfully, setting off in a very different direction then the young man had pointed out to me.

"Hey! Where are you going now?" he asked, confused.

"Well I've been told the Barron will be having his afternoon tea around this time. So that means he'll be in his lounge, not his office." I explained simply.

"Oh right... I knew that." The stable boy answered in embarrassment.

I grinned to myself as I left him behind, confused and embarrassed. I had learned years ago that if I used the right tone with people who were older than me but not yet adult, it would produce interesting results. I knew instinctively that the young man wouldn't report me to the guards now, because he'd feel silly to admit that he didn't understand my actions, when my tone had suggested that they should be obvious.

I wandered over to the kitchens in a carefully casual way, looking out for guards. There were none near the kitchens. I entered silently and looked around. The castle kitchens were as big as my father's whole house including his workshop. The metal counters were practically mirrors in their cleanliness, and the ovens were big enough for my father to have used in his workshop if they could be made hot enough. I couldn't resist looking around in some awe at the huge kitchen. I spotted several trays of tarts cooling near the ovens, and went over to these with interest. There were no cooks around, as there was no cooking to be done at this hour, so everyone was on break. I touched the tarts to see how hot they were, and found that they were cool enough to handle. I helped myself to a selection of them, since I had more or less been invited by the Barron to roam about the castle during my challenge. 'Besides,' I told myself as I slipped back outside again, 'it's not like I ate any desert at the feast, so in the end it all evens out'.

I sat amongst the barrels outside munching on my treats, and waited for the cover of darkness. As I waited, I studied the guards' routs, learning their patterns. At nightfall there was a change of shifts, and I used that opportunity to make my move. Silently I slipped in the deep shadows over near the heavily guarded entrance. While the last shift of guards was still busy chatting with their replacements, I climbed up the wall a few yards so I was out of reach. I stayed still for a while, waiting patiently for the guards to settle into their watch. The guards faced away from the door, looking out at the courtyard, so they didn't see me as I carefully climbed up the tower. The window was locked, but locks had never been a problem for me. I took out a wire Joseph had agreed I could use, and soon, the lock of the stained glass window was open.

I slipped into the dark office, and closed the window most of the way, just in case someone did happen to look up. I crept to the door, tapping in to the magic to intensify my hearing and listened for sounds out in the hall. I could hear the Barron moving in his personal rooms, and I slipped silently over to the desk. I listened carefully for anyone approaching, and silently began to search through the drawer Joseph had told me I was permitted to look in. In the back, under several documents I found the bag. It was a money bag with a silver dagger painted on it. I took the bag and slipped it into my pocket, closing the drawer softly. I winced as the money inside clinked with the bag's movement. I pressed my hand firmly against my hip, making the bag stay silent, and turned to leave.

I heard footsteps approaching, and hastily moved the chair, slipping in to hide under the desk. I pulled the chair back so it wouldn't look moved, and stayed very still. The door unlocked and opened, as someone checked the office. He paused in the doorway for a moment, and then left again, locking the door behind him. I stayed where I was for a while, waiting until the guard was far away. I scolded myself for not considering the fact that if the outside of the tower was guarded; the inside was likely to be as well.

I was twice as cautious as I made my way back out of the castle grounds. I had come far too close to being caught in my opinion, and that was not good. I got back to the ranger's house by the twentieth hour, and everyone look up in surprise bordering on amazement when I entered alone so early in the night.

"You made it already?" Mark asked amazed.

In answer I pulled the money bag out of my pocket and handed it to Joseph. Joseph grinned at the amazement on the other ranger's faces. "Now you know why he is Haldor's gem." He said cheerfully.

"How many times has he played the games?" Jack asked as I sat down to eat the dinner Mark offered me.

"None officially before tonight, but the reason Lord Haldor first took an interest in Peter was because he watched him sneak through town every night when he was a small boy. Peter was a quite adventurous and defiant child. Lord Haldor told me Peter refused to stop even after his father literally locked him up at night." Joseph said grinning at me.

I grinned back, remembering the many times my father had beaten me and locked me into his workshop for disobeying him, and how stubborn I had been in my refusal to stop roaming at night. "I was very bored at night. All anyone ever wanted to do was sleep, so I had nothing else to do with my time." I explained.

The rangers laughed at my explanation. "Here Peter, this is your prize." Joseph said, handing me the money bag. As he passed it back to me, I heard the coins inside clinking again. I opened it curiously, and gasped in amazement at the wealth I had been given.

"There are at *least* twenty five pieces of silver in here!" I exclaimed. I had never held so much money before, much less been given it as my very own. "That's TWO and a half a gold!" I stated in amazement.

"Well, you did pass a level ten challenge with four hours to spare. Mark thought Lord Haldor was making a mistake in giving a first year apprentice such a hard game. Obviously Lord Haldor knew what he was doing. You earned the money Peter." Joseph told me, smiling in satisfaction at my reaction.

# CHAPTER 19

Joseph and I left Woodward and headed east to the town of Rockwood. It was a good ten hours walk from the city to the small logging town, and it had begun to snow. Before we left Woodward; Joseph had brought me to a cloth weaver, and had purchased leather winter gloves and a liner for my cloak. As we set off, I was glad of the cold weather gear. The liner was made of soft wool, and was a pure white color. Joseph had a similar liner of his own that Mark had given him as they were around the same size and build.

"Why white? I mean, won't that show up against the background, making it harder to blend in?" I asked as we left town.

"It is a type of camouflage. With the combination of dark green and white, we will be able to blend into the winter background once there are several inches of snow. Until then, the white stays on the inside, and just keeps us warmer."

"Sir, I have been wondering something for a while now." I said once we were a mile or so away from the city.

"What's on your mind Peter?" Joseph asked, looking all around as always.

"What has Lord Haldor been saying about me? Every ranger I meet already knows so much about me, and I've never even seen them. I've still only known rangers existed for a couple months or so, yet the whole guild knows my own past better than I do."

160

"Do they indeed? So you've met the whole guild and had them tell you so?" Joseph asked; his tone slightly amused.

"No I haven't! You know I haven't met them all. Yet all the one's I have met know who I am!" I said, my voice testy in frustration at Joseph making fun of me.

"Lord Haldor has been watching you since you were young. He's kind of adopted you as his new project you might say." Joseph paused to consider what to say and what not to say to me. "Peter, most rangers are a prodigy; that's why they were chosen. But out of the rangers there will sometimes appear people like you, me, and Thelmer. Sometimes there are people whose skills before they even get the magic are as powerful as rangers skills become after years of training. Thelmer's father was a knight. He brought Thelmer up learning battle skills since the boy was old enough to walk. I don't know if Thelmer ever told you this, and I beg you to never tell anyone else, but Thelmer was marked down to be a ranger since he was just a baby. Thelmer's father was a night of Askia who worked hand in hand with Sir Lucas, and he asked Lord Haldor to accept his son as a ranger, because he wanted Thelmer to have the best life possible, and he was wise enough to remember how important rangers are to the country. When he died in battle against a raid of swamp trolls, Lord Haldor went to check on Thelmer and his mother. He saw Thelmer's amazing skills, and took him in at once without hesitation.

Because Thelmer is a prodigy who has spent his whole life learning how to be a ranger, his skills were adequate before he even received the magic. You have similar skills, more actually. Thelmer excels at archery and tactics, but I have yet to find anything we commonly teach apprentices your age to teach you that you don't already have skills in. Magic can make a ranger an expert at their skills to the point of being unable to fail, but it works on what skills you already have. We train you in new skills so that you have more uses for the magic to help you. But I am at a loss as to what skills you could use development in that your year mates will study this year." Joseph explained.

"What do you mean by adequate?" I asked.

"I mean that you would pass the final exams given to ranger apprentices in order to graduate and become a full adult ranger. When I say someone's skills are adequate, I mean that they are adequate for a ranger, not an apprentice." Joseph answered lightly.

I stopped walking and stood in shock. Joseph turned around and paused, waiting for me. "You mean… that day you were testing my archery skills… I would have passed the final exams given to *rangers*?" I gasped.

"Yep, oh that reminds me." Joseph said, looking at me sternly. "If I ever hear that you hold back on your skills just to get someone to like you again, I'll twist your ears raw. You have no right to be ashamed of your gifts, and I don't care if Gene and the girls never speak to you again, you will NOT hold back. You were handpicked by Lord Haldor to be a ranger. He has only ever selected two other people in all his life. If you want to deny your abilities, then I guarantee you, Lord Haldor will discharge you from his ranks faster than you can blink, understand?"

"Yes sir." I said quietly, feeling ashamed that I had held back because of Gene.

"I just wanted to be his friend. Gene, well he kind of dismissed me when I told him my dad was a blacksmith. I thought that maybe if I showed him that we were equals he'd like me better." I admitted as we were walking again.

Joseph sighed softly, looking up at the sky. "Peter, anyone who does not accept you for who you are is not someone who would make a good friend. Would you rather have Gene be friends with a lie, or ignore you?"

"Neither sir, I want him to be friends with who I am." I replied.

"If you had to choose, would you rather have Gene be your friend because he thinks you are a lesser person than you truly are, or would you rather find a friend who accepts you?" Joseph pressed.

"The second one sir." I agreed, understanding what he was telling me.

"Peter, Lord Haldor has much bigger and better plans for your life than the (in comparison) simple life of a common ranger. You are destined for greatness. Even the rarest of magical creatures come to you. You are the first human who has seen a Lammasu in hundreds of years! That is why most people thought they were just a legend, because no one at all has caught so much as a glimpse of them for many generations. There isn't a man alive today who can remember their grandparents ever having seen one. Yet one came to you, of all people. Perhaps you are too young to understand, but..." Joseph trailed off suddenly.

"What?" I asked, looking and listening hard, wondering if I had missed something I should have seen.

Joseph shook his head, and we walked in silence for a while. I couldn't help but wonder what Joseph had stopped himself from telling me, but then I remembered the conversation I had overheard at the healing house. Perhaps Joseph had stopped himself from telling me what he and the other rangers had decided might be dangerous for me to know. I walked with him in silence, not having any desire to press the issue and loose my friendship with Abiyram.

"You still haven't really told me what Lord Haldor has been telling people about me." I said after an hour or so of traveling through the snow in silence.

Joseph tilted his head to one side. "Basically he's been telling everyone how pleased he is with your raw skills. Once in a while he will oversee the apprentices in their training exercises to check on their progress, and he has been scolding even Thelmer for not trying hard enough. You've become his standard for an ideal apprentice. Anyone whose skills aren't up to par with yours were before you got the magic is considered to be not trying hard enough to develop their skills. You've set a whole new standard for what is adequate in an apprentice. I feel sympathy for your year mates, who are no doubt being run ragged trying to become as good as you were." Joseph was smiling slightly at me, and I smiled back remembering how hard just one day of training had been for Gene when I hadn't felt tired out at all.

"But Peter, listen closely, because what I have to tell you is very important, and you must never forget it." Joseph paused and waited for me to give him my full attention.

I looked up at him curiously.

"To those who more is given, more will be expected in return. You have been blessed with amazing abilities, but that does *not* make you better than anyone. It makes you the servant of your people. You are their caretaker, just as the king and Lord Haldor and I myself are. A position of leadership makes it your duty to care for those under you, not look down on them. To be in command is to take care of people, to protect and love them. Can you understand that?" He asked, looking at me closely.

"I think I do, sir. You're saying that I need to use my abilities to help others, not to embarrass them, right?" I asked, nodding slowly.

"Close enough yes; don't forget that fact. It is one of the most important lessons you may ever learn, and I hope that you take it as a way of life rather than a suggestion." Joseph agreed, leading the way through the woods.

\*\*\*

When we were about three miles away from the town, there was a broken wheelbarrow in the road. Beside it was a figure slumped in a sitting position, with the snow piling on his backside and his wide brimmed hat. Joseph and I hurried over in concern, wondering if he was hurt. But the man raised his head as we approached, and rose to greet us. He was an old man, with his wrinkled skin brown from years of sun exposure. "Are you hurt sir?" Joseph asked, looking the man over for injuries. The man shook his head and gestured to the cart. The wheel had snapped off and the cart had tipped over, the potatoes inside spilling out onto the road.

"No ranger, I am unhurt. I was bringing my produce to sell in town when my cart broke, and tipped over. I tried to lift it, but I haven't the strength for such things anymore." The man looked down at his withered hands. "I'm a stubborn old fool, insisting on doing this instead of leaving it to my grandson like my daughter asked. But I just can't..." The man's voice caught in his throat, and he cleared it roughly to keep speaking. "My daughter wants me to stop working, but I just can't. How can I resort to sitting on the porch all day, every day with nothing to do? I'm seventy three years old, far too old to be treated like she would want me to be. But..." The man trailed off, looking at his spilled potatoes in despair.

Joseph put his hand on the old farmer's shoulder. "Let's just get you to town before the snow gets any worse." He suggested, glancing up at the darkening sky where the snow was falling heavy and slushy to the ground. Joseph helped the man gather up the spilled produce, and he asked me to inspect the wheelbarrow and see if it could be fixed. I felt anger building up inside me as I recognized some of the deceptive tricks that dishonest blacksmiths used to take shortcuts and cheat people out of their money. The welding job on the wheel had been done with an inexpensive metal that was not meant for bearing the weight of stuff that one would commonly put in this kind of farm equipment. The metal was supposed to be used for things like hand tools and equipment. It wasn't meant to hold more than twenty or thirty pounds of weight. The fact that some dishonest man had in effect stolen money from a poor old farmer made me feel hot with anger.

"Well, can it be fixed?" Joseph prompted me.

I stood up, and brushed the snow off my pants before answering, trying to calm down. "Sir, this wheelbarrow was made badly on purpose. A blacksmith would have to be mentally daft to make the wheelbarrow with the metal used on this one and actually expect it to work. It was a setup. My father told me about this kind of thing, he said it would work fine for long enough for the blacksmith to not be blamed, but it is set up to fall apart. This man was cheated out of his money." I told Joseph, who nodded as if he had suspected as much.

"Is your farm closer, or is the town closer to where we are now?"

Joseph asked the old man, whose shoulders sagged as he heard that he had been cheated out of his money.

"The town is closer Mr. Ranger, but all my potatoes…" The man trailed off as he realized he'd have to leave most of them, as there was no way for us to get the large wheelbarrow to town without a wheel.

Joseph loaded me up with as much of the produce as I could carry in one of the largest of the farmer's boxes that he had brought to display the potatoes at the market. Joseph considered trying to carry a large box himself, but I reminded him that Lord Haldor didn't want him carrying anything too heavy. I did my best to make my voice sound humble, but Lord Haldor had essentially told me that it was my job to make sure Joseph didn't get hurt. Joseph looked at me and seemed to understand why I was reminding him of Lord Haldor's orders. So Joseph and the farmer carried a box between them, and we set off for town, leaving the rest behind. It was a very slow three miles as I had to rest every few minutes because the box was so heavy, being stacked to overflowing with what felt more and more like rocks each time I lifted the box after a rest. By the time we got to town my arms were burning in agony, and my hands were covered with sore spots that were threatening to blister.

Joseph and I helped the farmer bring his potatoes to the storehouse where people kept their goods for the market days. Joseph gave one of the other farmers some money and requested the farmer help the old man retrieve the rest of his goods. The farmer gave the piece of silver back to Joseph, saying that he was more than willing to help his neighbor. Joseph asked the old farmer for the name of the blacksmith he had bought the wheelbarrow from, and then Joseph and I left to find the head of the town guards.

We found the head of the town guards (who was in this town a retired ranger) in the barracks, in a back office that was set up very much like Carl's office was in my father's town. On one wall was a detailed map of the town, and on another wall was a map of the kingdom, with tagged pins in various different places marking the known location of various people of interest. An older man was sitting at the desk reading through an official document with a silver ribbon marking it as military business. The man stood up to greet us, and Joseph and I bowed to him in return. "The town knights and I have already tested the men's skills, and would like your input on my decisions for where to send them." The man Stanly said to Joseph after the introductions took place and we all sat down.

"That is just as well, because I have something else to discuss with you." Joseph said calmly.

Stanly raised an eyebrow slightly. "Indeed? Pray continue then my Lord." He invited, spreading his hands out in invitation.

I started in surprise and looked at Joseph. Since when was he a lord?!

Joseph seemed just as surprised at the new form of address, and looked questioningly at Stanly, his face paling slightly.

"Lord Earl is dead. He died this afternoon from a heart attack (which at his age was bound to happen sooner or later). That makes you an official Lord now, since there is an opening in the number of ranger lords. Haldor declared you a lord in Earl's place. Of course, the ceremony won't happen until you reach the capital, but the title still holds."

"Why did Lord Haldor not contact me?" Joseph asked softly, his brow furrowed.

Stanly raised his eyebrow again, folding his hands on his desk calmly. "You were supposed to be here a couple hours ago. When you didn't show up; Lord Haldor told me to give you the message for him as he is very busy." Stanly paused and smiled slightly. "Also I think he figured if I give you the message and he signs you up before you are informed, you won't be able to turn down the title again, like you've done the last few times it has been offered to you." Stanly lowered his voice, his slight smile disappearing. "It would not do for the head of the guild of rangers to be anything less than a lord you know. As second in command, it is only a matter of time before you are given the position. You might as well get used to being a lord now,

167

instead of it being yet another thing to adjust to."

Joseph nodded reluctantly, and pulled his hood off, signifying acceptance of his higher rank.

"What was it you wanted to talk to me about my Lord?" Stanly asked.

Joseph told Stanly about the farmer who had been cheated by the faulty wheelbarrow. As Joseph talked, Stanly opened his desk and began to search through his papers. He pulled out a scroll on the blacksmith, and opened it, skimming through the notes he had on the man.

"Well, I gave him more than enough warning. He's been fined twenty silver total in the past three years. I've had enough of his dirty dealings." Stanly muttered to himself. He looked up from the document. "I'll take care of him my lord. Eighteen months in the mines should hopefully be enough to cure his swindling habits."

Joseph and I went to the inn, as there wasn't enough room for us to stay with Stanly in the barracks. As we walked through town, I thought back to the brief encounter I had with the dead ranger lord. He had praised me and spoken to me in a kind voice. I remembered Lyle telling me that he was a very strict father, and wondered how Lyle was doing coping with the Lord's death. Lyle had said his father didn't praise him no matter how well he did, but he still gave off the impression that he and his father had a good relationship.

Once Joseph had paid for a room for us and we had entered the room to freshen up before going down to eat, I broke the silence that had grown between us. "Joseph, ah…sir…my Lord?" I stammered.

Joseph raised an eyebrow and waited for me to continue. "I… how do I address you now my lord? I mean…" I stammered as Joseph looked up at the ceiling in something resembling despair, "Everyone calls Lord Haldor 'my lord' and bows to him dropping to one knee when he appears, should… am I to do that with you sir?" I asked, feeling uncomfortable in my efforts to not be offensive now that Joseph was a lord. The lords of the kingdom were to be given all

THE RANGERS OF ANDOR

the respects possible. A lord was one of the leaders of the country and, as Thelmer had told me, a soldier could be reprimanded or even discharged if they failed to show proper respect. Lords were considered almost royalty as most of them excluding the rangers were of the king's bloodline in one way or another.

"This is exactly why I turned down the title in the first place." Joseph muttered under his breath. "Alright Peter, if you and I are going to work together we're going to have to set a few ground rules. First of all, the proper address is 'my lord' or 'Lord Joseph'. But I don't want you to feel you have to call me that all the time. When it's just the two of us, call me Joseph please. Things will get uncomfortable for us both if you keep worrying about what to call me. When we are around other people, then you use the lord title, but not when it is just us two, or when its people I say are ok to be informal around." Joseph gave a weary sigh. "As for bowing, you would bow to me the same way you'd bow to Barron Rice. Only to the head of the guild do you need to get down on one knee. The royal family too of course." Joseph said, adding the last part as an afterthought. "You bow when you are summoned and dismissed, or when I give you an order. But again, since you and I need to work together, you get the special treatment, so you don't have to worry about formality when it is just us two, ok?"

"Yes my lord." I agreed, and then blushed when I realized my mistake in Joseph's preferred form of address. Joseph raised his eyes to the ceiling again with a sigh.

# CHAPTER 20

Joseph brought me to the pub area of the inn, muttering directions to me in a low voice that only my magically intensified hearing could pick up. "I want you to learn how to listen in on conversations. So I borrowed a book on tactics from Stanly, and I want you to pretend to read it. But what you will really be doing is listening to various conversations going on. The magic can help your focus on not just everything around, but it could also be used to zero in on certain conversations, even if they were all the way across the room." Joseph instructed me to listen a bit too each conversation and report back to him everything of interest I could remember. He said it would be a good way to practice.

So while Joseph sat at the bar telling the men around him about an encounter he once had with a troll, I sat staring at the tactics book, and letting my focus glide from one conversation to another, flipping the page every now and then to give off the impression that I was studying. For the most part, people were just talking about the life they lived out here. This area of the forest of Brune was apparently a big logging community, so most of the talk was about the orders that were pouring out of the capital for wood to be used for crafting weapons. There was a lot of laughter suddenly from over at the bar as Joseph was imitating the troll's small vocabulary.

"I hate them rangers, all of 'em. You can't trust those rangers any further than you can trust a bandit. Filthy little spies they are, always sneaking around getting into our business." An angry and heavily slurred voice muttered. I couldn't help but look up to see who had spoken. Over by the door leading outside a thick bearded man was sitting, grumbling to himself. His face and hands were smudged with soot, and I realized as I looked at the black work apron he hadn't bothered to take off that he was a blacksmith. He had the anvil and hammer symbol painted on the apron, I could just make it out through the soot that so often got all over people as they wielded metal.

The blacksmith glanced at me suddenly; and I turned away quickly. Too quickly I realized, as the man made his way over to me; staggering in his drunkenness. The drunk blacksmith put his face close to mine, and I leaned back so far that I almost fell out of my chair. His eyes were fierce and wild, and I almost gagged at the strong smell of ale on his breath. "You want something ranger boy?" He snarled at me, grabbing the front of my shirt to stop me from getting away.

"N...no sir." I said hastily, wishing I hadn't let my fear show through. The first lesson Fletch had taught me was to never let your opponent know you were nervous or scared. Always look like you are in control, even if you're not.

"You were a-spying on me, weren't you?" The blacksmith growled, shaking me roughly.

I opened my mouth to answer, but a calm patient voice spoke up from behind the man. "What seems to be the problem here gentlemen?" The blacksmith released me and turned to face Joseph, who was standing calmly, one hand resting casually against his sword hilt.

"You and your little spy brat should be run out of town. We don't want none of your kind sneaking around here no more." The blacksmith said, swaying slightly as he tried to make himself look taller than he really was.

"Then you have picked the wrong country to live in sir. The rangers have been here for over seven hundred years, and we have no intention of clearing out any time soon." Joseph said calmly.

The blacksmith spat on the floor at Joseph's feet. "Here's what I think of you ranger spies!" he snarled. Without another word, he shoved his way out of the inn, and staggered out into the streets.

"I think Stanly is looking for you." Joseph called after him.

There was silence in the room for a moment, and then slowly the conversations picked up where they had left off. The cheerful atmosphere returned gradually, until the room was lively once more.

Joseph and I made our way back to our room. My lesson in listening in on conversations had been more or less brought to an end, as everyone would now be focusing on watching me curiously after the incident with the drunk blacksmith.

"I'm sorry sir." I told Joseph as we prepared for bed.

Joseph looked at me confused. "Sorry for what Peter?" He asked.

"For causing a scene like that. I realized as soon as I turned too quick that I had given myself away. I failed your test sir." I explained, not understanding why Joseph was confused.

"Peter, that wasn't a test! That was just a lesson, a practice for you. For goodness sake, not everything I have you do is going to be a way for me to judge you! Relax son, you worry far too much about letting people down with your indiscretions." Joseph said with a slight laugh.

"Besides," he added as I was about to ask a question, "We got the information I was looking for. So all in all, you acted just like I needed you to."

I stared at Joseph, not having the slightest idea what he was talking about. "I was wondering who the blacksmith Stanly was looking for was. By you acting as you did, it brought him out in the open."

"So, you were using me as bait?" I asked.

Joseph laughed softly. "No Peter, I was using you as a lookout. In towns like this, the inn is a common place for people to come after working all day. It's a place to relax, and to not have to worry about cooking dinner, perfect for unmarried men. You can learn the most interesting things by listening to people in an inn or tavern, where the good food and ale makes them feel relaxed and open enough to discuss things they wouldn't say on the streets."

"But… you were talking and making so much noise at the bar, how could you possibly hear what anyone was saying?"

"I did that to pull their attention away from you Peter. If the men focus on me as the potential threat, they will ignore the real eyes and ears of the situation. That's also why I had you on the other side of the room, because any shifty people would want to be as far away from me as they could sit. Like I said, it was just practice for you. There may come a time one day when having skills at listening unobserved may come in handy." Joseph said, putting a reassuring hand on my shoulder.

The next few days were a time of great happiness for me. I knew that the war was a serious matter, and that it was the reason Joseph and I were traveling on the road from one town to another. But all the same, as there had been no word of attacks or battles yet I couldn't make myself worry too much. By now the news of war had spread throughout the kingdom, and so Joseph's job in the towns and villages we stopped at was just to check to make sure the conscripts were well on their way. This left Joseph and me lots of time together, and I learned a lot of fun things from him. I learned how to survive in the wild, how to fight with my daggers, how to navigate at night by following the stars, and I practiced the skills I already had such as sword fighting, archery, and silent movement.

One night when we stopped on the side of the road, Joseph taught me how to keep my weapons razor sharp and ready for use. I knew how to sharpen weapons, being the son of a blacksmith who had a lot of underrated skills in the craft of knife and dagger making. But Joseph taught me that after each sword fight I needed to rub the sword down in a certain way that would bring it back to the exact sharpness that was demanded of a ranger's weapon. He taught me how to oil my sheaths with a special oil the rangers used so the sword and daggers would come out smoothly and never rust. Joseph also showed me how to sharpen the tips of my arrows. I sat there working on my own weapons as Joseph did his.

I kept glancing curiously at his long arrows that were designed for the heavy bow he used. My arrows were small and light and would work well against such creatures as orcs, but Joseph's arrows were a different design. They were made of dark wood, and black feathers. They were over three feet long, where mine were just one and a half feet in length. Joseph noticed me glancing at them, and he handed one of them to me to look at. I turned it over in my hands inspecting it, very impressed with the skills that would be needed to make such perfectly designed arrows. Bows were a common enough tool. People used them for hunting all the time in the smaller villages near the woods and plains. But Joseph's bow and arrows were something else all together. The arrow I held was obviously a well designed weapon.

"Impressive isn't it? You won't find arrows like that in the regular army." Joseph said softly.

"Why not? It's obviously a powerful weapon, so why doesn't everyone use arrows like this?" I asked, handing it back to Joseph.

"Because the arrows are expensive to make, requiring high skill… for one thing, if it's not done correctly than the whole thing has to be scraped and started over. The regular army doesn't have the time or the people to make arrows of this caliber. So they just use normal arrows, which are much easier to make in bulk supply. Also there is the problem with the bow being so strong." Joseph said, standing up and handing me his bow to try out.

I took the offered bow and arrow uncertainly. Not for the first time in my life I wished I was taller, as the long bow was hard to hold for me, and I had a feeling that I looked downright silly holding a bow that was much taller than I was. I notched the arrow to the bow and looked at Joseph, wondering what he was expecting from me.

"Aim for the tree there." He suggested, pointing to a pine tree a few yards away from us.

I took aim, and started to pull the string back. The heavy chord resisted, and I pulled harder, straining my arms in my attempt to bring the string back as far as I could.

"Use your back muscles, it makes it easier." Joseph suggested lightly.

I did as he suggested, and found it a bit easier, but not nearly enough to pull the string back half as far as I had seen Joseph do it many times. Of course, my arms were too short for the bow anyways. When the string was as far back as I was able to pull it, I let it loose, and the arrow flew away from me without the speed that it would have if I had been able to use the bow properly. The arrow wavered in the air as it traveled, until it hit the tree with a soft thump, barely penetrating the wood.

Joseph took the bow from me, and fitted another arrow, pulling the string all the way back to his ear, which was the more common distance for an archer of any skill. The arrow took off like a hummingbird, and penetrated into the tree so deep that half the arrow was buried, going almost the whole way through the thick old tree. I stared in silent admiration as Joseph retrieved the arrows. The one he had fired was broken in the shaft, and Joseph tossed into the campfire casually, obviously used to having to dispose of arrows once in a while if they got damaged. He put the arrow head into his money bag for later.

\*\*\*

When Joseph and I were walking through the village of Flora, something happened that I would treasure forever. We had just finished talking to the knight in charge of the guards, and were heading back to the inn. The knight had told us that a whole host of archers from the east side of the great river would be coming through the village soon on their way to Stoneriver. I had listened, but not understood the significance of the situation. My heart leapt into my throat as I recognized an all too familiar face leading the new recruits to the barracks. "Lord Joseph!" I gasped, stopping in my tracks as I stared at the man who was leading one of the groups.

"What is it?" Joseph asked, instantly on higher alert at my sudden change in mood.

"It's Kevin! My lord, it's Kevin!" I gasped, tugging on Joseph's sleeve like a child.

"Kevin your brother?" Joseph asked, looking at the men passing by with a lot more interest.

"Yes, it's him! Joseph, it's Kevin, he's one of the men in charge. Joseph, they gave him a knighthood, he's finally a knight! Just like he's always wanted." I said softly. I longed to rush to my brother, but I forced myself to hold back. I knew better than to bother him when he was busy. He had obviously been given an important job in being one of the leaders of these men, and after many years of watching his determined climb in rank I knew that he took his job very seriously. It would not do now for me to distract him. "Waite, if Kevin is here than that might mean…" I trailed off searching the lines of men desperately for some sign of another of my brothers. There were so many men, and they were all marching behind their leaders, carrying their packs and ignoring me as I searched desperately.

Joseph took control of the situation. He made a signal to someone at the end of the line, and a soldier mounted on a warhorse approached, bowing low in his saddle to Joseph when he reached us. "Have the son's of the blacksmith Richard come to the inn tonight after the men have eaten. Tell them that there is a lord who wishes to speak to them. Don't tell them that I'm a ranger, just a lord." Joseph told the soldier.

I couldn't stay still. When Joseph and I were eating dinner, I kept glancing from my food to the doorway. I was kicking the legs of my chair unconsciously until Joseph put a hand on my knee, silently asking me to stop. I tried to stay still, but I couldn't help myself, I had to be doing something, anything! I moved from kicking my chair, to constantly over chewing my food. I felt sort of like a rabbit constantly shredding my food, but no one else seemed to notice. Except for Joseph, who gave me a patient smile as he reached for another roll.

"What's taking them so long?" I asked in frustration as we were served after dinner tea.

Joseph gave a weary sigh and looked up at the ceiling. "Peter, will you relax? The men would have only started eating half an hour ago. Kevin probably has duties to do before he can leave the men. Sit still and be patient!"

I looked at Joseph and realized that I was probably getting on his nerves. It suddenly occurred to me that I had been restless for the past few hours, and I was likely wearing through the store of patience Joseph had for such childish behavior. I sagged back in my chair and stared into my tea, determined not to annoy Joseph further.

Joseph looked at me, gave a nod to himself, and then addressed me. "Peter, don't feel chastised, I want to teach you what younger rangers need to learn from their superiors. The magic that heightens our senses can cause us to over react as well. When this occurs, it is far safer for us if we train ourselves to keep calm under any conditions. Even in the height of battle, a ranger is still observing his surroundings, adjusting his tactics, and putting his resources where they can best be used.

Even though we don't usually teach beginners until their third year or so, I suspect that you'll be capable of picking it up in no time… you seem to have a knack for doing such things." Joseph smiled at me again.

For my part, I was unconsciously nodding and looking at him, eager as always to learn anything and everything possible. Joseph continued, "Ok, close your eyes lightly… I said lightly, not tightly! Take a deep breath through your mouth; breathe out through your nose. Then take a deep breath trough your nose, and let it out slowly through your mouth. While you're sitting there, continue to breathe slowly while mentally seeing all the tension go out with your breath. Later on, I'll teach you how to relax your entire body in addition to using the breathing technique. Those of us who've been doing this a while, can actually get to the point where we relax our bodies almost at the same time that our first breath goes out of our noses. But that's going to take you a while to learn yet."

After what seemed like a day, but was really only about twenty minutes since Joseph had taught me to calm down, the door to the inn opened. I felt a leap of joy in my chest as I saw Kevin and John looking around for whatever Lord had requested their presence. Joseph raised one hand in the air and waved them over. They came over and bowed to Joseph, not seeming to recognize him, until they had finished bowing and looked over at the slouched figure sitting across the table from the ranger lord. Kevin and John stared at me dumbstruck for a while. I put my cup down slowly, and stood to greet them. Then I tossed aside all formality and hugged my brothers, trying not to let them see the tears of joy that had sprung to my eyes.

"Peter!" Kevin gasped, dropping to one knee so he could see me better. "Look at you! You look so grown up! It's only been a few months, but you look more mature than ever. Peter, you've become a man! Our little baby brother who would tag along and get in our way has become a man!" Kevin held both my hands in his and gazed at me in wonder.

"I'm not so different. I'm just the same as I always was." I protested gruffly, trying hard not to cry with the emotion I felt at seeing my brothers after so long a time.

John dropped down to his knees and looked up at me too. "No, you've definitely grown up. There is a new look in your eye baby brother, you truly have become more mature." He agreed, brushing my hair out of my eyes.

"Well, look at you!" I countered. "Where's your beard?" I remembered vividly that John had spent years impatiently waiting to grow a beard like my fathers. I remembered his frustration when he finally did get facial hair but found it to not be nearly as thick. Father had tried to assure John that it would get thicker with age, but John had just become more frustrated. He wanted to be a man, and having a beard would make him look older.

John smiled slightly. "They make us shave in the army." He explained.

"There's so much to tell you guys! You won't believe some of the stuff I've seen, and Kevin, you're a knight! How did that happen? You must be thrilled!" I told my brothers.

"Why don't you all go to our room to talk? That way you have some privacy." Joseph suggested. As I was about to lead my brothers away Joseph put a hand on my shoulder. "Make no mention of the M word, or any of our secrets." He said, smiling at me kindly.

I nodded my understanding. There were many things that the rangers didn't share with just anyone, even their blood families. Only the royal family had access to the ranger secrets. If the secrets got out, it could mean disaster for the guild. I assumed that the M word was magic, so I was careful to not talk about that. There was still plenty to tell. Kevin told me that Carl had put his name down as a recommendation for promotion into the knighthood for the general army. Since his rank was already equivalent to a knight as a town guard without the official title, the recommendation from the ranger and the other knight from our village guards, plus the sir knight Kevin had once trained under was enough for Sir Lucas. Kevin hadn't known the promotion was even in the works, but when he had gotten to Askia, Sir Lucas promoted him and put him to work right away.

Then when they had updated me on the bit that had happened since I left, I began to tell them about my adventures. My brothers were eager to listen, and they made a good audience. They laughed softly when I told them how Lord Haldor had tricked me into trying to climb the dead tree to get a leaf, and they were interested as I told them about my experience with the draft dodgers. I left what Lord Haldor had told me about my past for last. I had been sitting on one bed while they sat on the other, but now I sat down between them as I told them what Lord Haldor had told me. "He said you might have been told, but that he didn't think father told John or Andrew." I told Kevin. Kevin had put his arm around my shoulder as I talked, and now he sighed as John and I both looked at him.

"Father told me that you had been chosen to be trained by a lord. When he kept encouraging you to practice knight's skills and bought our family that archery kit, I assumed he meant someone like Sir Lucas. Sir Lucas isn't a lord, but he is second in command to the army."

I nodded, accepting that explanation.

"What I don't understand is why he had father lie to us in the first place." John said with a dark scowl.

"He wanted to protect me." I explained softly.

"Protect you from what?" John almost snapped.

I cringed slightly at the venom in his tone. "Rangers are feared by people John. They think we are bandits and spies. Lord Haldor didn't want anyone to know that he had taken an interest in me because he saw how much I tried to hide from the older guys. Remember the Carpenter's boys? Think how much worse they would have been if they knew I was actually training to be a ranger. They would have been horrid!"

"Hey, you know that whenever those jerks caused you trouble you had three older brothers to pound them. You were perfectly safe; Kevin was a town guard for goodness sake!" John protested.

"I agree with Lord Haldor, John. Peter would have been harassed ten times as much as he was if the boys his age thought he was a ranger." Kevin said in his firm, big brother tone. John subsided at once, recognizing the tone. For some reason I felt a deep surge of homesickness at hearing that tone once more. So many memories came flooding back of when Kevin used that tone of voice to make us obey him. Since he had taken on a role of a sort of parent for us, my brothers and I had grown use to his authority. He used that tone when John and Andrew would argue, or when John would fight with the carpenter's twins, or when I was caught by him or one of the guards as I roamed at night. I grinned as I remembered the game Lord Haldor had set up for me.

"Oh man Kevin; I HAVE to tell you this!" I said with a laugh, proceeding to tell my brothers about the game.

Joseph came into the room as I was finishing talking about the explanation I had given the rangers as to why I used to roam at night. "It's getting late, Peter. Your brothers are moving out first thing in the morning, so they need to get back to their camp now." He explained gently.

When my brothers had hugged me, I pulled out my money sack and gave it to Kevin. "Here, send this to father for me. I keep forgetting to do it." I said, pushing it into his hands.

Kevin shook his head and pushed it back at me. "No Peter, this is your money! You earned it, you just told us so." He protested.

I frowned frustrated. I hadn't expected him to protest. "What am I going to do with two and a half gold? I never have anything to spend money on, and I KNOW father and Andrew could use it! Wouldn't it be nice if Andrew could have new snow boots, or how about a new blanket? Last I remember, you three were sharing this moth eaten thing. How can you expect me to spend money on sweets or something if Andrew is shivering under an old blanket, or walking around in winter with Dad's old boots that blister Andrews feet since his feet are too small for them?"

Kevin looked from me to Joseph, a plea in his eyes. Joseph just shrugged slightly, not willing to get involved in my blood family's business.

"Look, I said, thinking fast. I'll keep one silver, and you send the rest. One silver is still more money that I had ever had all to myself, and this way, I can spend it knowing that my family benefited too."

Kevin was about to protest further, but Joseph spoke up. "Peter will have other opportunities to earn money. The apprentices are given such challenges quite often. It's one of the only parts of their training that offers them the chance to be rewarded with leisure time benefits. It is not uncommon for those with Peter's financial background to send money to their families."

Kevin considered for another moment, than nodded. "Alright Peter, I'll send the money to Father first chance I get." He promised, emptying my money bag into his own, and making sure I kept one silver for myself.

It wasn't until we were on the road the next morning heading for Askia that the reality hit me. I hesitated slightly in my movement as it occurred to me suddenly that my brothers might very well die in this war. I found myself pausing for a half a second as the realization hit me. But I continued on, not wanting to show my emotions. "You ok Peter?" Joseph asked me, immediately aware of the hesitation in my step. If I hadn't been traveling with a ranger, no one would have likely noticed, but I realized after he spoke, that being aware of everything around him, Joseph would immediately see a change in my regular rhythm of jogging that I always used to keep up with his almost running pace.

"Well sir, it… I just realized that my brothers might die in the war." I said quietly, unable to keep my sadness out of my tone.

Joseph and I stopped, and he put his arm around my shoulder. "I lost my best friend in battle, he had just passed the final exams and become a ranger. He kind of adopted me as his little brother, and when the fort was attacked, he was put in charge of the apprentices. Two Kronlords found where we were hiding and…" Joseph swallowed hard and I could feel the hand on my shoulder trembling slightly. "At least you can rest assured that your father and Andrew are safe. There are so many towns all around them that they will get loads of advance warning of an attack. It is for your father and brother's sake that Kevin and John are going to war, their sake and yours. You have much reason to be proud of them."

"I am, believe me I am." I promised. "I just…" I trailed off, unsure how to explain`. "It's just that…" I tried again.

"I know Peter, I know." Joseph assured me softly.

182

# CHAPTER 21

Joseph paused at the sign announcing Askia was five miles down the road, staring at it in distress.

"What's wrong?" I asked, looking up at him curiously.

"My family lives in Askia. I haven't been to Askia since I joined the rangers." Joseph said distractedly.

"You haven't been allowed to see your family since you became a ranger?!" I asked, surprised and slightly horrified at the thought.

"Allowed?" Joseph asked, as if the concept was foreign to him. "Allowed to yes; encouraged to... no. This... is Sir Lucas' city, remember?" He told me.

"So he told you to stay away from his city?" I guessed.

"No, not exactly." Joseph said softly, gazing down the road. "But this being his home has kept me away none the less. Come on." He said, walking firmly down the road, his face determined. He was clearly distracted though, because he didn't notice the rabbit darting across the snow as we passed too close to its hiding place. Seeing he wasn't paying attention, I resolved to watch the surroundings more closely, just in case.

My curiosity was still burning in my brain, and I couldn't resist asking more questions. "Couldn't you come when he is gone? Knights are often away from home." I said, looking up at Joseph, wondering how I'd know if I was asking too many personal questions.

"There was one time I had resolved to come home, whether Sir Lucas approved or not. But then I was given a huge promotion that Lord Haldor refused to let me turn down, so it was impossible for me to go at that time. By the time I had a free moment to request permission to go home, the event was long over, and I didn't want to be anywhere near Sir Lucas. So I just sent a letter, and left it at that."

"I can't believe Sir Lucas managed to keep you away from home for so long! I suppose he has no choice but to let you see your parents now; after all, you're here on official,"

"Peter," Joseph interrupted me suddenly. "Drop it. The last thing I want to do right now is talk about Sir Lucas. I'll have to pay my respects to him soon enough. So for now, be silent." He said; his voice strained.

I did drop it. I could tell Joseph was upset, and I couldn't blame him. It was a horrible thought that just because of one man with a grudge, Joseph had been forced to not visit his family for so many years. When we got to the city gates and paid the travelers tax, Joseph requested a quill and parchment. He wrote a quick message, and gave it to one of the gate guards. "Deliver this to Lady Rose. Tell her to meet me here, at the gate. Then tell Sir Lucas that the king's messengers will pay respects to the lord of the city tomorrow." The guard bowed, and hurried off to the stables to get a horse.

Joseph and I stood waiting. Joseph didn't speak to me; his mind was still lost in thought. There was a definite look of distress on his face as he looked around. After twenty minutes or so I couldn't resist asking more questions. "So what IS your family like?"

Joseph hesitated before answering. "My father died fifteen years ago. My mother and older brother are alive still, and live here in Askia. I can't really say what my mother is like, since it has been so long. But my brother is the same as he always has been, if my meeting with him at the harvest fair is any indication." He replied.

"Well, you got to see some of your family then. At least you saw your brother at the fair." I pointed out, trying to cheer Joseph up.

Joseph looked down at me, his face full of even more sadness and pain. "Yes, that is true."

I wondered about what I had said that was making him feel worse, and stood for a moment, wondering how to ask about it.

"Joseph!" I looked up to see an elderly woman in a rich green dress scrambling out of the carriage that clattered to a stop in front of us. The horses' sides were heaving; apparently they had been driven here with all speed possible. "Oh, Joseph! My dreams have come true!" The woman cried, flinging her arms around Joseph's neck and embracing him.

"Mother." Joseph murmured, hugging the old woman as if she was made of delicate glass.

His mother pulled away and stroked Joseph's cheek tenderly. "My dear son, my poor little boy. At last you have come to see me. If I had known that you'd avoid this city like the plague, I might have had second thoughts about letting you go. You didn't even come to your father's funeral! I know he didn't want you there, but you still…"

"I would have been there Mother, but Lord Sidney died the day I got the news. I couldn't leave. When Lord Sidney died, Haldor took command, and made me take on the role of his second, even though I was so young and inexperienced. I had too many responsibilities to take time off, even for my blood family. I am so sorry Mother; I really did want to be there for you." Joseph explained sadly.

The old woman reached up and kissed Joseph's brow. "It doesn't matter now. None of that matters now. What matters is that you're here, just like my dreams. Oh, Joseph!" The woman hugged Joseph again, tears of joy rolling down her cheeks.

"But who is this? Don't tell me you've gone off and gotten married and had children without telling me?" She asked after she had embraced her son, smiling down at me.

Joseph laughed softly. "This is my apprentice Peter. I have written to you about Thelmer, this is who I have now that Thelmer is grown."

Joseph explained.

"Well, it is very nice to meet you child. I'm sure your mother is very proud that the rangers have chosen you. But I hope you visit her more often than Joseph here has visited his poor mother! You write to her at least, yes?" She said, offering her hand to me to bow over, which I did, unsure of how to begin to explain about my past.

"Peter, go to the inn and get us a room for the night. I have to go arrange a meeting for the soldiers of the city." Joseph said distractedly, handing me his money bag, and pointing me in the right direction.

I nodded, and set off down the street, relieved to be away from the responsibility of having to explain about my mother, and more than happy to let Joseph have a moment alone with his own mother. As I was walking, I heard someone call out to me. "Hey, Ranger squire, come here!"

I looked ahead to see four young men striding down the street towards me. "Hi, my name's Peter." I said with a friendly smile.

None of the young men smiled back. My smile faded as I suddenly felt like something was very wrong. They were wearing cream colored shirts that reached down to their knees with a knight's family crest on them. That meant that they were obviously squires. The tallest of the guys looked like he might be my brother John's age, and I could see the beginnings of facial hair on his cheeks and lip. He was very muscular, and his upper arms looked tight in his shirt. The other guys looked like they might be a couple years younger, but just as muscular. All this I took in within a second, but what made me nervous was the fierce look in their eyes, and the quarter staff the tallest squire was holding.

I took a step back as they continued to advance. "Why do you back away ranger brat? We have a message from Sir Lucas for you and your master." The taller boy jeered.

In my head I could hear Fletch's lessons to me as we trained in front of the healing house. "Never let anyone you don't trust and know very well get close to you. If their intents are friendly they will honor your personal space. If they insist on advancing, get out of there, especially if you don't have back up."

I held up a hand, signaling them to keep away. "What is the message?" I asked, already suspecting what the answer was going to be.

"The message is this!" the taller boy shouted, rushing at me and swinging his weapon.

I took off running back down the street. If I could get back to Joseph, back to where adults were, then I'd be safe. The squires would never attack me in front of grown-ups, right? But in my haste and panic I took a wrong turn, and found myself in an unfamiliar part of town. I stopped and looked around wildly, trying to get my bearings. My heart leapt into my throat when I saw the smallest boy had somehow gotten ahead of me using a short cut. Looking behind I saw that the other squires had caught up, and I was trapped in a narrow street with no means of escape.

I stood with my back against a wall and braced myself for the fight. Seeing this, the taller squire laughed. "Baby wants to play. I bet you think you're special don't you ranger brat? I bet you think you're so great, just because you have a cloak, and a toy archery kit. Ok, we'll let you play, it will be more fun this way anyways, right?" he jeered, advancing slowly, his quarter staff held in both hands and swung over his shoulder, ready to strike.

My mind was racing. I really didn't want to use my weapons, knowing how deadly they were. These squires may be bullies, but they were still human, children really, not a whole lot older than me. I tossed my bow aside, and took off my quiver. I didn't want them to get damaged, but even more, I didn't want to instinctively use them against the squires.

Doing so was a mistake. As my hand was busy with the task of removing my weapon, the older squire struck, swinging his stick hard against my shoulder. I cried out in pain, dropping the quiver and clutching my upper arm. The smallest boy (who was still more than a head taller than me) grabbed my arms and pinned them behind my back, leaving me vulnerable to the older boy's weapon. I kicked back and up, and heard the squire holding me grunt in pain, but he didn't let me go. I tried to wretch myself out of his grip, but his hands got tighter and tighter as I struggled. When I couldn't bear any more pain from him I gave up trying to escape his hold on me.

Meanwhile, the tallest squire jabbed his quarterstaff hard into my stomach, causing me to double over, my eyes watering as the wind was knocked out of me. I closed my eyes, and took as deep a breath as I could. I knew from experience that it would stop eventually; I just had to be patient. I gritted my teeth, and determinedly tried to think of something good about the squires. It was hard to do when they were beating on me, but the last thing I wanted to do was hate these guys. I told myself what I always did when I was beaten up by the local boys, that they just didn't have the same honor and morals that I had grown up with. It didn't make them bad people, just uneducated.

The next blow from the quarterstaff went against the side of my head, leaving a bruise under my eye that lasted for almost a month, and making my ear ring as the stick smacked against it. The world around me seemed to burst in my eyes, and I groaned, feeling very sick suddenly. The fourth blow was the staff slammed down hard on my back, as I was still bent over double. All the time I was being hit with the staff, the other squires were punching and kicking me, their fists and boots pounding into me in what seemed like a hail storm of assault. I was quickly becoming battered and bruised. I went limp and waited for the attack to stop; there really wasn't anything else I could do as far as I could see. Maybe if I acted unconscious, they'd stop sooner and leave me alone.

"That's enough!" A deep voice roared.

I fell to the ground as I was let go unexpectedly. Looking up I saw all four squires standing at attention and staring straight ahead. A tall, well built man strode forward and pulled me to my feet, practically lifting me off the ground with the strength of his arm.

"Anything broken lad?" he asked me, looking me up and down

with mild concern. I shook my head looking at him in wonder. I had seen Sir Lucas at the fair before, competing with the other knights during the tournaments, but up close he looked far more powerful then I remembered him. He was tall, easily above six and a half feet tall. He had black hair, and a thick black beard. He was muscular, as all knights are, but on him the muscles seemed to look somehow bigger, stronger. He had the same aura about him that Joseph did, as if he was wise and mighty. Where Joseph preferred to have this aura hidden in his ranger uniform and wild shaggy hair, this man wore it like a badge of honor. Just looking at him it became obvious why he was the second in command of the army, answering only to the king.

"It's Gene, isn't it? Your father is Lord Covington, isn't he?" Sir Lucas asked, frowning at me, trying to figure out who I was.

"I… my name's Peter sir, Gene is a friend of mine, a year mate. I'm Kevin's little brother, Kevin son or Richard who you promoted to the knighthood recently." I explained weakly.

Sir Lucas turned from me and glared at his squires, who were still staring straight ahead. "Well?" he barked. "What is the meaning of this appalling display? Four battle trained young men against a much smaller and younger boy? Explain yourselves!" he demanded.

When the squires lowered their eyes to the ground without speaking, Sir Lucas became angrier. "So, you have nothing to say do you? You think attacking a small ranger apprentice is fun? Do you think this is a good use of your free time? I suppose you think that sleeping with the pigs for the next month will also be fun too? Is that where I should have you swine sleep from now on?" he shouted, glaring at his squires.

"No sir!" The four squires answered in unison, their eyes snapping up to stare straight ahead again.

"Then what the hell WERE you thinking?! Did you WANT to get yourselves killed?" Sir Lucas barked.

The squires looked up at their teacher in confusion.

"He could have cut you to ribbons, and would have been well

within the law to do so, you fools!" Sir Lucas shouted, pulling my cloak back to reveal my belt where my sword and daggers hung.

The squires looked at me horrified. Apparently they hadn't expected a ranger's apprentice to travel so heavily armed.

I saw Joseph running up the street towards us, and I went to him, shaking slightly. I was sore all over, and my head was throbbing, making me feel dizzy and slightly disoriented. I staggered, unable to walk straight. I reached out to Joseph, and grabbed at the air, looking for his arm. That blow to the head was apparently more serious then I had thought. Joseph wrapped his arm around my shoulders to reassure me and calm me down, and addressed Sir Lucas. "What happened?" he demanded, seeing the bruises on my face, and noticing the quarterstaff still held in the tallest squire's hand.

"Nothing that matters now ranger, it's over. No broken bones, no death, no need to press charges." Sir Lucas said, his voice filled with contempt. "You four," he shouted, turning to his squires, "Get your worthless rears back to the castle at once! Twenty demerits a piece for your stupidity, and be glad you're still alive!"

The boys took off at a sprint, eager to get away from their angry teacher. Sir Lucas picked up my bow and quiver of arrows and handed them to me. "Thank you for not killing them. Fools though they be, they're the only squires I have right now, thanks to your *friend* here." He said, adding the last part with a tone of obvious hatred in his voice.

Before I could reply, Sir Lucas headed off in the same direction his squires had fled.

"Lucas, please talk to me." Joseph pleaded, leaving me where I was and stepping forward after the retreating knight.

Sir Lucas turned back to regard the ranger with contempt. "That's SIR Lucas to you, ranger." He barked, his voice full of loathing and spite.

"In that case, it's LORD Joseph to you, *Sir* knight." Joseph said firmly.

Sir Lucas' face flashed with surprise, and then turned back to loathing and anger.

"When will this quarrel end? Why can we not get along, as equals who have chosen different paths in life?" Joseph asked his voice full of sorrow, and pain.

"Our quarrel will end when you are dead, and your head is brought to me on a silver platter, *Lord* Joseph." Sir Lucas growled spitting at the ground in front of Joseph's feet.

Joseph did not speak as Sir Lucas left. When the angry knight was gone Joseph turned to me, putting his arm back around my shoulder leading me away.

I was feeling more dizzy and nauseous by the second, but was taking great pains to not show it. I didn't want Joseph to worry about me, not when he was finally able to see his family again after so long. He was clearly distracted, and I didn't want to worry him. But my curiosity and desire for answers was burning in me. "My lord?" I asked hesitantly.

"What is it Peter?" Joseph asked sadly.

"What was all that about? Why does he hate you so much, is it because you took Gene from him?" I asked, wondering if I was overstepping my boundaries by getting into a subject that was personal.

For several seconds we walked towards the inn in silence, and I gave up, deciding that he wasn't going to answer, but he did. "He's my older brother." Joseph explained. Before I could ask why that equated to the situation I had witnessed, Joseph continued. "Every man in my family has been knights, for hundreds of years. This city was named after my ancestor, and his descendants always managed to secure residency of the knights castle here, being sir knights high up in the army. But Lord Haldor, who was just Haldor at the time, saw that I was a prodigy in archery and hand to hand combat. So he approached me at the fair, after the tournaments and before the choosing ceremony, and offered me an apprenticeship as his personal aid (this was back when squires were chosen at age eleven not thirteen by the way). I knew Lucas had convinced the knight he was working for; my Uncle, to claim me, like my father told him to. But I also knew how much more powerful and mysterious the rangers were then the knights could ever be. To be honest, I was also tired of putting up with my brother's often mindless violence towards me. I wasn't looking forward to being a squire beside him, with him being superior enough to me to make my life even more miserable. So I accepted Lord Haldor's offer, and didn't go to the ceremony.

When I didn't show up at the knights' choosing ceremony, Lucas came looking for me. He saw me talking to Haldor, and shaking his hand as he welcomed me into the guild. Lucas waited for the ranger to leave to talk to my parents and then he came over to yell at me. He called me a traitor to the family, and beat me until I was barely conscious. That was when Haldor came back, and told Lucas that if he ever laid hand on one of the ranger apprentices' again; Haldor would cut off his ears. Lucas is more or less mindlessly violent in regards to me; he always has been... one might almost say he was brought up to be so. So he wasn't about to give up so easily. He started picking up stones and throwing them at Haldor, cursing and screaming, so Haldor grabbed him, dragged him over to a well, and threw him down it, standing there for three hours refusing to let anyone help Lucas get out, insisting the boy needed to cool down his hot head.

Ever since then, Lucas and my father and Uncle as well, have hated me, and I have avoided this city knowing that Lucas has inherited ownership of the castle here. My father disowned me when I joined the rangers, I don't even have a family treasure. At the fair; I was told by my father that if I left with the rangers, he would never again look at me as his flesh and blood. I made my choice, and was disowned. So while I did indeed have opportunities to visit my family, I had no desire to, and wasn't really welcomed here. I do regret not being able to see my mother, the one person in my blood family who was kind to me, but just thinking of this city reminds me of old hurts, hurts that took a very long time to heal. It's hard to explain to you who grew up loved, but I have little from my childhood worth remembering."

"If you were good at hand to hand combat, why was Lucas, Sir Lucas, able to beat you up?" I asked, confused.

Joseph looked down at me strangely. "He's my brother. I can't fight back against my brother, no matter what he does to me! That's why Lord Haldor said for you to be ready to back me up."

I nodded as if I understood, but really, I couldn't imagine just standing there and putting up with violence like that over and over again. Most people would fight back, defend themselves, so why didn't Joseph? Nodding had made me feel even more sick, so to distract myself from my almost overwhelming nausea, I pressed on, hoping I wasn't going too far with my questions.

"But why did Lord Haldor send you after the newcomers in September when it was common knowledge that Sir Lucas would be looking for squires there?" I asked, shocked that Lord Haldor had made such a judgment error after seeing that Joseph didn't have a good relationship with his brother.

"What happened between my brother and me the night I became a ranger was over thirty years ago. Lord Haldor and I had both thought he was over it by now. I've been the one sent after new apprentices for years, but ever since Lucas became so influential he has apparently done his best to thwart me. But never before in my adult life had he openly attacked me like he did in September." Joseph explained, the sadness becoming more pronounced in his voice.

"Sir?" I asked weakly, unable to hide how sick I was feeling any more. We were walking at the usual ranger, almost running pace, and I felt like I was dying.

Joseph looked down at me in concern at my tone.

"I don't feel so well." I choked out, trying not to get sick.

"That's what I was afraid of." Joseph muttered, sitting me down on a stool outside of a shop.

Joseph took off my hood and looked me over in concern. I sagged down so my elbows were resting on my lap, and closed my eyes, wishing the dizziness would pass.

"Is he alright?" A female voice asked. I looked up to see the shop keeper had come outside and was talking to Joseph. I also noticed that several other people had stopped their business to stare at me. I looked away, I hated when people stared.

"Would you kindly send word to the closest doctor or healer to come to the Red Griffin Inn? I'd appreciate it." Joseph said to one of the boys who had stopped to stare. Joseph gave the boy a coin, and the boy ran off.

"Come Peter, you'll be fine." Joseph soothed, lifting me into his arms and carrying me away, followed by some of the curious onlookers.

"But...your ribs... Lord Haldor said you shouldn't be carrying much." I said quietly as Joseph brought me down the street.

"My ribs feel fine, better than ever." Joseph assured me.

"I didn't know ribs healed so quickly." I commented.

"They don't. Not usually." Joseph answered as he carried me into the inn, the innkeeper holding the door open for him.

Joseph put me down and turned his attention to the curious crowd. He raised an eyebrow, and everyone started to back away, as if they had just realized that their presence was inappropriate.

Soon after Joseph and I were brought to the room Joseph paid for, the innkeeper came back with the doctor in tow. "Thank you; that will do for the moment. Stick around in case we need anything." Joseph said, handing the innkeeper some money, and closing the door on him.

"What happened here?" the Doctor said, gently examining my head. He was an older man, with gray hair, and soft withered hands that weren't use to hard labor.

"Sir Lucas' squires," Joseph started to explain.

"Ah, say no more. I figured as much from the pattern they took to batter but not maim." The doctor said grimly, checking my eyes. "But by the looks of it, they got completely carried away this time. What were they after from you lad; money, or just sport? I take it you tried to resist their demands?"

"So this has happened before then?" Joseph asked darkly. I looked over at him. He was standing against the wall half hidden in shadow, his arms crossed, and a look of firm anger in his eyes.

"Yep, and it will probably happen again. Lucas, SIR Lucas, has the bad habit of turning even the most decent squires into bullies. All squires fight with the local boys, it's what young people do. But these squires know that they can get away with it, and so they are dangerous. Sir Lucas refuses to let them be punished, insisting that boys will be boys, and that they will grow out of it. HA! Sir Lucas obviously didn't grow out of it, if the rumors I've heard are true. He was quite the bully to his sickly baby brother, until his brother ran off to join the rangers in order to escape him. The stories I could tell about that family... then this September, rumors started running wild that he found his long lost brother, and attacked him AGAIN!"

"Did he indeed?" Joseph said softly, ducking his head further into the shadows from the late afternoon sun.

I glanced at Joseph wondering why he didn't tell the doctor who he was. At first I was surprised that the doctor knew Joseph's childhood, until it occurred to me that Joseph hadn't been home in so long, he probably looked nothing like his eleven year old self. Of course his family would recognize him, but Askia was a big city. I probably shouldn't be surprised if no one else did. I closed my eyes, thinking was making my head hurt.

"Well, he is far better off then I had feared from the way the messenger you sent was talking. He took some bad blows to the head. I recommend he stay in bed for a few days at least. If he starts to get any worse, send someone to get me, and I'll come running. But a couple weeks of bed-rest and he should be ok." The doctor said, gently laying me down, putting the covers over me, and addressing Joseph.

"We are on something of a schedule." Joseph replied.

The doctor glanced at me, and then led Joseph into the hall, shutting the door behind them. I tapped into the magic to intensify my hearing, and listened. By now I knew that eavesdropping always ended up badly when I was the one being discussed, but they were talking about me, so I couldn't resist wanting to know what they were saying. "I didn't want to say it in front of the boy my lord ranger, but he is badly hurt. I don't know how he kept from being knocked out, but he is very sick. To be honest, he shouldn't be able to sit up at all right now, much less be aware of what is going on around him. I fear that if he doesn't be careful, he may not do well at all. You'll have to modify your schedule, or else carry him on a stretcher. Head injuries are serious business, my lord. He needs to stay in bed, and not move too much. I am simply amazed that he is even able to talk right now, much less sit up, but he needs to rest." The doctor said in a hushed voice.

"I see." Joseph said with a sigh. "What should I do for him?"

"Keep him in bed, and keep him calm. No excitement, and no unnecessary head movements. Make sure he drinks plenty of water, and I'll come back to check on him again in the morning. Make sure you keep a close eye on him for the first couple days at least."

"Doctor," Said Joseph in a patiently amused tone, "Have you ever tried to keep an energetic thirteen year old child confined to a bed before?"

The doctor laughed, apparently understanding the joke. "Well, if he wants to get better he'll stay in bed like you tell him to. Maybe I can find some young lad who will keep him company from time to time. This is a serious injury we're talking about. I doubt it would do any good, but I recommend you try to press charges against the squires. It's never amounted to anything when other victim's parents have tried, but maybe Sir Lucas will listen to a ranger."

"Oh, I have every intention of pressing charges, I have little choice in the matter anyways. But I'm going to have to be careful how I do so. The penalty for attacking a ranger is death. I'm going to have to find some way to save their lives. Oh by the way, since you're here, I wanted to talk to you about a small sickly boy you once knew."

Joseph's voice and the doctors were getting softer as they retreated down the stairs.

I stared up at the ceiling, I felt guilty that I had thrown us completely off schedule by getting attacked. Why hadn't I paid more attention? Why hadn't I tried harder to fight back? I could have done more than just close my eyes and wait for the assault to end, so why didn't I?

# CHAPTER 22

"How foolish can your decisions get Joseph?! Of all the places in the kingdom to let Peter wander the streets alone, Askia is the worst you could have chosen!" I opened my eyes weakly, and looked over to the other side of the room. Joseph was sitting on the other bed, the message basin in his lap. Lord Haldor's voice was loud and furious. I had never heard him like this. Lord Haldor seemed even more livid then he had been the night Joseph had come back with my year mates. "Of all brainless things you could have done, sending Peter unguarded into Askia takes the lead. What if they had killed the boy? What if he had killed THEM?! Do you really want to have Peter's hands stained with human blood at thirteen years of age; you, who preach about the importance of childhood innocence?" Lord Haldor lowered his voice. But it didn't seem like he was calmer, if anything the low tone had even more anger in it. "Enlighten me, Lord Joseph. Tell me what insane thought was in your head that made you put that boy into such danger. Give me even ONE reason I shouldn't be mad at you for this."

"My Lord, I wasn't thinking at all. I would *never* intentionally do something so irresponsible. There is no excuse for my act. I am unworthy of this assignment." Joseph said softly.

I frowned. Joseph had been distracted by what was going on with his mother. It wasn't his fault; none of this was his fault! I sat up quickly to say so, but my head started to spin horribly, and my eyes went dark.

When I next woke up, Joseph was pacing back and forth in the room, his hands clasped behind his back. I lay there and watched him, my head throbbing horribly. He glanced over at me, and seeing that I was awake, he came and sat down on the bed next to me, examining my head gently.

"My lord, Sir Lucas' squires… what happened to them?" I asked, trying hard to ignore the pain that was threatening to make me physically sick.

"Right now Sir Lucas has them confined to their quarters, pending investigation. I am going to go down there soon to talk to Sir Lucas, but I didn't want to leave you until I knew you'd be ok." Joseph hesitated for a moment. "Sir Lucas has personally invited you and your teacher into his home so you can receive all the care possible. It was his mother's idea."

"She's your mother too." I said frowning.

Joseph shook his head. "I am banished from the family. I have no right to call her my mother now."

"Yes you do, I HEARD you call her mother!" I insisted.

"Yes, and Sir Lucas is angry enough about that, let's not make matters any worse for you or your teacher." Joseph said firmly.

"My teacher meaning you, his brother?" I more said than asked.

"I am not his brother, not in any way that matters to him."

"But it matters to you! Can't he just get over your decision and love you? You're related for God's sake!"

Joseph looked at me in concern. "Peter calm down, right now. You heard the doctor, no excitement. This conversation is over. You will take some deep breaths, and calm yourself down, or I will have no choice but to call for the doctor and have him bring a sleeping potion."

I lay there, and looked at Joseph, realizing that he was serious in his threat. As soon as I stopped thinking so hard, I realized that my head was throbbing so it felt like it was going to burst like a sack that was too full. I did my best to calm down, and waited for my heart to settle back to a normal pace. "Please, let *me* talk to Lord Haldor about the squires, maybe I can make him understand." I pleaded weakly, thinking of a change of subject.

"We have no way of contacting him right now, the message basin was destroyed." Joseph said, gesturing over to the floor near his bed.

I looked over to see that there was a huge burn on the floor rug. "How did that happen?" I asked in surprise.

"When you sat up and started getting sick all over yourself a couple nights ago I was talking to Lord Haldor; I jumped to my feet to get to you, knocking over the basin." Joseph stood up and went over to a table. He came back to show me the silver bowl which was pitch black, and badly bent out of shape.

I looked at the ruined bowl, feeling hopeless. There was nothing I could do, no way for me to contact Lord Haldor, no way for me to try to help the four squires. "I don't remember getting sick."

"Well with a head injury as bad as the one you have, that is what is going to happen when you sit up too fast." Joseph said, raising an eyebrow slightly.

"The doctor didn't tell ME my head was so bad. He said I wasn't nearly as bad as he had thought by the way the messenger had spoken." I pointed out.

Joseph frowned slightly at me. "Don't take me for a fool Peter. I know you well enough to know that you were listening in on the conversation I had with him in the hall."

"Forgive me my lord." I answered, lowering my eyes, suddenly realizing that what I had said could easily be misinterpreted to come across as a lie on my part.

"I just said it to ask why he thought I shouldn't be told how bad off I was. I didn't mean…" I trailed off, unsure how to continue. My head really was hurting a lot, and I could barely see through the pain, much less think easily.

Joseph put a hand on my arm. "Go to sleep Peter, let your body heal. I promise, I haven't given up on the squires yet, I am going to talk to Sir Lucas about them soon. Just get better, ok?"

I tried to tell Joseph that I'd be fine, but I'm not sure if I ever got the words out, because darkness took me yet again, and I sank down, feeling like I was gliding deep into a dark well, with no end in sight.

Sir Lucas was sitting at a desk that was styled much like Barron Rice's desk was in Woodward. He folded up a letter, poured a few drops of wax on it so it would seal, and pressed a ring on his finger onto the hot wax. There was a knock on the door, and Sir Lucas' head snapped up.

"Come in or go away!" He barked.

An elderly servant woman stepped in nervously. "Sir, Lord Joseph is here, he insists on an audience with you. He says he has a matter to discuss that is of interest to you both." She explained.

"Well then send him in! What are you waiting for?!" Sir Lucas asked, glaring at the servant under heavily lidded eyes.

"Sir... your father ordered that Jos... Lord Joseph was forbidden to set foot inside the castle grounds. I had the guards stop him at the drawbridge." The woman explained apologetically.

"My father's orders were that Joseph was forbidden to set foot inside HIS castle grounds. But my father has been dead fifteen years, and retired out of the knighthood four years before that. This is MY castle, and I say; send Joseph up to me at once! How dare you try to stop a Lord of the kingdom from going wherever he chooses old woman?! Do you not know the laws that were set in place hundreds of years ago? Lords of the kingdom have the right to go anywhere they wish, and speak to anyone they wish, and the likes of you will NOT hinder them!"

The woman fled the room as Sir Lucas began to rise to his feet in his anger. Vaguely I found myself wondering how such a violent and angry man could have ever become second in command to the army. That was when I realized that I must be experiencing dream magic again. I braced to watch whatever catastrophe was about to unfold, knowing there was no way for me to stop it. All I could do was talk to Joseph about it as soon as I saw him again.

Sir Lucas stood up and started to pace back and forth in his office, his hands clasped behind his back. As the time went by, he seemed to become more agitated at the delay. He went over to his stained glass window, and opened it so he could look out and down at the courtyard. He searched the yard for a moment, and closed the window again. He paced a few more times, and then he stopped, taking a deep breath to calm himself down. "Ok Lucas, it's time to put the past behind you. You've always known in your heart that what your father said and did to you and your brother was wrong, time to own up and let it go." Sir Lucas was muttering, staring at the door.

Joseph gave his usual three knocks, and Sir Lucas threw the door open, stopping himself just short of literally pulling his brother inside. Sir Lucas glared once more at the old servant, and slammed the door in her face. He went over to his desk, and sat in the chair behind it, gesturing to the chairs in front for Joseph to use if he wanted. Joseph looked at the chairs, a haunted look crossing over his eyes as if recalling a bad memory that had to do with the antique wood and velvet chairs. The quick flash of pain that was suppressed in a second wasn't lost on Sir Lucas, who got to his feet at once. "I've redecorated some of the castle in the past few years; we'll talk in the new parts." He offered.

Joseph nodded automatically, still staring at the two chairs. When he didn't follow, Sir Lucas came back, and touched Joseph's shoulder. Joseph started in surprise, his hand going to his dagger faster than conscious thought. Joseph's hand relaxed as his mind caught up with his reflexes; and he turned to his brother. "Sorry, didn't mean to startle you." Sir Lucas said in a much softer voice than I had even thought possible from the big angry man.

"We can talk here. Thirty four years is long enough to be afraid of those chairs." Joseph said firmly, sitting down in one of the chairs, and taking a slow shaky breath.

Sir Lucas sat back down behind the desk, and stared at Joseph's hands who's knuckles were white with the amount of force he was using to clutch the arms of the chair.

"Joseph... Lord Joseph; I am sorry, truly sorry for what I did to you. I was your big brother, I should have been the one who..."

"I'm not here to talk about that. My apprentice is at death's door because of your squires. Lord Haldor has agreed that the matter can be left to us, but only if we can come up with a suitable reprimand for the young men. Apparently Lord Haldor has the jurisdiction to alter the law, since he helped write it. I am here to tell you that I have had enough of this nonsense. Beating me like you have always done is one thing, but I will NOT stand by and let your squires get away with bullying and terrorizing youths, especially rangers apprentices." Joseph pulled a scroll out of his cloak pocket and handed it to Sir Lucas. "I have here a list of the victims of the past few years, and what your squires took from them. In total, your squires owe the young men of this city three gold, four silver, and three copper. Plus an additional three gold that has been paid by the victims' parents and the poor funds for medical care for their injuries. As the latest victim is still in critical condition, I do not yet have a total amount owed in his case."

Sir Lucas looked up from the scroll at Joseph. "He was fine when I left him with you." He said, his voice cracking in surprise. I was surprised too. Was Joseph talking about me? Was I the one who was in critical condition? I certainly didn't feel well, but that didn't mean I was dying, did it?

"He is a ranger who is protected by celestial beings. Peter is the first human in hundreds of years to be visited and aided by a Lammasu. When he was first inspected by the doctor, the man was amazed that Peter was even able to sit up, much less be aware of what was going on. He told me to make sure Peter stayed still for a while, which didn't happen. Peter sat up on the first night for some reason, and it almost killed him."

"A Lammasu?" Sir Lucas gasped in disbelief.

Joseph didn't answer that, he continued with what he had been saying. "Peter's first question on waking was what had happened to the squires. I promised him that I would do what I could for them. By the law put into place last October; they are to be executed, but Lord Haldor agrees with me that there is still a chance the boys can be redeemed. Besides, we're at war and will need every man at arms that we can get. The only good thing about the squires you train is that they end up being killer fighters who are an asset in war that we cannot afford to lose."

"What kind of punishment do you recommend my lord?" Sir Lucas asked, his face pale.

"You will show them that their actions have consequences. You will have them do manual labor until they have paid back every copper they have bullied people out of through their antics, each one of the squires will pay the price in full, the extra money will go to the poor funds. They will be paid the same amount as your lowest paid servants, and will not be given any breaks or special treatment.

Their free time privileges will be revoked completely. You will forbid them to leave the castle grounds without you present, and you will have them give proper apologies to every victim they have had who still lives within the city. When I say proper; I mean on one knee with heads bowed, like the honorable knights that they once dreamed of being. If they truly are one day redeemed, than Lord Haldor said they may still graduate and try to join the knighthood. But if they don't show enough improvement in one year's time, you will dismiss them from your battle school and send them to their families in disgrace. If at that time they have not paid back their share of the money, they will continue to work for you, being dismissed once they money has been paid in full.

Sir Lucas nodded thoughtfully. "It sounds reasonable. Please send my personal thanks to Lord Haldor for his mercy." He agreed.

"It would sound better if it came from you. Unfortunately, Lord Haldor doesn't hold a very high opinion of you Sir Lucas. If I were to deliver your apology for you, he'd be likely enough to reject it."

Joseph said calmly.

Sir Lucas nodded, looking resigned. "Joseph, the boy, will he make it?"

Joseph stood and went over to look out the window, unwilling to let his brother see his emotions. I recognized the look, I had seen it on Joseph's face before, when he had been with Lance at the healing house. "I honestly don't know. He keeps drifting in and out. I've rarely seen head injuries like this. Doctor Nick is doing all he can, but we just don't know yet. Peter's life hangs by a thread. I have no idea if he will be able to hold on or not."

I longed to reassure Joseph that I wasn't going to give up, that I wasn't going to die. But it being a dream, he didn't hear me. I knew then that the dream was about me, *I* was the disaster that the magic was trying to help me avoid.

"I had no idea Doctor Nick was still alive, he must be at least eighty years old by now! Well if anyone can help the boy, it's that man. After all, he cared for you as a child, and look how healthy you are now." Sir Lucas said, trying to reassure his brother.

Joseph's answer was lost to me as the dream faded out of focus, apparently over.

# CHAPTER 23

When I woke up, I found myself in a grandly decorated room. There was a tapestry on the wall above the fireplace, and it showed a scene of a hunting party with dogs and horns and everything. I felt a soft cloth dabbing my throbbing forehead, and I turned to see who was with me. Lady Rose was sitting next to my bed, taking care of me. She had a basin of warm water and a soft cloth, and she was gently washing me. "Please my lady, you don't have to." I said weakly, embarrassed that she had obviously seen me naked.

Lady rose smiled gently at me, and I saw Joseph's smile had come from his mother. "I've had two sons and a husband child; you have nothing I haven't seen before. Don't worry though, you've been washed by my son Joseph. He's been caring for you for a while now. I am just washing your face for you since he had to leave so suddenly a minute ago. How are you feeling?"

"My head really hurts a lot my lady." I admitted through gritted teeth.

Lady rose looked at me kindly, and I was reminded again of Joseph. "I have a pain reducing potion here, just give me a moment and I'll get it for you." She assured me, rising to her feet.

I tried to stay awake, but my eyes were going dark as Lady Rose looked at the labels of the various potions, looking for a certain one. I found that I didn't have the strength to fight against it. I tapped into the magic to stay awake, and the darkness took me at once.

When I woke up next and looked around, Lady Rose was nowhere to be found. Instead, there was a young man who looked to be about John's age sitting on the cushioned stool she had been using, and staring at the fire, looking bored out of his mind. "Hey, who are you?" I asked weakly. The boy turned around, and jumped to his feet.

"I'm Lax. Well actually, my name is Laxworth, but if you ever call me that I'll give you another bump on your head." He said, rummaging through a bag that he had slung over his shoulder.

I stared at him, trying to get my brain to work. "What are you doing here, where's Jo... Lord Joseph?" I asked.

"Lord Joseph is at the barracks, official ranger stuff I think, but I have no idea. All I know is that my grandfather (your doctor) told me that you can't be left alone, so I was sent here to keep an eye on you. I'm a healer in training you see, so I get jobs like this from time to time. I must say, you're really boring to watch, you've been doing nothing but sleep for three days now! I told my grandfather, because it seems really odd, and dangerous with a head injury. But he talked to some Lord Hal-thingy who said you were fine. Apparently you rangers sleep a ton at your age. It's weird, I don't understand it, but I'm just in training, I don't need to understand everything yet, not for a couple months when my tests happen. The time I met you was kind of exciting, in a bad way. My grandfather brought me with him to help out. You almost died you know; but we saved you, and you're getting better really fast now. But really, I'm not complaining, I'm being paid half gold a day to watch over you, and that is a really generous amount at my age and level of experience..."

The healer in training continued to ramble on, but I found myself unable to keep up with his rapid speech, so I stopped trying, it was making my head swim.

After several minutes, Lax finally found what he was looking for in his bag. He pulled out a small potion bottle and gave it to me to drink, not stopping his chatter. "What is this?" I interrupted.

Lax paused in what he was saying, and helped me pull the cork out of the top. "It will help with the nausea. We need to get you to be able to drink some water; you haven't had any at all in far too long. Your blood will be as thick as soup soon, and that will kill you."

I swallowed the potion, and couldn't suppress the urge to gag. Lax laughed lightly. "I know its nasty stuff. But it works wonders, you'll see." He reassured me.

Lax spent the rest of the day taking care of me. He gave me water to drink every half hour or so, and he had brought potions to help with the nausea and pain. The whole time, he kept up his rapid chatter, telling me all about the things he had learned as a healer in training. I lay there silently listening to him. He had some interesting things to teach me, and I was more than eager to learn, I loved learning anything and everything. By the time it was getting dark, I was too tired to take in any more information. I was wondering how I could tell Lax to be quiet without sounding rude, but Joseph came back before I had to.

"My lord, he's awake now." Lax informed Joseph as he packed up his bag.

"I can see that Lax, thank you for your services." Joseph said patiently.

"Same time tomorrow sir?" Lax asked, his hand on the door.

"I'm not sure yet. My superior is arriving some time tonight, so we may not need your services any more. If we do, someone will let you know." Joseph promised, gesturing for Lax to leave.

"Shame, he was just starting to get interesting. Did you know…"

"Lax." Joseph interrupted before Lax could get into the swing of his chatter. "Thank you for your services. I need to talk to Peter before he falls asleep on me again. You should go home now. Your mother no doubt has your supper waiting for you."

Lax bowed, realizing that he was being dismissed. He waved to me, and shut the door behind him.

"Did you say Lord Haldor is coming here?" I asked, starting to sit up, but catching myself in time.

"Yes, he will be here any minute."

"Why? Does he want to talk to me about the squires?" I asked, trying to get my head to work better, willing it to heal faster.

"Talk to you, and take you back under his care. I have proven myself to be unfit to protect and teach you, so Lord Haldor is coming to take you as his own."

I looked at Joseph, trying to see his reaction to what he was saying. But he was facing away from me, straightening the cushion on the stool, which had been ruffled as Lax had used it as his seat. His voice was soft and even, giving me no hint as to his thoughts.

"Lord Haldor was wrong." I said firmly.

Joseph turned to me, frowning slightly in what might have been surprise, but could just as easily have been disapproval. It was hard for me to read him, I was too tired. "You haven't seen your mother in thirty years, and the one time you did talk to your brother, he attacked you. Of course you were upset and distracted. Anyone would be under the circumstances, even Lord Haldor himself. He was wrong to call you unworthy; he had no idea what you've been going through."

I tried to listen to Joseph's reply, but the darkness was dragging me back down again, and I knew better than to try to fight it. If the magic demanded I rest; then it would make sure I rested, fighting against it would accomplish nothing. I knew that had been why I had been sleeping so much since my head injury, because I had tried to resist.

# CHAPTER 24

I woke up to the familiar feeling of being stared at. I blinked, and my vision cleared a bit, showing me blurry shapes in the room. A few more blinks, and I could see that Lord Haldor was sitting by the fire waiting for me to wake, watching me with his unwavering gaze. There was an empty bowl and spoon on the floor beside him, and I wondered how many meals he had sat here watching me.

"My lord, I have so many things I want to talk to you about, but I have no idea where to begin." I said weakly.

Lord Haldor frowned slightly as he considered what I had said. He brought his chair over, and sat down next to my bed.

"Let's start with the reason I am here. Has Lord Joseph talked to you about what is going to happen to you now?" Lord Haldor asked, his grey eyes piercing into me, as if he was looking into my soul.

"He told me you were taking me away from him, because he was unworthy." I said; lowering my eyes, unwilling to look at Lord Haldor's piercing gaze any more. I felt undeniable anger at Lord Haldor for what he had said to Joseph, and I didn't want him to see it, knowing that it would be the height of disrespect for me to let on what I thought.

"Did he tell you what he did that made him unworthy?" Lord Haldor prompted, unwilling to let the matter rest.

"Well its obvious isn't it? *You* were the one who was yelling at him for his mistake in having me go off alone into Askia! It wasn't his fault he was distracted by his family. You would be too if you hadn't seen them in thirty years." I could feel my cheeks starting to burn, and I stared at my blanket, looking at a loose thread. I knew that I was getting angry, but something about my anger didn't feel right. I felt as if there was some fact missing, and so I was unwilling to look at Lord Haldor if my accusations were somehow false.

Lord Haldor cupped his hand under my chin, and turned me so I was looking him in the eye.

"Peter, it was not I who declared him unworthy. That was a decision he made on his own." Lord Haldor told me, forcing me to hold his gaze.

"No, he would never do that! Why would he want to leave me now of all times? He would never do that to me! I've learned more from Jos… Lord Joseph then I've ever learned from anyone else in my life! He's my guide, my mentor, my…" I trailed off, surprised at the word that had almost escaped my mouth.

"Your second father?" Lord Haldor suggested gently.

I swallowed hard, willing myself not to show emotion. Now that it was out in the open, I realized that the reason I hadn't felt homesick was because Joseph had taken on the role of a parent to me. He had become more than my mentor, he had become my extended family. The only family I had access to right now.

"Peter, that is exactly why Lord Joseph feels that he needs to distance himself from you for a time." Lord Haldor said softly.

"I don't understand sir." I managed to choke out through the tears that were taking all my willpower to suppress.

"Joseph feels that he has failed you. As far as Joseph is concerned, he put you into danger because he was blinded by the prospect of seeing his blood family. If you had grown up in the situation he did, you too would have adopted the rangers as your only family. Because Lord Joseph sees you as his family far more than he ever did his blood relatives, the fact that his blood family distracted him to the point where you; a member of his true family; was in danger is in his mind unacceptable.

Lord Joseph has done fine for years now, as long as I have permitted him to stay far away from his hometown. But I knew that he could not hide from his past forever. Sooner or later he would have to face what his brother and father had done to him. I couldn't afford to wait any more for him to take initiative on his own. Joseph has requested time away so he can sort through his thoughts. The most I am able to offer him while we are at war is solitude in his travels between towns. Since Joseph feels that he let you down; he asked that I look after you until he feels worthy of being in your presence again. Have you noticed that he is no longer here?"

I blinked back my tears, nodding slightly, my eyes downcast as Lord Haldor had withdrawn his hold on my face.

"I promise you Peter, he will take you back no later than the end of the winter. Give him time to sort out his life; he *will* come back for you." Lord Haldor assured me, standing up to leave to do official business.

I waited until Lord Haldor's footsteps disappeared down the hall. Then I turned around and buried my face into my pillow. Alone in the room; I let loose the tears I had been trying so hard to suppress. I felt completely miserable, and all I wanted was to be with my father and brothers. I cried harder as I remembered that two of my brothers were gone off to training camps. I had no idea if they would live or die, and I longed to be with them again. But I was far away from them, in a strange city where I had been almost killed, and now; the one person who had become like family to me had left me in what I couldn't help but feel as an act of abandonment. I had never felt so alone in my life; and for the first time since I was a small child, I cried myself to sleep.

When I woke up, I saw a familiar face sitting at the table, busy writing on a piece of parchment. Gene was so focused on his work that he hadn't noticed me wake up yet. I lay and watched him. His brow was furrowed and he was muttering to himself, trying to focus. After a few minutes, I began to be amused. It had occurred to me that

Gene was probably there on Lord Haldor's orders, which meant he was supposed to be paying attention to not just his work, but also to what was going on in the room.

"Lesson number one, a ranger must always pay attention to everything around him. Failure to do so will cost you your life." I recited softly.

Gene whirled around in surprise. When he saw me watching him, he got up and came over, looking slightly guilty. "Hey Peter. Sorry about that, I was trying to do a tactics scenario, and I guess I got distracted for a moment or two."

I tried hard not to smile, but Gene saw the look on my face. "Err… just how long have you been awake?" He asked uncomfortably.

"Ten, maybe twenty minutes." I said with a grin. I wasn't sure why catching my year mate not paying attention cheered me up so much, but it did. Then I realized that I was just happy to see him. I'd spent so much time with adults lately that it was almost refreshing to have Gene around.

"Oh man, Lord Haldor is going to kill me!" Gene moaned, running his hand through his short hair, knocking off his hood in the process.

"What does happen if you forget a lesson?" I asked, more talking to myself than actually seeking an answer from Gene.

Gene gave out a noise of exasperation as he put his hood back on, and sat down on the stool beside the bed. "Well, when you learn it, you recite it a dozen times, right?" He asked, checking to see if I knew that much.

"With you so far." I agreed, remembering my stints of reciting.

"Right, well if you are caught with your guard down it becomes reciting two dozen times. After the second time, they add punishments to the mix." Gene made a sour face. "Lord Haldor gave me two days worth of demerits last time he caught me not paying attention to my surroundings. He had a ranger there with me, making me recite lesson one over and over again the whole time! I've never washed a dish in my life before joining the rangers, and I had to wash all the dishes in the ranger's headquarters for TWO hours, breakfast lunch and dinner, reciting lesson one the whole time!"

"Ouch." I muttered in sympathy. "I had no idea ranger punishments for mistakes were so harsh."

Gene shot me a strange look. "Oh please, you can't tell me you've *never* gotten punished for anything! Thelmer told us Lord Joseph is one of the stricter rangers alive. He was trained personally by Lord Haldor you know." Gene snapped in disbelief.

I shook my head, regretting the action immediately as a wave of nausea and dizziness hit me. "He's lectured me, but I've been really careful to not do anything he'd punish me for. I don't really forget things easily, so I've had no trouble making sure to remember the lessons." I said softly, holding my head with both hands, willing the dizziness to pass.

"You're a liar. Every ranger apprentice is punished; it's part of being an apprentice." Gene said, crossing his arms across his chest and glaring at me.

I closed my eyes and didn't answer. I was feeling far too sick to try to defend what I had said, even though I knew that I was right. "Let's just drop it, ok? Tell me what else you've been studying." I said once the dizziness had passed and I could open my eyes again.

"All sorts of stuff, all the apprentices have their own training program, and it works on improving those things we aren't good at. For me, it's been mostly archery and moving without being heard. Can you run silently? I know I still haven't gotten it down yet. Robin has been working on her hand to hand combat, and Sara has been learning how to use a sword, which she had never done before. We do those things one day, and the second day we have formal studies after exercises, with lessons in tactics and history and geography and stuff. Sara isn't with us for that very often, because she has to learn how to read first. Did you know that farmers are never taught how to read?! Apparently gypsies aren't either, but Robin taught herself how to do so when she was little."

"Well, most people aren't taught how to read Gene, not until they become apprentices. My brother John could never get good at it, because he was so old when I had learned and could teach my brothers. But father always said reading only helps a bit. He always said if you had a good eye for your craft, there was no need to learn your letters. I think most of the kingdom thinks like that." I explained patiently, remembering suddenly that Gene was a noble's son and so wouldn't understand the lower classes that well.

Gene shook his head in disbelief. "I've been learning my letters since I was six years old. Hey, if you're a blacksmith's son, how did you learn to read anyways, especially if your brothers didn't even know how?"

I hesitated, wondering what to say and what not to say. I didn't want to sound like I was bragging, but at the same time, I remembered Joseph saying I had no right to be ashamed of my gifts. "Lord Haldor took custody of me when I was eight years old. He let me continue to live with my father and brothers, but only under the condition that I be given an education in more than just blacksmith duties. He had me learn reading, archery, geography, sword play, all sorts of stuff. I've been training to be a ranger most of my life."

Gene glared at me again. "You are such a liar! Ranger apprentices aren't claimed until they are thirteen, just like every other craft. I'm not talking to you any more if you won't stop lying. Besides," he added as I was about to protest, "I've seen how little skills you have with a bow. You and I were tested at the same time, remember? It's obvious that you don't have any more skills in archery than I do."

"Yeah, well I was holding back for YOU!" I snapped, feeling suddenly hot with anger.

"You're mental! Why the heck would you hold back for me? Face it Pete, I caught you in two lies today. Now you're just lying to cover for your lies, just like all liars do." Gene snapped, his own face red with anger. His hands were balled into fists, and he raised them into a fight position.

"You want to fight?" I asked furiously, raising myself up into a sitting position carefully. "You really want to have a physical fight over your delusional beliefs that I am lying?"

"You ARE lying!" Gene shouted.

That was when Lord Haldor chose to make his presence known. He had been standing outside the door listening to our raised voices, and he came in now, a look of cold anger in his eyes, the usual frown on his face. I felt nervousness grip me, as he looked from me to Gene. Both of us looked at Lord Haldor, all anger forgotten as we wondered how much trouble we were in for fighting. Lord Haldor regarded us thoughtfully, me sitting on the bed with one arm holding the blankets to shield my nakedness, and Gene standing next to the bed, his arms hanging loosely at his side, as he had dropped them in shock at Lord Haldor's sudden appearance.

"Did you hear me approach, Peter." Lord Haldor asked me.

"No my lord, I didn't." I admitted, my voice calm despite the nervousness I felt as Lord Haldor studied us gravely.

"So then you don't know how long I've been listening to you?"

"No sir."

"Then I ask you now, have you said anything that is a lie, bearing in mind that you don't have any idea how much of the conversation I have heard?" Lord Haldor asked grimly.

"I didn't lie my lord, why would I? Gene just,"

"So then you vouch before your Lord, the head of your guild that you have told nothing but the truth?" Lord Haldor interrupted.

"Yes sir." I said firmly.

Gene made a noise of disbelief, unable to help himself. Lord Haldor turned to Gene now, and regarded him gravely. "What did Peter say that you consider a lie Gene?" He asked softly.

Gene was trembling as he answered. Apparently Lord Haldor's eyes had the same effect on Gene as they did on most people, Joseph being the only exception I'd ever seen. "Well my lord, first he said he has never really been punished while an apprentice,"

"He hasn't. Next 'lie'." Lord Haldor interrupted.

"Then he said he was holding back during the archery test."

"He was, next 'lie'." Lord Haldor interrupted again.

Gene's resolve was wavering now as Lord Haldor confirmed everything I had said. I could tell that he had been caught off guard by Lord Haldor's presence and his confirmations of what Gene had taken as lies. "Next 'lie'!" Lord Haldor demanded as Gene didn't say anything.

"M... my Lord, he said that you've been having him trained as a ranger since he was eight." Gene said in a quiet voice, knowing that he was going to be told that he had made a mistake again.

"Why did you consider what he said to be lies?" Lord Haldor asked.

Gene lowered his eyes, unable to look at Lord Haldor anymore. "I don't know sir, my lord. I... what he said just sounded unbelievable."

"Why did it sound that way?" Lord Haldor prompted, not satisfied yet.

Gene stared at his boots, unable to think of a good answer. "I don't know sir, it just did..."

Lord Haldor continued to stare at Gene, who began to shift uncomfortably under his gaze. "You have accused your year mate of lying, a *very* serious charge for a ranger's apprentice. Being caught in a lie will get an apprentice ten demerit per lie. Is that what you wanted, for Peter to be given ten demerits for each lie you accused him of?" Lord Haldor asked, his voice soft with suppressed anger.

"No sir! I had no idea that the punishment for lying was so harsh, I would never want him to go through that!" Gene protested looking up at Lord Haldor, his eyes wide in horror at the thought.

"Then from now on, you will find the truth behind a claim BEFORE you accuse one of my apprentices of lying." Lord Haldor said coldly.

"Yes my lord, I will." Gene promised, his voice humble and subdued.

"As for you," Lord Haldor said, turning to me with a sharp glint of anger in his eyes. I swallowed hard, wondering what was coming. "Who said you could sit up?"

I lowered myself back down onto the pillows carefully and watched Lord Haldor, waiting for him to speak. "You almost died the last time you decided to sit up. If you try it again I will have you flogged and then strapped to the bed. Do I make myself clear young man?"

"Yes my lord." I said weakly.

"You were supposed to be taking care of him, not driving him into causing himself more damage." Lord Haldor scolded Gene. Gene lowered his eyes to the floor, ducking his head into his hood.

"You boys are rangers. You need to work together, not fight like dogs over a piece of meat. Gene, you hardly know Peter so have no reason to believe he, a fellow ranger, would lie to you. Peter, I expected you to be mature enough to not take offence at claims you know to be false." I stared at my blanket in shame. I hated letting Lord Haldor down like this. He was right; I should be mature enough to have not let Gene get to me so easily. "Both of you shake hands and make up. Next time I find you two fighting I promise, there will be consequences." Lord Haldor ordered.

# CHAPTER 25

Gene stepped forward, and I grasped his hand. We let go and looked at Lord Haldor, waiting to see what his next order was going to be. Lord Haldor looked down at us, and seemed satisfied that the event was over. "Peter, there are four young men who request an audience with you."

I looked at Lord Haldor in confusion.

"Gene, go open the door and invite them in." Lord Haldor ordered.

Sir Lucas entered, followed by his four squires. I watched them hesitantly. I knew why they were here, but seeing the squires really made me want to run out of the room and keep on running until I was a thousand miles away from this city. I felt helpless lying there in bed with nothing between my naked, wounded body and the squires except for a few layers of bed coverings. I glanced over at Lord Haldor nervously. But his eyes were focused on the squires.

One at a time, the squires got down on one knee and bowed their head to me, reciting their apology. "I am sorry for my wrongful acts against you. I solemnly swear before you and before my knight that I will never again do anything to bring harm to you or your family. I will work hard to pay back any money that was spent for your medical care due to my actions. I ask for forgiveness, but will understand if you wish to withhold said forgiveness due to the amount of pain you suffered at my hands."

I told each of the squires that they were forgiven. I truly didn't hold what they had done against them. I had never held what happened against them. To me, they were no different than any other young men who hadn't been brought up with the same morals that my father had brought me and my brothers up with. They enjoyed causing pain to others, but since they were swearing in front of Sir Lucas and Lord Haldor to never do it again, that was good enough for me.

After the four squires had apologized to me, they moved on to Lord Haldor, altering the words slightly so their speech was an apology for harming one of his apprentices.

"My apprentice may be willing to accept your word as sufficient, but I am not inclined to be so generous." Lord Haldor told the four squires once they had all apologized to him. "Those who attack rangers are supposed to be executed as traitors to the kingdom. You have been spared your lives only out of the goodness of the king's heart, and the fact that we don't want to waste your training when we need you in battle. But this is your one and only warning. If ever you harm a ranger again, your lives will not be spared."

The squires went pale as Lord Haldor spoke to them sternly. Lord Haldor dismissed them, and they bowed and left silently.

Sir Lucas stayed behind, and waited for the squires to leave before he spoke. "My lord Haldor, I wish to speak to you." He said formally.

Lord Haldor frowned slightly. "Then speak." He said.

Sir Lucas glanced at me and Gene. We were both staring at the knight, curious to know what he was going to say.

Lord Haldor gave a weary sigh, looking suddenly very old. "Gene, go wait in my room for me. I'll be there soon to check on your tactics scenario." Gene had a disappointed look in his eyes as he bowed and left. He was obviously bummed that he didn't get to know what Sir Lucas was going to say. "Satisfied?" Lord Haldor asked Sir Lucas, his frown deepening.

Realizing that he wasn't going to get a better deal, Sir Lucas nodded. He got down on one knee to Lord Haldor, adjusting himself so he wouldn't have to look at me. "My lord, I have brought pain upon my brother, and so upon all who know him. As his older brother it should have been my job to protect him against my father, not join my father in terrorizing him."

"This is a discussion you should be having with your brother, not me." Lord Haldor interrupted.

"Believe me my lord, if he was capable of listening to my apology, I would have told him a week ago. I tried to tell him, but he wasn't ready. Anyways, I have more to say to you."

Lord Haldor nodded acceptance, leaning against the wall as he listened.

"I wish to personally thank you for your mercy in altering the law to spare my squires. I have failed to train them properly, and will do all I can to rectify the situation. Lord Joseph made me realize that the way I have been living is harmful not just to my squires, but also to myself. I swear my Lord; I will do everything in my power to heal the damage I have done, especially to my brother."

Sir Lucas kept his head bowed as he spoke, staring at the floor as he was down on one knee. He didn't see what I saw, which was the quick flash of approval and relief in Lord Haldor's eyes. "Rise Sir Lucas." He invited. When Sir Lucas had risen to his full height and was standing at attention, his face determined, Lord Haldor continued. "It is a true sign of wisdom that you have realized the errors of your young life. I accept your apology. You may go now."

Sir Lucas bowed to Lord Haldor, and left the room.

Lord Haldor crossed over to the table and sagged down into Gene's chair, rubbing his eyes with his hand, looking exhausted and ill.

"My Lord, are you alright?" I asked in concern, turning over on my side so I could see him better.

Lord Haldor opened one eye to glance at me. "I am fine Peter, just tired. I'm a very old man you know, and old men like me don't have a lot of stamina."

"But…" I started to say, very confused. "But my lord, when I saw you a few months ago you were as fiery as any ranger."

Lord Haldor gave an exhausted laugh. "That was a few months ago Peter. A lot has happened since then." Lord Haldor paused, considering what to say. "The magic has left me. I am too old to use it, and so it has left."

I looked at Lord Haldor horrified. "But surly, the magic understands that you are old, that it isn't your fault if you can't practice with it!"

Lord Haldor got to his feet, and sat down next to me on the bed, taking one of my hands into both of his. "A human is a human Peter. Sooner or later, we all have to do things that the magic will not help with. There are many things that the magic will not do, such as interfere with natural death. One day when you are old and withered the magic will leave you too."

"But…" I said, choking back the tears that had sprung to my eyes. "But without the magic you'll…"

"I'll eventually die of old age, yes."

"Peter, there is no need for that!" Lord Haldor said as I couldn't suppress my tears any more. "I am not dead yet, I still have a bit of life left in these old bones. I told you because I don't want you to be taken by surprise. But I have lived a very wonderful and very long life. Believe me lad, when a person dies of old age, it is like finally being able to put your feet up after a very long day of hard work."

When I looked at Lord Haldor not understanding, he squeezed my hand gently in his and sat there silently with me, letting me sort things out on my own.

After several minutes I looked up at Lord Haldor again. "How long… did the magic tell you when you'd…"

Lord Haldor frowned slightly at me. "What are you talking about Peter?" He asked.

"The magic, when it left you did it say how long you'd have to live?" I asked, wondering if I was out of place asking for personal information of such a sensitive nature.

Lord Haldor stared at me silently. I looked into his piercing grey eyes for a bit, and then looked away feeling ashamed. Obviously the question was far too personal; I had kind of suspected it would be.

"Peter, I am going to ask you an extremely personal question, so do not feel that you are obligated to answer if you desire not to. When the magic talks to you, what does it sound like?" Lord Haldor asked softly.

I looked back up at Lord Haldor, not understanding why he'd ask. "I don't know sir. It's… not exactly words… it's more like… feelings." I said, thinking hard.

"What kind of feelings? Give me an example." Lord Haldor prompted, his eyes becoming even more focused.

"Umm, well when I overheard something I wasn't supposed to, I asked the magic to help me keep whatever qualities I needed to stay friends with Abiyram. The magic responded by making me feel a sense of… comfort. I felt a sort of reassurance that everything was going to be fine. It was like when I was really little and I'd wake up from a bad dream to find myself in the bedroom of my Father's house with my father and brothers all around me. I… I'm sorry sir, I don't know how else to explain it." I said quietly.

Lord Haldor frowned slightly in thought. "Peter, when you tap into the magic to help sharpen your skills, how long does it take for your skills to get better?"

I stared at Lord Haldor, becoming more and more confused. Where was all this leading? "It happens really fast sir."

"How fast exactly?" Lord Haldor prompted, leaning forward slightly, his frown deepening.

"I… I don't know exactly sir, my lord. It is almost instant." I said nervously.

Lord Haldor sat back and considered what I had said. His eyes became less intense as he stopped focusing on me so much. Lord Haldor stroked his chin in silence for a few minutes. Then he returned his focus to me. "Peter, it is essential that you stay with me as much as possible. For the moment, I need to discuss with the other ranger lords and we must decide what will happen. But from now on, you will take orders just from me and Joseph, no other rangers. Consider yourself my personal assistant. When Joseph takes over, you will take orders from none but him and Thelmer. Do you understand?"

"Well yes my lord… and no." I admitted.

"Why no?" Lord Haldor asked.

"Well, I understand your orders, but I don't understand WHY."

Lord Haldor sat back considering what he should tell me. "Out of rangers, there will sometimes be people like you and me. Once in a great while there will be people who take to the magic like a duck to water. We develop a sort of… relationship with the magic. Your bond with the magic is above and beyond the usual bond of rangers. Because of this, you need to learn the skills needed to be a ranger lord of a certain class that is not spoken about to many."

"So Lord Joseph also has this bond with the magic then?" I asked curiously.

Lord Haldor nodded. "As does Thelmer. The last time the Lammasu visited humans was when the guild was first established, when the present ruling family took over the country. When the elves gave rangers magic as their peace offering to humans, the Lammasu told us to make sure that we found those with the right bond with magic to be the heads of the guild. Unless the right kind of person was in charge, the magic would not work for rangers properly, and eventually it would die out. So since you have this bond, you need to be trained to one day be in charge, when Joseph and Thelmer have passed on."

"But sir… why haven't the Lammasu been here is so long? Why did they choose ME of all people? I'm no one special, just a blacksmith's son!"

"I don't know Peter. I don't have any of the answers to that since I've never met a Lammasu, and so only have the stories from the old days, and your own word to go off of."

"But you've seen my bottle before, or one just like it! You told me so, well sort of." I said, starting to sit up.

Lord Haldor pressed me down firmly. "There are four of those bottles being kept in the royal treasury. Ranger lords have access to see them. But we are forbidden to touch them, and no man can handle them except the one to whom they were given over seven hundred years ago. They have powerful magic in them that normal humans can't touch."

"But I AM normal! I'm just like anyone else, so why can I touch them?!" I pleaded, desperate for an answer.

"I don't *know* Peter. As I said, I've never met a Lammasu. Abiyram said he would see you again, so when he does you can ask him." Lord Haldor rose to his feet. "My travel companion is waiting for his tactics practice to be graded, and as I said, I need to consult with the other ranger lords. I will send Gene in to you shortly. Will you be alright until then?"

"Yes my lord." I said, feeling distinctly unsatisfied with the answers I had been given.

Lord Haldor turned and looked at me intensely. "Peter, I need you to hurry up and heal yourself, just like you healed Joseph." He said with one hand on the door.

Before I could ask about what he had said, Lord Haldor was gone, shutting the door behind him. I lay there puzzling about that. What on earth had he meant? I hadn't healed Joseph. Maybe he meant Lance? But no, the juice only worked when the damage was caused by the touch of evil. The squires weren't evil, not in the same way as the Kronlords were. So how could that possibly be it? With a sigh I closed my eyes, and willed my body to heal faster. Lord Haldor didn't understand the juice's powers, but how could he? He had just been confused. But I willed myself to heal faster anyways. I didn't want to disappoint Lord Haldor any further. If I wished really hard, than at least I could truthfully tell him I tried.

# CHAPTER 26

Three days after Lord Haldor and I had our talk about Abiyram, Doctor Nick agreed that I was healed enough to go to the capital. Lord Haldor had reserved a carriage to bring us back, as it was too far for him to walk now that the magic had left him and he was getting rapidly weaker. Doctor Nick gave me some instructions before he would let me leave. "You are to lie down for an hour to rest some time during the day for at least one week. No running or other strenuous exercise for at *least* three weeks. If you feel dizzy, sit down and wait until the dizziness has passed by for at least five minutes before you continue on. Take it slow and easy for a while. Don't try to push yourself too far too soon. If you start seeing double, or your dizziness doesn't pass within a few minutes, get yourself to the nearest doctor."

"Yes sir, I will." I promised as Gene climbed into the carriage behind Lord Haldor.

I turned to follow Gene, but Doctor Nick put his hand on my arm. "Please be careful lad. I can't come with you, and I want to know that you will take care of yourself." He said softly when I turned back to him.

"I'll be careful sir, I promise." I assured him, smiling in thanks for all he had done for me.

I entered the carriage; and sat down next to Gene, across from Lord Haldor. I felt as if a great tension was released once we had passed through the city's east wall, and got on our way. I sat back against the leather cushion of the carriage, and released a breath I felt like I had been holding ever since entering that city. Lord Haldor's lips twitched into the closest I had ever seen him give to a smile (even when he laughed, Lord Haldor always seemed to be frowning). "I suppose we know one city you won't be in any hurry to visit again." Lord Haldor said softly.

I blushed and ducked my head into my hood. "Forgive me, my lord; I shouldn't think that way." I muttered.

Lord Haldor waved his hand dismissively. "Just because you are a ranger to the country doesn't mean you have to like every aspect of it. There are almost always going to be places or people that rangers wish they never had to deal with again. Ranger's aren't perfect you know."

"Yes my lord, I know." I agreed. But I still felt guilty for some reason that I never wanted to be near Askia again. Surely there were plenty of good people there, like Doctor Nick and Lax. So to hate the whole city was unfair of me.

"No, it wasn't hate I was feeling. It was just reluctance to return there." I thought to myself.

It took us six hours of riding before we reached the town of Latit. I sat calmly and listened to Lord Haldor lecture about history since the beginning of King Stephen's family's reign over the country. Lord Haldor explained that after several years with no sign of a Lammasu, people became offended and tried to convince themselves that they were just a myth. After a few dozen years, people really did start to believe it, especially the more uneducated villagers. Lord Haldor talked about how even the rangers began to wonder if it had not all been a dream as another hundred years went by with not even a whisper from the celestial beings. The kingdom eventually realized that they would have to survive on their own, and learn how to cope with the little magic they had been given. I soaked the information in, eager as always to learn everything and anything.

Beside me, Gene was listening a bit less enthusiastically. He had a look of polite boredom on his face. It occurred to me that since he had never met Abiyram, of course the history lesson wasn't going to have the same impact it did on me. Lord Haldor often fired questions at us to make sure we were paying attention. He would describe some law or policy, and then ask us questions about what we thought should be the wording of such a law so that it wasn't misunderstood by anyone. He also described different wars against the southern and western countries, and told us the tactics the rangers and the king used, asking us to predict the outcome.

I was surprised when the carriage stopped in Latit. The hours had flown past a lot faster than I had expected them to. We had stopped for a dinner break. Lord Haldor told us that he planned to ride through the night and so reach the capital by sunset tomorrow. We had stopped to get fresh horses, and to get a break from sitting and riding all day. Lord Haldor took Gene and me to the inn, and talked to the innkeeper, requesting a private lounge with a couch for us to stay in while we had our meal. When we got to the room, Lord Haldor had me lay down on the couch and rest. I lay there and watched Lord Haldor have Gene do pushups and sit-ups. Gene was use to exercising like this, as he had been traveling with Lord Haldor the past few months, and Lord Haldor was keeping his young charge in top physical shape. It occurred to me that in the capital, Gene would probably have gone running like we had done at the fortress, but when he was in a carriage all day with Lord Haldor, the pushups were probably the most he was able to do for fitness. Gene's face was red and shiny with sweat when our meal came and Lord Haldor gave him permission to stop. Gene went over to a wash bin and tidied himself up as Lord Haldor divided the meal onto three plates. I lay on the couch, half fearing Lord Haldor would make me stay down. But he held the plate out to me, and I joined him and Gene sitting by the fire with a sense of relief.

"My lord, how is Peter going to exercise if he's still injured?" Gene asked curiously as he waited for the large amount of butter he had taken to melt onto his fresh dinner roll.

"There are exercises that he can do; he just has to be careful. Peter can't run, but he can still walk if he watches his pace. Also he can strengthen his arms and legs by holding them out to his sides." Lord Haldor answered, not looking up as he cut his meat.

Gene and I glanced at each other in confusion. How could holding our arms out to the side be a form of exercise? Lord Haldor looked up to take a roll from the basket and saw the look on my face. "Don't believe me Peter? You hold your arms out; see how long you can do it." He suggested lightly.

"Yes my lord." I said uncertainly, holding my arms out to either side so they were stretched out. Soon I came to realize what Lord Haldor had known. It was easy at first, but eventually, my arms did indeed get tired, and it only took a few minutes for that to happen.

"Eat your food boys; we have a long way to go yet." Lord Haldor ordered once I had to let my arms drop, unable to hold them out any more.

There was a lit lamp inside the carriage as we set off again. Lord Haldor didn't lecture us anymore. As soon as we were off, he nodded off to sleep, his head resting against the wood wall of the carriage. Gene and I chatted in low voices, making sure that our words were no louder than the noises the carriage was making.

"I must say, it's nice to have someone else to talk to for once, being Lord Haldor's travel companion makes for very dull conversations." Gene said lightly.

"He wasn't the most talkative person to travel with when I was with him either. Most of the time, we just walked in silence. Lord Haldor is a man of few words." I agreed, smiling slightly.

"Oh yeah; I forgot that you knew him way before I did. You've known him all your life practically." Gene said.

"No, actually, I never even knew rangers existed for years." I said, and then began to explain a little about my past. I didn't want Gene to think I was lying or bragging, so I made it sound more like I had just been the lucky selection Lord Haldor happened to make when he was looking for new apprentices. I didn't tell any lies, but I left most things unsaid since I was unsure how Gene would react.

Gene was especially interested in hearing about my family, and he seemed awed at the fact that we only had two beds in my father's house to share among us in one bedroom that didn't fit much besides the beds and our pile of clothes. He also seemed to not mind me telling him about other things I had taken for granted, such as second hand clothes held together with patches of cloth. He smiled slightly when I told him how amazing it felt to me to have footwear that was made especially for me, and the new clothes Lord Haldor had bought for me in Askia when he saw that I had grown so the ones from home didn't fit right any more. Unlike the one other rich youth our age I had met in Woodward, Gene was kind about the obvious differences of our upbringings. When I mentioned this to him, he smiled in understanding.

"I've always hated those parties. The rich youths in my father's city were so dull. There was this one boy named Henerik who my mother kept trying to encourage me to socialize with. He seemed to consider anyone who wasn't as rich as his father to be not worth talking to. The problem was, he was one of the more poor families out of the rich. We all know he's a snob, and a foolish one at that, so no one ever gives him so much as the time of day anymore." Gene's smile widened. "Don't worry; some of them grow out of it. Those who don't are looked down on by the rich and poor alike. They can snub their noses at the common folk all they want, but at the end of the day, it's them who are all alone, not you guys."

I smiled back at Gene, touched by his understanding.

"Oh, by the way, I've been thinking a lot about what you said." Gene said casually, some minutes later.

I turned to look at him. I had bunched my change of clothes into a pillow and was resting my head against the side of the carriage. Gene had done the same against the other side. "What did I say?" I asked, wondering what he was referring to.

"When you said you were holding back because of me, remember?"

"Yeah…" I said, unsure where he was going with this.

"Well, I kept wondering why you would do that. We hardly knew each other, so why would you feel the need to hold back?"

I hesitated, unsure what to say. But Gene wasn't looking for an answer.

"Then I started going over everything that had happened between us since we first met. I knew something must have happened, something I had said or done that would make you act so strange."

I ducked my head further into my hood. Why did my face always have to blush when I least wanted it to?

"So I was going over our conversations, and that's when it hit me." Gene sat up and looked at me seriously.

"I'm sorry. I realize that my reaction to you saying your father was a blacksmith was highly offensive. I should never have reacted like that. I know I'd be offended if you dismissed me for my father being a Barron, and I should have realized that it would go both ways. I really don't have anything against blacksmiths, or any poor people. Sara's a farmer's daughter and I still…" Gene cleared his throat, and continued on his original track. "I'm sorry for what I did."

Gene offered his hand to me, and I shook it. Then Gene wrapped himself up in his cloak, and went to sleep. As I rested my head back against my side of the carriage, I glanced over at Lord Haldor. I had been sure for the past few minutes that he was watching me with one eye slightly open, but when I looked back again, he was still asleep, snoring softly. I watched him for a while as I waited to fall asleep, but he didn't stir from his position except for the movement of the carriage under him. As I was drifting off, I glanced once more at him suspiciously; I had been so sure I had felt his piercing gaze on me and Gene as we talked. Finally, I shrugged and closed my eyes; obviously I must have just imagined it.

# CHAPTER 27

We went to an area of the capital that I had never been in before. The harvest fair always took place right inside the first wall of the city, where everyone in the kingdom was welcome to be. The land behind the second wall was used mainly for those who had business and trading of some kind to conduct in the capital. Behind the third wall was where those who lived in the capital full time had their homes. The fourth wall, which was over two meters thick, was where the carriage took us. This was where the official business of the kingdom took place. This was where the knights and lords had their second homes (the head knights always had multiple ones to use when they retired), and held their meetings. This was where the ranger lords and apprentices were staying in the case of a need for a last stand. Here in the fourth wall, close to the castle Andor itself.

I watched in awe as we rode along. It took a lot of my willpower to not press my hands and face against the window like a child, so eager was I to see the capital city. The city soldiers wore black leather and half armor, with the symbol of the royal family painted on their chest with silver paint. They had a look to them of pride and power. I knew from Kevin that this was where several squires ended up, as soldiers of the capital. They were the last to be able to pick squires out of the boys at the tournaments, but the squires got the same training as any other squire, more sometimes since the boys still got to live in the capital with their masters and so had access to a lot of educational benefits the squires who learned far away didn't.

The soldiers were just one thing to see. The very buildings were worth looking at. In comparison to the simple straw roofs of the villages and towns, the roofs here were wood or grey stone. The buildings often had paint on them, and some of the social buildings such as the inns and taverns had designs carved into the wood walls, especially around the windows and doorway. The result was beautiful to see, especially with the piles of snow against the walls and on the roofs. I watched the people as we passed them. They all were dressed well; there were no patched or torn clothes here. The clothes were casual, but definitely nowhere close to the shagginess I had grown used to seeing from the villages and towns. Many people were going about on horses, or in carriages like we were. Very few people in comparison were actually walking from place to place on foot.

We stopped outside of a building with a silver dagger painted on the door. My heart leapt in excitement as I saw who came out to greet us. Part of me wanted to call a greeting to Joseph, but then I stopped and hung back, letting my companions leave the carriage before me. I still felt somewhat hurt by what had happened in Askia, I still felt like Joseph had abandoned me there. I couldn't help but wonder what it would have been like if I had arrived here in the capital with Joseph instead of Gene and Lord Haldor. Joseph would have understood my excitement I knew, and I wouldn't have felt the need to stay still and not let myself give in to my emotions. Lord Haldor was always so serious; I didn't feel comfortable being overly excited around him. I stood behind Gene as Joseph bowed in greeting to Lord Haldor. Then Gene and I bowed to Lord Joseph, and Gene went forward to greet him excitedly. I backed away and focused my attention on Lord Haldor who was counting out money to pay the carriage driver; I didn't want to look at Joseph just now. But he put a hand on my arm and pulled me away from Lord Haldor and Gene.

"What's on your mind Peter?" He asked me softly.

I looked down at my boots without answering. I couldn't figure out if I felt hurt, or angry, or both.

"Peter, please talk to me." Joseph pleaded.

I looked up at my friend, pain filling my chest as I recognized the tone to be similar to the one Joseph had used when he had pleaded with his brother.

"I'm not mad at you my lord, I swear. None of this was your fault." I said earnestly.

Joseph attempted to smile, but I could see that he was anything but happy. He got down on one knee in the snow and held both my hands. "Peter, I didn't mean to abandon you in Askia. I had no idea you'd take it that way, I swear. I thought I was helping you by distancing myself. I didn't want you to have to suffer any more because of my feelings towards my blood family. I thought that by having you stay with Lord Haldor you'd have someone who could give you the attention you deserve. The thought never occurred to me that you would want me there. I thought you felt like I had let you get hurt, and in that case wouldn't want to see me. That's why I left before you were fully awake each time. I was trying to protect you, not hurt you."

I had no idea what to say to that. I was surprised that Joseph had thought he was helping me by staying away from me. I didn't understand why he would think like that. Joseph was my best friend, my second father. Why would I not want him there when I needed him most? Finally I found something to say. "Who said I felt abandoned?" I asked.

"Lord Haldor told me when he was talking to the ranger lords about you, making your entry into prodigy training official. He had me keep the message basin open after the others had left, and told me. Peter, I truly am sorry." Joseph said, his face tight with earnest.

I took my hands out of Joseph's and threw my arms around his neck, embracing him. I closed my eyes as all the hurt I had felt was soothed away at last. When Joseph stood up and I turned around, I felt it again. I felt as if Lord Haldor had been watching me, but when I looked, he was busy paying the driver, who bowed his head in thanks for the tip Lord Haldor gave him for his extended services.

Inside the building with the dagger painted on it, there was a long hallway. The sounds of a lot of chatter were coming from behind one of the doors, and Lord Haldor led the way to the room. As soon as he opened the door and entered, there was a flurry of movement as everyone stopped what they were doing and got down on one knee. Besides the ranger lords and apprentices, there were also several other rangers in the room. When Lord Haldor gave the signal, everyone got to their feet and tried to find somewhere to sit in the overcrowded room. The apprentices and several of the rangers ended up on the floor, and Gene and I went to join them. Sara beamed at me in greeting, and Robin smiled shyly. Gene sat between the girls and slipped his hand into Sara's, who looked at Gene with adoring eyes. When Robin saw that I had seen Gene's actions, she rolled her eyes up to the ceiling. Apparently Robin wasn't nearly as amused as I was about Gene's behavior.

"Now that all the lords including our unofficial one are present, we can get back to business." Lord Haldor told the room. Robin turned away from me and gave Lord Haldor her full attention, so I did the same. "Tomorrow will be Lord Joseph's ceremony, but that is tomorrow. Tonight there is work to be done. You children will all work on your lessons for now. Ranger lords, I want a full update."

Everyone got to their feet, and the ranger lords started to file out of the room. I turned to my year mates to ask what I should be doing, but then I heard Lord Haldor's voice rise over the chatter of the apprentices. "Peter, come on. What are you waiting for?" He demanded.

I blushed and hurried after him, suddenly remembering that he had told me to stay with him. Apparently I was expected to accompany him even to meetings. Gene looked at me and Lord Haldor uncertainly. Lord Haldor frowned slightly at him, realizing his confusion. On the road Gene had been his travel companion, going with him wherever he went. Gene didn't understand why all of a sudden, the positions had shifted. Lord Haldor approached Gene, and laid a hand on the boy's shoulder. "Peter is a special case Gene, like Thelmer. I am training him myself." He explained patiently.

Gene nodded, but his face showed that he didn't really understand. Lord Haldor didn't stick around to explain either, he was already half way out of the room by the time Gene had finished nodding.

Lord Haldor led me to a meeting room. There was a large map of the kingdom spread out on the table, taking up almost all the available space. Lord Haldor took the seat that would put him so he was facing the map right side up. I stood two paces behind him, waiting for someone to tell me otherwise. I wasn't surprised when no one did so. Two steps behind my teacher had become what I was use to as the proper position for an apprentice. Everyone took seats except for Lord Joseph, who was the speaker, being second in command.

"There has been no sign of trouble yet in the fortresses. We sent some of our newly trained archers to help out there, just in case. There has also been no more word of kronlord attacks. The kronlords seem to have withdrawn, or else they are biding their time. We suspect that they let Lance go, wanting the alarm to be raised. Why else did they not kill him? If this is the case, then Kron is playing with us. He wants to wait for us to crack under the pressure of wondering where and when he will strike next." Joseph said, catching me up on the news.

"What of the elves, have they made contact with us yet?" Lord Haldor asked.

Joseph shook his head. "Not a word my lord. We've tried to contact the ones in Maltron in person of course, but so far, there had been no answer from the rangers we sent there yesterday. If the centaurs knew of Kron's attack plans, chances are the elves know as well. But why they haven't at least answered our messages, I'm not sure."

There was an uncomfortable shift from the lords. "It's not like the elves to not answer. They've always welcomed our help in the past." Lord Walter stated.

Lord Haldor sat silently, deep in thought. "Maltron you say?" He murmured to Joseph.

"Yes sir." Joseph said, looking at the map and the dark forest Lord

Haldor was pointing to. Maltron sat right at the border of the country on the south, just about half way down the border line.

"Lord Walter, did you notice any problems when you left?" Lord Haldor asked.

Lord Walter shook his head firmly. "No more than the usual, my lord."

"Are you POSITIVE that there was NO more than the usual? There was no sign of more activity, or anticipation from any of the forest dwellers?" Lord Haldor asked, leaning forward slightly.

Lord Walter thought the question over, not making a hasty answer. He considered for a while before answering. "If anything, things were a bit quieter than usual sir. Not noticeably quieter, but perhaps a small bit." He said at last.

That was all Lord Haldor needed to hear. He quickly got to his feet, and went over to a table by the window where a message basin and a jug of water stood. The lords got up and joined him, Lord Joseph pausing long enough to tell me to stay where I was. Lord Haldor called out the name Stonecat, which seemed a very strange name to me. When several minutes passed without answer, Lord Haldor spoke the name again, with even more urgency than before. Finally, the light grew brighter and a soft voice answered.

"Rangers, we are very busy at the moment, so if you don't mind…" a voice said in a tone that reminded me of an overworked parent who was trying to be patient with a pesky child.

"What's happening?!" Lord Haldor demanded, refusing to be dismissed.

There was a weary sigh from the speaker, and I could hear a lot of noise behind him. "We have quite a raid of orcs to deal with right now. Plus four Kronlords are here. They've already managed to get past our first two rows of traps, but your men are here with us, and we should be able to get rid of the rest of them. We've already killed one Kronlord, and the others are hanging back letting the orcs do the dirty work. But don't worry; this is just a testing party like what happened a few months ago in the western mountains. Kron is still trying to find out how tough we are. So there's only a couple thousand, easy for us to manage unless you keep bothering me! I'll make sure the rangers get in touch with you later."

The light died away, and everyone returned to their seats wordlessly. Everyone's face was grim at the news of this new development. "How is this possible Lord Haldor?" I asked weakly.

All eyes turned to look at me. I wanted to shrink away at the sudden attention, but I didn't. I really wanted to know the answer to my question. I swallowed nervously and continued. "In order for Kron to attack from the south he would have had to first conquer Suvia wouldn't he? But if Suvia was under attack, wouldn't we have heard of it before now? After all, we supply a large chunk of their army. Wouldn't they have tried to call on us for help? Carl told me that all the surrounding kingdoms protected Suvia since they don't have their own army because of their religious beliefs. So if there was trouble there, wouldn't they have told us?" I could feel myself blushing as everyone continued to stare at me. Apparently I must have said something foolish to have everyone stare at me like this.

Finally everyone turned to look at Lord Haldor instead, waiting for him to answer my question.

"How indeed?" Lord Haldor murmured thoughtfully. He was frowning fiercely at me, deep in thought.

"I…I'm sorry." I stammered into the silence.

"For what Peter?" Joseph asked me softly.

I opened my mouth to answer, but could think of nothing to say. Why did he ask that? Joseph knew that I had asked a foolish question, so why was he asking what I was sorry for right afterwards?

But as I looked at the ranger lords I realized that no one found my question foolish or obvious. Everyone was thinking over my point, wondering the same thing I was.

"That will be something we will have to ask the king in the morning, right?" Lord Yves asked Lord Haldor.

Lord Haldor shook his head and got to his feet. "The king will want to know about this right away. If Suvia is indeed taken, then the king needs to know."

"But that's my point sir, it hasn't been taken." I said quietly.

All eyes were on me again. I blushed, but continued on determinedly. "I saw Suvian traders in the markets when we passed by in the carriage earlier. They certainly didn't act like anything was wrong. I realize it would have taken the traders a couple weeks or so to get to the capital, but Suvia is huge, and Kron would have had to conquer the whole country before he moved on to us. He couldn't have managed that in the short time since the traders left, could he?"

Lord Haldor considered the fact thoughtfully. "Lord Joseph, go see if you can find some of the traders Peter talked about, and meet us with them at the castle." He decided.

I was trembling with fear as Lord Haldor took me with him and the ranger lords to the castle. I had never thought that my questions would lead to me talking to the king himself! If I had known that Lord Haldor would bring me to see the king because of my questions, I would never have had the courage to ask them. Lord Haldor had me wash up and change into fresh clothes before we left. He also had me brush my hair, since it was disrespectful to have your head covered in the king's court, so I would have my hood down. As I walked into the castle behind the ranger lords, I suddenly wished my father was there. He would never think twice about having an audience with the king, he was brave and bold. All I felt was small, and very much out of place.

The grand hall where the king held audiences was breathtaking to me. The walls, floors, columns and ceiling were made of a smooth shiny white stone with some strange grey lines in it that I learned later was called marble. There were banners hanging down from the ceiling which was far above my head. Along the walkway were statues of the former kings, and people approached the throne by walking between them as they stood like sentries with their swords in parade rest, their eyes seeming to follow us as we walked. The throne sat upon a stage, and there were three steps leading up to it. On the first step, there was a smaller throne to either side, where the prince and the queen would sit. The two smaller thrones were made of silver, with black velvet cushions. The king's throne was made of a weaving of both silver and gold, and had blood red velvet cushions on it. On each side of the stage was a statue of a Lammasu, and they sat with the same kind of posture that Abiyram had sat at the healing house, with their wings folded against their back, their human-like faces calm and wise.

The ranger lords dropped to one knee before the king, and I did the same, staring at the floor hoping that I could stay unnoticed. The king invited us to rise, and ordered his servants to bring seats for us. I sat down at the end of the bench that was brought, and tried to make myself unnoticeable. For a while I succeeded as Lord Haldor told the king what had happened at the meeting. But eventually he got around to me telling about the traders I had seen in the market.

"Are you sure they were Suvian son?" The king asked gravely.

"Look up at the king when he addresses you." Lord Locke whispered to me.

I looked up nervously. The king had black hair, a thick beard, and piercing grey eyes that were staring hard at me. "Yes sir, I recognized one of them from the harvest fair a few years ago. He came to my father's stall to look at horse shoes, his pony had lost one." I said quietly.

"What did the boy say? Speak up lad, I can't hear you." The king said.

I swallowed hard and repeated what I said louder. I clutched the bench on either side of me, willing myself to stop trembling.

The king sat back thoughtfully, frowning slightly. "This just doesn't add up at all." He murmured to himself.

"What do you make of this Lord Haldor?" The king asked.

Lord Haldor was already frowning. "I have nothing to base speculations off of at present your majesty. I have sent my second in command to find the traders, so perhaps we will get some answers when he brings them here.

The king nodded. "Very well, we will wait." He agreed.

It was almost half an hour before Joseph came. During that time the king had his servants bring us refreshments. I was too nervous to eat the cheese and fruit given to me, but made myself do so anyways, knowing that it would have been rude to refuse the king's hospitality. When Joseph finally arrived he was leading the two traders in, surrounded by a group of soldiers, the Suvians hands bound with chains. The king got to his feet in surprise. "What is the meaning of this Joseph?! Why do you have them escorted as if to trial?" He demanded.

Joseph was calm as he answered. "Your majesty, my apologies for displeasing you. The two men tried to attack me when I told them that their presence was requested here. Under the circumstances I felt it best to ensure they could not try to put another knife in my back."

The king sat down slowly and regarded the two traders. The men looked at the king fearfully, their eyes filled with despair. "Why did you attack one of my rangers Suvians?" The king asked calmly.

One of the Suvians took a step forward, bowing so low that his head was level with his waste. He didn't straighten up to speak, so his voice was a bit muffled. "Your pardons, oh gracious and powerful king. Our actions were done in the panic of the moment. We would NEVER try to betray his majesty's treaty with our country under normal circumstances, never. It is a bad habit of our people, oh wise and noble king; to act first and think later when we are panicked. A most regrettable action on our part, valiant sir, most regrettable. I would never think to harm such a handsome and brave ranger as was sent, but as I said oh courageous king, it was the heat of the moment, an action done out of panic."

"Why would you have reason to panic? What were you afraid I planned to do with you?" The king pressed on, frowning deeply.

"Oh glorious and kind and…"

"Enough of that just answer the question!" The king said, tired of the flattery the man was using.

"If you please, your lordship… we feared that you wished to punish us for the devil Kron's plans." The man stammered.

The king sat pondering those words. "Why would I punish YOU? You're not working for him, are you?" he asked, looking hard at the traders.

"Oh no, most gracious and handsome king, never! We don't work for the devils, I assure you!" The man gasped wide eyed.

"Very well, then why would I punish you?" The king asked.

The Suvian's face paled, and he looked fearful. He shut his mouth tightly, and looked at the king in horror. Behind him, his companion actually gave out a whimper of terror. I felt a deep sympathy for the men. They were obviously terrified, but by what? I sat and wondered about that, what was causing such terror for them?

"Well?" The king prompted. But the Suvian shook his head fearfully, refusing to answer. "I demand you answer me. As it stands you are already in violation of a serious breach of contract between our countries, don't make matters worse for yourself." The king stated firmly.

As I looked at the man whose eyes were showing more despair by the second, an idea occurred to me. I bit my lower lip, unsure how to bring up my suspicions during what had turned essentially into a trial. But Joseph, ever aware of my slightest changed in attitude, spoke up. "The ranger Peter has something he would like to say your majesty." He announced to the king.

The king gestured for me to speak, so I did, choosing my words carefully. "Your majesty, my lords; I don't think they can tell us. I think… that perhaps they are being threatened into silence, perhaps by Kron. I think maybe they were told to pretend that everything was normal. But that is just speculation." I said, adding the last part with emphasis, not wanting to make it sound like I knew anything I didn't know. But my heart went out to the two men. The despair in their eyes and the hopelessness was plain to see, and if my idea was right, it would explain everything.

The king considered my idea, and regarded the traders, who were looking at me horrified, as if wondering how I knew what they had refused to say. "Is this true? You can just nod, that will be sufficient. Is it true that you have been sworn by Kron or one of his followers into secrecy?"

The traders glanced at each other in fear, and then they turned to the king and nodded. They closed their eyes cringing, the looks on their faces suggesting that they were waiting for fire to rain down on them where they stood.

"Very well, you may go." The king said, waving his hand to dismiss the prisoners, knowing that he would get nothing more out of the men.

# CHAPTER 28

The king and the ranger lords talked for several hours, speculating what Kron might be up to. The most likely theory they had come up with was that Kron had decided to build his army in Suvia, where there were no elves or centaurs, and very few humans who could actually put up a resistance. The Suvians were interested only in trading. They lived simple lives, and the country had no standing army. They relied on the countries around them and their rangers for protection. Since the Suvians were expert miners and craftsmen, not to mention peaceful and kind, we and the countries around us were more than happy to protect them in exchange for goods and services. The Suvians loved working in the mines, so we let them do so, it saved other countries from having to bother with the task. But it was the Suvians peacefulness and lack of army that had apparently led them to be ideal for Kron's uses. They had apparently not been able to put up any sort of resistance, and Kron had taken over, forcing the Suvians to continue on as always, with threats hanging over their heads if they dared speak.

It was decided that rangers should be sent to the other countries around, to warn them of the problem. We had expected Kron to wipe out Andor first, since it was our country that had beaten him back last time. But apparently Kron had other plans in mind, and had attacked humans where they were weakest before moving on to take out the elves. When Lord Haldor told about the elf mentioning the battle of

Hulim as having been an attack by Kron, the king nodded. He's had the same speculation the past few weeks, especially after hearing that the Kronlords had managed to sneak into the country.

When the meeting with the king was over, Lord Haldor led us back to the ranger's base. Everyone went inside exhausted both physically and mentally. But something was holding me back, like a nagging doubt in my mind. Joseph turned inside the door and looked at me curiously. "What's on your mind Peter?" He asked softly.

Lord Haldor turned around as well. "My lords, may I take a walk? I want to be alone for a few minutes." I said, unsure why I wanted to be alone, but knowing that the desire was burning urgently in me.

Lord Haldor considered for a moment, and nodded his consent. "Be back in one hour, no later." He agreed, shutting the door behind Joseph and himself.

I wandered around for a bit until I found a spot where no one would see or hear me. I was in a garden on the side of one of the social buildings where casual parties were held. I sat down on the stone bench which was icy cold since it was winter, and wondered why I had wanted to be away from everyone so much. The answer appeared in front of me. Abiyram landed softly, and closed his wings against his back. "Well done little human." He said simply, a satisfied smile on his face.

"For what sir?" I asked; all the questions that had sprung to my mind upon seeing him forgotten as he spoke.

"For your good use of your magic." The Lammasu said, sitting down to face me.

I tilted my head to the side, considering what he had said. "What exactly did I do?" I asked, truly not understanding.

"Your love of all humans led you to finding a crucial answer at a crucial time. Your heart went out to the Suvians, and because of that, the magic gave you the answer you needed."

"Well, wouldn't the magic do that for any ranger? We all love humans, after all, we are human."

Abiyram smiled slightly more. "Not all humans love all humans as much as you do child. Your compassion even for those who almost killed you in Askia is one of the reasons we decided you are worthy of our help. Very few people can forgive even while they are in the process of being beaten to death. But resentment never even reached your battered head. When the magic found out just how good you were, it became willing to help you do what I had hoped you would do, which is stand up for any and all humans when they need an advocate. Do you remember me telling you to take good care of your people, little human?"

"Yes sir, I remember. But I had thought you meant Lance and the other rangers."

"I did. But you took the initiative to extend your love and compassion to all humans, and so I say again to you, well done little human."

I smiled at the praise. Hearing Abiyram say "well done" felt to me to be more thanks and praise than I had ever received for anything in my life. My questions came back to me, and I wondered how to ask them, or even if I had any right to ask.

"Abiyram, I have some questions, but I don't know if I should ask them or not… I don't want to offend or anger you." I said hesitantly.

"Yet sadly, unintentional offences are all too easy to say. Best to say nothing than to offend your friends little human." Abiyram said with a touch of humor in his voice.

I considered what he had said, but my desire for answers was burning in me. "Please, may I ask it with you knowing I'm not trying to offend you?" I asked.

"I doubt very much that you have an offensive thought in your still bruised head, Peter. I have often seen you dismiss such thoughts and scold yourself harshly for thinking them."

I stared in surprise. "Have you been following me, and reading my mind?" I asked.

"That is your possibly offensive question?" Abiyram asked,

grinning so much that his pointed teeth showed.

"No! It was something else." I said hastily.

"Well to answer your questions, yes you may always ask and know that I won't hold your innocently asked questions against you. Yes I have been following you and listening to your thoughts. I've been doing it since the day you were two years old." I opened my mouth in shock, but Abiyram continued speaking. "As for why you were chosen and no one else has been for seven hundred thirty five years, which is the question you fear to ask; I like you. You're smart and loving and have all the qualities that I admire in humans. But unlike most of your kind, you actually have the ability to benefit all of humanity with the help I can offer. Very few humans would have been able to enter my friend's garden you know."

I shook my head in protest. "But I'm no one special, just a blacksmith's son." I said, raising the same objection I had given to Lord Haldor.

"Exactly. Because you are no one special, you know what it is like to not be special. You understand what it is like to go through winters wondering if you and your family would starve to death before spring. You know what it's like to have your feet blistered and bleeding because your father can't afford to buy you proper shoes. You know what it's like to be teased and bullied by other boys. You know what it is like to be the underdog, to be looked at as an ignorant child despite the understanding of situations you know you have. The "special" people have no idea, and so they are no use to me. I needed someone like you, someone who had enough experience to know what people are going through, and enough love to help those who are going through it."

"But sir, I don't know how to end poverty or anything." I protested.

"I never said you had to. I didn't come to you to help you fix the problems of the world, but to guide you in how to help people accept the world, and still be happy." Abiyram stretched his front legs and extended his claws, as if he was tired. "When we had given the humans all the help they needed, we left to do other things. But your people became offended when we stopped coming. Eventually, they forgot that we existed almost entirely. We became a bedtime story for small ears. When we came back, it took us a while to understand what we had done wrong. Then we realized that the humans had grown dependant on us. Well we can't have that happen again, and so we have stayed away."

"But sir, why have you come to me then?" I asked, feeling more and more confused.

"I already told you, I like you. I miss having small humans like you to talk to. We've waited for a very long time for someone like you to come along, someone who would let us help, but not expect us to do everything for them. Humans are far too easily addicted to having others solve all their problems for them. When you came along, we figured the time was ripe for us to try again. We chose you because you have proven yourself to be worthy."

"How? What did I do that made me worthy when no one else had been so for seven hundred years?" I asked, sitting forward, desperate to understand.

"You told the truth, knowing that you would get punished."

I sat back confused. Abiyram saw my confusion and explained further. "When you were two years old, you stole your brother's cream cake. When your father asked if you had taken it, you admitted that you did, and accepted your punishment. Almost all children your age would have lied, they would not have known any better, and would have simply wished to get out of trouble. But the thought of lying never occurred to you. Even when you were too young to remember, you loved your family so much that you were unable to even conceive of lying to them. All your childhood I watched you get into one bout of trouble after another. I saw you develop almost a craving for defying rules, for pushing your boundaries. But never once did you try to lie, or beg your way out of punishment. You have always accepted whatever came your way with courage and honor. That is why I chose you."

"So you chose me because I tell the truth, and accept punishments?" I asked.

"You accept punishments because you know they come to you out of love. You understand that punishments are supposed to correct wrong behavior, not harm you. But far more important than that, you have love even for the humans who tried to kill you. You cast aside your weapons, letting them do what they wished with you. You did try to pull free, and you kicked one of the men, but you accepted what they were doing with nothing but compassion for them. You are no one special in the eyes of some humans Peter; but you are special to me, and that is why I saved you from the death they would have inflicted. You're my friend, and I plan to ensure that you are around for a very long time." Abiyram rose to his feet and spread his wings. "I will see you soon little human. In the meantime, take good care of your people, and don't forget to love them."

"I will and I won't." I promised as Abiyram took off into the air once more.

# CHAPTER 29

Joseph's promotion to a fully fledged Lord of the kingdom meant a holiday for the ranger's guild. All the apprentices were given a piece of silver, and given permission to roam the city, doing as they wished. Lord Haldor had told us that we had worked hard, and deserved the money, and the break from studying. At first I had been reluctant to go. The rangers in Maltron had yet to get back to the lords, and I wanted to stay around and see what had happened. But Lord Haldor told me quite firmly that there was a time for me to work, and a time to play. Today was a time to play, since there was nothing I'd be able to do about the situation anyways, and so not taking time for recreation would be pointless for me. When he saw that I was trying to think up another protest, Lord Haldor decided to make sure I got the picture. "Peter, you are ordered to go and enjoy yourself. You will report back here at one hour past noon for your rest period, and then you will go back out and enjoy yourself again."

I swallowed hard, knowing that I couldn't argue a direct order from Lord Haldor. "Yes my lord." I said softly, bowing in acceptance.

I wandered around the city for a while, wondering what to do with myself. I wasn't familiar with the capital, and so was unsure where to go or what to do. As I was passing a bakery; Robin, Gene, and Sara came outside. They all had pastries with them, and were munching on their treats happily. Gene smiled when he saw me. "I thought you said you were going to stay with Lord Haldor." He stated; his mouth full of maple sugar.

I smiled thinly. "I wanted to, but he wouldn't let me."

Gene swallowed and gave me a slight smirk. "That's a bummer, mate. But really, I can't understand why you'd want to spend your free time with the grownups anyways. We've been given the WHOLE DAY to do whatever we want! No exercises, no lectures, total freedom! How can you not be enjoying yourself?"

"I didn't say I wasn't enjoying myself." I pointed out.

"Hey I have an idea, why don't you let Robin show you around? Then you two can get to know each other." Sara suggested.

Robin narrowed her eyes at her friend. "Yes, and while I am showing Peter around, you and Gene will have lots of time together without having to worry about me. This is your way of politely telling me to bugger off isn't it?" The girl demanded, her hands on her hips.

"No, I just thought maybe you and Peter could…"

"Not everyone is as interested in having a boyfriend as you are Sara!"

"Um, yeah, I'll… see you guys around." I said hastily, starting to back away.

I started to walk rapidly, but stopped within five paces as dizziness hit me. I closed my eyes, and waited for the dizziness to pass. I felt a hand on my arm, and looked over. Robin was looking at me in concern. "Are you alright?" She asked.

"I just need to sit down." I told Robin, lowering myself to the ground against the bakery.

Robin sat down next to me. "Sorry about her. Ever since we got to the capital all she ever talks about is Gene, Gene, and Gene. Brave Gene, wise Gene, Strong Gene. She's completely lost in what my grandmother calls puppy love. I get so tired of it."

I attempted to smile, but I felt rather uncomfortable with the conversation. I had no idea how to react to Gene and Sara; and Robin fighting with them certainly wasn't helping me figure out what to say.

When the dizziness was gone for long enough, I got carefully to my feet. Robin and I walked slowly down the street, not having any particular destination in mind. I cast my mind for some sort of conversation. "So… you're a gypsy huh? What's that like?"

Robin shrugged. "We go from place to place, and perform. When we're around, people take a break from work and watch us. Then we get paid and move on."

"Is it true that gypsies use magic?" I asked.

"NO."

That was the end of that conversation. After a few minutes, Robin attempted to start up the talking. "So what was it like to travel with Joseph? When we were with him, he was quizzing Thelmer like crazy, because Thelmer's tests were coming. I think he was almost showing Thelmer off to us, showing us all the skills we would learn."

I smiled a bit. "That sounds like Joseph. He seems to like to show people my skills too. When we were in Woodward he was almost laughing at how amazed the rangers there were at how easily I played the game. He really has a bond with apprentices; that's why Lord Haldor often sent him to the fair."

Robin nodded thoughtfully. "I bet things are going to change after he's sworn in as a Lord. He'll have to be more serious now, won't he?"

"Yes, I suppose so." I said sadly. That thought hadn't occurred to me. All the ranger lords were so grim, so proper. It was hard to imagine Joseph like that, constantly serious, rarely smiling, always judging instead of praising.

Robin seemed to sense my feelings, and switched the topic to family. We chatted about our siblings, comparing stories about Robin's older sister vs. Kevin; laughing at how similar they were, even though they were five years apart in age. We stopped at a tavern and had lunch, still talking away. I was amazed how easy it was to talk to Robin. I had so little experience with girls, but Robin was just as easy to talk to as any of the boys I use to play with in my father's town. When I mentioned this fact, Robin laughed so hard she sprayed me with the milk she had been in the process of drinking.

"I was just thinking the same thing about you!" She managed to tell me through her coughing fit.

"What, that I'm as easy to talk to as a girl?" I asked, dabbing my cloak dry with my handkerchief.

"Yes!" Robin exclaimed, and then she doubled over in laughter.

I looked at her, trying hard not to laugh, trying to pretend to be offended at the suggestion. But I couldn't help it, her laughter was contagious.

When we had finished laughing, my head was swimming slightly. So we paid the bill, and headed back to the ranger headquarters. Robin offered to stay with me while I rested, but I reluctantly turner her down, admitting that I needed to sleep for a bit. I went into the large room that was full of several rows of bunk beds. I found mine, and fell asleep almost instantly.

I woke up to the touch of a hand on my back. A ranger I didn't know was there, and he smiled as I woke up. "We figured that you might want to get up soon. Lord Joseph insisted we let you sleep, but Lord Haldor seemed to think it should be up to you. Lord Joseph is going to be sworn in soon, we thought you might want to be there."

I nodded and sat up, trying to rub the sleepy blurriness from my eyes. "How long have I been asleep sir?" I asked as I made my bed.

"My name's Tim. I have no idea how long you've been asleep, I just arrived an hour or so ago. It's the eighteenth hour of the day, if that gives you any information."

I looked up in surprise. "I've been asleep five hours?!"

Tim shrugged casually. "If you say so, you're a first year aren't you?"

"Well, yeah I am." I said.

"So that explains it then. You must have not gotten the hang of pacing yourself right, yet." Tim said simply.

I shrugged in reply, deciding not to mention that I hadn't been doing anything that put a strain on me. Tim seemed satisfied with his answer, and I saw no reason to even try to argue the point. I'd talk to Lord Haldor about it later.

Joseph was sworn in to Lordship in the King's conference hall where I had been taken last night. I was relieved when I was told to stay with the apprentices and squires, just one young person among several, inconspicuous in my cloak. The apprentices were sitting in the last row of the people assembled to watch Joseph take the vows of Lordship. Besides rangers, there were quite a few of the knights who were stationed close by, as well as many of the soldiers of the capital. Sir Lucas and Lady Rose were both there, sitting in the front row where the ranger lords, sir knights, and Barrons sat. All the knights had brought their squires, except for Sir Lucas, which I was very relieved to see. The last people I'd want to see today were those four, and so it was an immense relief to discover that Sir Lucas refused them the privilege of coming to this ceremony. I knew from Joseph's lessons that squires went to these sorts of functions as part of their training. It was important for those who wished to be knights to know how to act at official army ceremonies.

Everyone rose from their seats and got down on one knee as the king and his two oldest sons entered the room. We all stayed in that position until the king had sat down on his throne again. The king made a signal, and the doors to the hall opened. Lord Haldor led Joseph to the king, and Haldor made a sharp right turn at the throne, walking to his set at the center of the ranger lords. Joseph got down on one knee and bowed his head so he was staring at the floor. His freshly washed and brushed hair fell around him, so his face was hidden from sight.

"I hereby swear undying loyalty to the king of Andor and to all his descendants. I accept the title and duties of Lordship with a thankful and humble heart. From this day fourth, all my actions, all my deeds shall reflect the wishes of my king, to whom I vow to look upon as my one true leader. I solemnly swear before witnesses to spend the rest of my days as a true representative of the king. I acknowledge that any actions on my part that are in contrast to the laws, wishes and ideals of Andor will result in immediate forfeit of my life. From this day fourth until death takes me; I swear to act as an extension of the king, bringing his word to the people." Joseph recited in a clear and calm voice.

The king rose to his feet and walked down to the first step, rising his hand to hover above Joseph's head. "I hereby declare Joseph, son of the guild of rangers; to become Lord Joseph. From this day forth, his word is my word. His actions shall reflect my wishes. He is hereby given permission to go wherever he choses, and speak to anyone he wishes at any time he deems necessary. No longer is he a ranger, from now on he is a ranger lord, and all the army is at his command unless his superiors override his orders."

The king lowered his hand onto Joseph's head and murmured something to him. Joseph answered back softly, and the king made a signal to his younger son, who rose to his feet and stepped forward, handing something he had been holding on a cushion to the king. The king held it up, and I could see that it was a medallion set on a silver chain. The king put the chain around Joseph's neck, and stepped back up to his throne, taking his seat once more. Joseph stood up and turned to face us. Everyone got to their feet and applauded. Joseph was hidden from view behind the many adults present, but I had a feeling that he was happy, even if he wasn't showing it. As I applauded, I couldn't think of anyone more worthy of the title of ranger lord than Joseph.

# CHAPTER 30

There was a reception and a banquet for Lord Joseph after he took his vows. Everyone who had been there as witnesses attended, including us children. I could see Sara and Robin felt distinctly out of place, so Gene and I did our best to help the girls feel more comfortable in the foreign situation. Gene kept us amused with his stories about parties he had attended back when he was living with his father. He talked mostly about how he had been bored out of his mind since there was no one interesting to talk to except his brothers and sister. By the time the banquet was over, Gene had convinced Sara that those parties were the most boring things in existence. He even made the food sound dull, talking about how it was tiresome to have to eat fruit between each dish, and how he was relieved to finally have people worth talking to, to pass the time along. I kept my head down to hide my smile. I knew from experience that those parties weren't half as bad as Gene made them sound, and I knew that he was trying to show off for Sara. Robin caught my eye, and we grinned at each other, both amused by the way Sara was hanging on Gene's every word.

There was no dancing, since the only girls in attendance were the ranger apprentices and Lady Rose. Instead, people just stood around and talked, relieved at the break from the seriousness of war. Everyone went to talk to Lord Joseph at some point in the night, to congratulate him and show their respects. I waited until the crowds around him had died down, and then I approached. Joseph turned and smiled at me, when suddenly I noticed Sir Lucas approaching Joseph from the side. Joseph shot me a curious look as he saw me back away. I tilted my head slightly in the direction Sir Lucas was coming from, and went back to Robin when Joseph turned to talk to the knight.

"Why didn't you talk to him?" Robin asked me curiously.

I gestured to where Joseph was talking to the knight, his face carefully void of emotion. "I think Sir Lucas wants to talk to him alone." I explained.

Robin frowned slightly, a look of worry on her face. "Are you sure it's a good idea to let them be so close? Last time Sir Lucas wanted to talk to him; he broke three of Joseph's ribs, didn't he?"

"Actually, he just cracked them, it wasn't a full break. Besides, I think they made up since then. Joseph and I stopped in Askia for a while."

"Yes, and then Sir Lucas tried to kill you as well." Robin said darkly.

"No Robin, it was Sir Lucas' squires who did that. Sir Lucas stopped them form beating me. He'd never try to kill a ranger." I said firmly, determined to make my friend understand the facts instead of the rumors she had obviously been exposed to.

Robin turned away from Joseph to look at me, noticing the seriousness of my tone. She regarded me in silence for a while, and nodded her understanding and acceptance of my correction.

"So what really happened then?" She asked.

Briefly I filled Robin in on what had happened between me and the squires. I left out the parts about the conversation Joseph and Sir Lucas had, and what Joseph had told me about his past. As far as I was concerned, Joseph had told me about his family in a moment of weakness, unable to shield his thoughts from me. If Joseph had wanted the others to know that he and Sir Lucas were brothers, he would have told them on the way to Stoneriver. Robin didn't press me for details about Joseph's interactions with Sir Lucas. She just listened silently, taking in the facts that I gave her about it having been the squires who had attacked, and what Joseph and Sir Lucas had decided to require of them as recompense.

We looked back at Joseph and Sir Lucas. The knight's face was firm, and he was obviously adamant about what he was saying. I had a feeling I knew what he was telling his brother. As I had suspected might happen, Sir Lucas and Joseph put a hand on each other's shoulders briefly. Then Sir Lucas dropped the gesture of friendship, and walked back to Lady Rose, who was watching with one hand over her mouth, trying not to break down in public. I watched the two leave, and then turned to look at Joseph. His face was still carefully not showing emotions as he watched his brother and mother walk out.

When they were gone, Joseph looked around, and headed over to where I was standing. "Thank you for being patient Peter. Sir Lucas couldn't stay long, and he wanted to talk to me before he had to attend to other business.

"What did he want?" Robin asked, still suspicious of bad intentions on Sir Lucas' part.

Joseph smiled slightly and put a hand on Robin's shoulder. "Nothing bad, I assure you. The confrontation we had in September is in the past, and definitely will never be repeated, ok?"

Robin nodded, satisfied with that answer.

The next morning as I was doing the light exercise program Lord Haldor had designed for me, my thoughts returned to Joseph and his blood family. Last night, the king had called Joseph "son of the guild of rangers". Why had he done that? Joseph had told me that his father refused to look at Joseph as his son, but that didn't change the fact that Joseph's father was still his father… did it? To be banished from one's blood family was extremely rare, almost unheard of in my experience.

All my life I had lived with the knowledge that your family was your family, whether you got along or not. I'd never heard of anyone actually being disowned to the point of no longer having their father's name be part of their identity. I had heard once of a baby who was born in our town to the girl who worked at the inn washing tables.

For reasons that I had been too young to understand at the time, she had no way of knowing exactly who the father was. Kevin had told John that she named twenty different men it could have been around the time the baby was conceived, but my father had told Kevin to shut up, pointing out that there were little ears present, meaning me and Andrew. Even so, the baby was still given a father who's name to take. He had ended up being named as his Grandfather's (his mother's father) descendant. That man had disowned his daughter many years ago, but she still had his name, and so did her son. So how did Joseph wind up with no real family name?

I was so wrapped up in my thoughts that I fell over from my balancing on one foot as Lord Haldor barked an order right next to my ear. "Lesson one, two dozen times, recite!" He ordered sharply.

I picked myself up off the ground and stood at attention, reciting dutifully. My face was red with embarrassment the whole time, realizing that I had been caught not paying attention. Apparently Lord Haldor hadn't approached silently, and so I should have been aware of his advance. When I finished reciting, Lord Haldor restated what he had been telling me as he came up to me a few minutes ago. "I figured you would be interested to know, the elves beat the orcs back into Suvia. Two rangers died in the battle, as well as twenty elves."

I nodded sadly. These were the first official casualties of the war, and twenty two people dead sounded like a lot to me.

Lord Haldor frowned slightly, not understanding my sadness. "The orcs were *beaten*. The elves also managed to kill two Kronlords, leaving ten left to deal with. Kron gambled, and he lost. He didn't send nearly enough orcs to deal with the wood elves, which are well use to dealing with far darker creatures than orcs. It is a victory Peter, not a defeat."

"Yes my lord, I know." I said simply.

"Then why are you sad?" Lord Haldor asked softly, his frown deepening as he tried to understand my thoughts.

"Two rangers are dead my lord, as well as TWENTY elves! That is a lot of people." I explained, unsure why he was so confused.

Lord Haldor's eyes softened considerably, and he put his hands on my shoulders. "Peter, twenty two deaths is nothing compared to the casualties we faced last time. During the last war, whole battalions were being wiped out, from all the human countries around, and those who did survive were dragged off to feed the kronlords."

"How did we win then? If he was wiping out our whole army, how did we survive?" I asked weakly, unable to even imagine so many people dead.

"Unity." Lord Haldor explained.

"Sir?" I asked, not understanding.

"The human countries had been fighting with each other for hundreds of years. Kron was using this to his advantage, and was wiping the army's out, knowing that his army could easily stand against any one country. That was when King Stephen the first realized that unless all the humans stood united, we would all fall. He got together with the other kings, and together they agreed to put aside differences and stand united as a single army. This increased our army by four hundred percent, and we were successfully able to defeat Kron, forcing him to retreat back into the underearth with what was left of his twenty Kronlords."

I nodded, understanding the wisdom that had guided King Stephen to that decision. "But why the elves?" I wondered, asking the question that had been bothering everyone for a while now.

Lord Haldor shook his head; he had no answer to that. "I don't know what the centaur meant. Like you, the magic responds to me, and to everyone else who has such a bond, as emotions, not words."

# CHAPTER 31

That night, I lay on my bed pondering. The centaur had told Joseph to ask the magic as if it was a simple and obvious thing to do. But it wasn't obvious to anyone, especially to me. How could a person ask emotions for actual worded information? For the briefest second, I wondered if I should try to make contact with Abiyram, but cast the idea aside at once. Abiyram had said point blank that his people didn't like humans to rely on them. He had also said that I had the ability to figure out the answers I would need with the qualities I had. I thought back to what abilities the magic gave me. There were the physical features, the heightened skills, and the dreams. Then there was what had happened with the Suvian traders, where I had realized what the problem was. Why they were so terrified of being questioned about Kron that the most peaceful men had tried to kill Joseph rather than be taken in for questioning. But how had that worked? I hadn't consciously asked the magic anything, I was too busy feeling sympathy for their fear. So why had the answer come to me?

I thought over the conversation I'd had with Abiyram. Hadn't he said the magic had helped me because it felt my love for the Suvians? I closed my eyes and thought over the twenty elves that had lost their lives. I let my sadness come out of where I carefully guarded it, and let my tears fall. I had never met an elf, but all the stories about them agreed that they were wise and kind. I ran through my head everything I had learned about elves. They were always willing to help the rangers, often comparing notes when tracking dark creatures through the forest. They had given rangers magic as a peace offering to the humans. The elves and Lammasu had taught the humans how to use the magic. The magic made humans more like elves, making it so we'd never get facial hair, and had superior eyes and ears. The elves gave humans the magic, and only the elves could control our magic against our will.

I sat up fast, my heart pounding as I finally understood. Kron wanted to get rid of the elves so he could get rid of the magic! After all, it had been the attack on the ranger's fortress where he had finally been defeated twenty three years ago. Lord Haldor had talked to Gene and me about the battle, and how the rangers had managed to hold him off for over twenty four hours until the main army made up of all the united countries forces arrived and wiped his army out. Lord Haldor had talked about how some of the kronlords had managed to sneak in, and had found where the apprentices were hiding. He told us that the apprentices had managed to use their combined powers to bring the two kronlords down, even after several of the apprentices had been killed as a threat and warning to the rest. Kron was not going to forget that kind of power, and so he wanted to get rid of it before he took another crack at the whole human race again.

I quickly got out of bed and rushed down the hall, towards the room where the ranger lords slept. They had to hear about this at once! I stopped and closed my eyes, waiting for the dizziness to pass. Then I looked over with a frown. The door was open, which struck me as odd. When I had gone to bed, the door had been shut, and all the lords were inside. I approached at a silent and slow walk, feeling that something very serious was going on. When I peeked into the room, my heart seemed to turn to ice in my chest.

The four younger ranger lords were all down on one knee in front of Lord Haldor's bed. Lord Haldor lay there, talking to them softly. He looked so weak, so frail. I can't say how I knew it, but I knew he was dying. I started to back away horrified, but someone came up behind me, and put a hand on my shoulder.

"Go to him son, he loves you. You're his gem, he's told me about you." I looked up to see the king had arrived to pay respects to his uncle. There was a resigned look in his eyes, and an acceptance of what was happening.

But how could he accept it? How could he or anyone be so calm? Lord Haldor was dying!

The king increased his pressure on my shoulder when he realized that I was unable to move, and he led me into the room. The ranger lords all backed away to give the king access, coming over to stand with me. Joseph put a hand on my shoulder, and we watched the king say goodbye to Lord Haldor. My throat felt like it was on fire. Why was everyone so calm, talking softly as if it was no big deal? How could anyone possibly be ok with this?! The king bent over and kissed Lord Haldor's forehead. Then he turned and left the room, pausing in the doorway long enough to tell Joseph to report to him immediately after the funeral.

At the word funeral, I felt like I had been splashed with a bucket of cold water. I wanted to run, get away from this place, and never come back. But Lord Haldor was calling me over to him, his voice weak. I stepped forward, trembling, going down on my knees when I reached Lord Haldor's bed. Lord Haldor touched my cheek with the back of his hand, brushing my tears away. "I thought I told you not to cry until I was actually dead." He scolded softly.

I let out a short breath, and rubbed the fresh tears away. "I'm sorry my lord." I managed to choke out.

"Peter, you need to stop doing that!" Lord Haldor said, his gaze becoming a little more focused on me.

"What, crying? I'm trying sir, honest." I said, trying yet again to stop my tears.

"No, not crying. You need to stop fearing judgment. You need to stop worrying about your actions being a letdown to those over you. If you never made a mistake, you wouldn't be human. So stop worrying so much that you are going to disappoint people. If people don't accept you for who you are, flaws and all, they aren't worthy of knowing you. You hear me?"

I nodded, not able to find the ability to talk. Lord Haldor took my hand into his, and whispered to me. "Peter, everyone dies in the end. But meeting you has made me complete. You are the most amazing person I have ever had the privilege of meeting. I can rest easy knowing that you will grow up to be an honorable man, one who everyone will be proud to say they know. Having you being here for the rangers makes me able to rest now, because I know you will be here. Take care of yourself, and do what Joseph and Abiyram tell you to. Always remember, you are my gem, and my love is with you, even in death." Lord Haldor lay back and closed his eyes with a relieved sigh.

# CHAPTER 32

Lord Haldor let out a soft breath, and became still. Joseph took Lord Haldor's hands, and rested them on the old chest, crossed peacefully. "Goodbye my father." He whispered softly, kissing Lord Haldor's brow. I backed away, recognizing the position as the same one they had put Lance in at the healing house. That could only mean…

I broke into a run and fled the building, blindly banging into walls as I ran. I was aware of someone chasing me, and I immediately slipped into the dark shadows of night, running silently and swiftly through the heavily falling snow. I didn't want anyone to follow me, not where I was going. After a few minutes I managed to shake off the pursuing rangers, and headed immediately for the garden where I had met with Abiyram. I burst into fresh tears when I saw him already there, waiting for me. He seemed to be letting off a golden light, illuminating the area around him. I rushed to him, and threw my arms as far around his neck as I could reach, sobbing uncontrollably.

Abiyram wrapped his right front paw and his right wing around me, and let me cry. The snow had stopped, and the sun was rising when I was finally able to control my emotions again.

"If I was not here, you would have killed yourself by now." Abiyram informed me softly.

I pulled away, looking at him in horrified confusion. "You would have ruined your feet, standing in the snow barefoot. You would also have frozen to death, dressed in just your pants and undershirt, with no warm clothes. But most seriously, you ran for a good half an hour with a half healed life threatening head injury."

I looked down at myself wordlessly. I had gotten out of bed to talk to Lord Haldor, I hadn't thought to get dressed or put on my boots, having had no idea I'd end up outside in the snow. I had run without any thought to my injured head, just wanting to get away as fast as possible. But I felt fine. My head didn't hurt at all, and I felt as warm as summer, including my feet, which were half buried in the snow, but looked perfectly fine.

"I'm sorry sir, I wasn't thinking." I admitted, ashamed at my obvious lack of common sense.

Abiyram nodded an acceptance of my apology. "You had never seen death before child. Under the circumstances, your lack of ability to think is forgivable. That is why I protected you instead of let you suffer the consequences that I would have otherwise. You needed me, and knew that I will not show myself in front of others. In your condition, there was no other way for you to get to me in time."

"In time for what sir?" I asked, fresh tears falling down my cheeks.

Abiyram leaned forward and touched his forehead to mine. "In time for you to not break down in front of witnesses. You needed someone to cry to, but couldn't bear to face your own kind, fearing that they would judge you, despite what young Lord Haldor had said to you in parting." Abiyram said softly.

I managed to laugh through my tears. "He's hardly young. He just died of old age!"

Abiyram smiled gently. "Yes, and yet he was young compared to me. That gives you an idea of how young I am not, doesn't it Peter?"

I laughed again, and brushed my tears away. The sun was fully visible now, and the clouds were thinning out, promising a clear afternoon. I looked up at my friend, feeling better now that I had cried enough. He was smiling down at me, his eyes full of love and understanding.

"I shall bring you back to your people, Joseph needs you near him. He has lost his father, and so will want his dearest of available friends at his side. You must remember to tell him what the magic helped you learn last night, do not forget it." Abiyram said, walking with me back to the ranger's headquarters.

"I won't forget sir, but why are you saying it like that? Lord Haldor isn't Joseph's father; Joseph is Sir Lucas' brother." I said as we walked.

Abiyram looked sideways at me. "I am going to bring you to a memory of mine that happened many years ago. I believe that it will help you understand Joseph, and Lord Haldor as well."

Before I could answer, I heard the sound of horses and laughter behind me. I turned around to find myself at what was unmistakably the harvest fair. It was getting dark, and there were lit holiday lanterns hanging from the stalls and trees. People were going in all directions, enjoying the festivities. I looked back at Abiyram in amazement and confusion. How had he done that? Abiyram pointed with his paw, and I looked where he was pointing. Unlike the many laughing people, there was a small group standing near the knights' camp area, deep in a heated argument.

One side of the group were three rangers, and a small boy, heavily bruised and deathly thin, who was cowering behind one of the rangers, clinging to his cloak. The boy had a sickly look to him, as if he was often ill. On the other side of the group was what I thought was Sir Lucas. But then I saw where Lucas was, standing soaking wet off to the side, a muscular boy of twelve years or so. As I looked closer, I could see that the man wasn't quite as tall, or as muscular as the Sir Lucas I knew. But he had a look of fury and even hatred in his eyes as he faced off against the rangers. Beside him was his brother, who was also a knight. I heard a suppressed sob off to one side, and looked to see a young Lady Rose, sitting on a barrel and watching. She looked in bad shape, as if she had been recently beaten by her husband.

I felt a burning anger in my heart. How could a man do that to his wife? I heard Lord Haldor's voice rise up over the two knights, distracting me from Lady Rose. "If he wants to be a ranger, the likes of you will not stop him! Every man has the right to choose his own future. You have terrorized this child long enough!"

"He is MY son and will do what I tell him to do! All the men of my family have been knights since before you rangers even existed. I will not have you elf loving fools break the strong traditions of my family tree. I'll kill the boy before I let the likes of you have him!"

The knight reached for his sword, but the three rangers were faster, and they had bows and arrows' pointing at the two knights before the sword was half way out of its sheath. "Put that away Sir Luke. I will not let you bring further harm on this child. You have done nothing but abuse him since the day he was born. He told me everything; how you make him sleep in your dungeon, how you often force him to go for days without food, how you constantly come up with excuses to punish him. The abuse of this boy stops now. I don't give a swamp troll if he *was* a mistake on your part; he is still a person who deserves far more love than you have ever given the boy and his mother, or your other son for that matter." Lord Haldor said in a soft voice that was full of fury.

Sir Luke's eyes flashed in anger. "You leave Lucas out of this; he's a good boy who does as his father tells him to." He growled.

"Yes I know he does. I've heard from three eye witnesses how well he looks after his brother for you when you're not there to terrorize the boy in person. I will say it again, the abuse stops here. Joseph has agreed to be a ranger, and that is exactly what I will make sure he becomes." Lord Haldor said in disgust.

"You won't! I will not have my family tree broken because of you!" Sir Luke shouted.

"It's too late. He has already been claimed. He's no longer forced to be at your mercy Luke; I have already signed him up with the king." One of the other rangers said.

"NO! I won't permit it, I won't! Joseph come here, *right now*." Sir Luke demanded, gesturing to the boy like one would do to summon a dog.

Joseph clutched Haldor's cloak tighter, and shook his head, looking at his father fearfully.

"I said come here! Get your filthy head over here before I lose my temper! COME HERE!" Sir Luke shouted.

Joseph shut his eyes tightly and shook his head again. His hands were trembling now, but he seemed determined to try to be brave against the terror his father was so obviously use to inflicting with his orders.

"You see Luke; already your hold on the boy is broken. He has no reason to obey you out of fear any more, and never once have you given him a reason to obey out of love or respect. Your son has chosen to be free of you." The ranger next to Lord Haldor said softly.

Sir Luke made a noise like an angry cat. "Joseph, if you do this to me, I swear that I will never again let you call yourself my son. You will be cast out as a no name, and no one will ever respect you again." He warned Joseph in a low and furious voice.

"That will never happen Joseph; your father is lying out of desperation." Haldor insisted, his grey eyes full of fury and loathing.

"You think so ranger? Who do you think is in charge of the book of names? I can easily write him off as a no-name, and no one will question my judgment." Sir Luke said, his voice triumphant, sure that he had gotten a win over the rangers.

"Well when you are pouring over your precious book of names, erasing your son from your family tree, I recommend you look up the royal family's tree. You might be interested in what name you will find there, under the late King Jacob III."

Sir Luke frowned, doing some quick mental searches of the archives. His eyes widened in shock as he found out who he was talking to. "Prince Haldor!" He gasped.

"Got to it at last have you?" Haldor sneered. "Joseph, I will personally ensure that you are given the name of all rangers. That way, your father will not have any right to write you out of the archives of the country, and you will have a new family." Lord Haldor looked at

Sir Luke coldly as he said the next part. "One who will love you, and not cause you harm. From now on, consider yourself *my* son. I will give you all the love you should have received."

# CHAPTER 33

I found myself alone standing outside the door to the ranger headquarters. I shivered in the sudden cold, and entered quickly, shutting the cold out behind me. "Thank you Abiyram." I whispered, thinking of the memory I had witnessed as well as my friend's loving understanding and protection in my time of need. I walked down the hall refusing to speak to any of the people who shot questions at me. I went to my bed and got dressed, and then went to find Joseph. He didn't seem to be anywhere to be found in the building. I walked around over and over looking for him, trying everywhere I could think of. Finally, I found him in the storage room. He was sitting between two large barrels, hidden from view. I wouldn't have found him if I hadn't heard him sneeze. I went to investigate, and saw him sitting there, staring dejectedly at the floor.

He looked up at me as I sat down across from him. "Peter, where have you been?! When you ran out into the snow with no cloak we tried to stop you, but you eluded us. Then we found out you had no boots or weapons either, and we feared the worst when you didn't come back for so long!"

"I'm ok, I promise. Abiyram protected me; he knew that I needed him, so he kept me from killing myself in my blindness." I assured my friend.

Joseph sat back in relief, and smiled slightly. "Thank goodness for that!"

"I'm sorry. I just… don't know what came over me. I guess I panicked." I said quietly.

Joseph waved my apology aside. "The important thing is that you're safe. If anything had happened to you…" Joseph trailed off, sadness coming to his eyes.

"I know why you called Lord Haldor father last night." I said quietly.

Joseph looked at me, a whole mix of emotions in his eyes, fighting for control. "Haldor told you?" Joseph asked, his voice strained.

"Abiyram showed me. He brought me to his memory or something, I'm not really sure. But I saw the fight your dad had with Lord Haldor. He really stood up for you against your father, didn't he? No wonder you were having trouble in Askia. You'd be insane not to have trouble being back there, even with your father dead for the past fifteen years!"

Joseph nodded. "That was more or less what Lord Haldor told me when he arrived to get you." He paused and considered. "How much did you see?"

"I saw the rangers and you faced off against your family. Your dad was shouting how he would never let you break his family's tradition and not be a knight." I paused, wondering how to say my thoughts. "Your father really did to you all that Lord Haldor said he did?" I asked quietly.

Joseph nodded, and shifted so he was sitting next to me instead of across from me. He put his arm around my shoulder. "My father hadn't wanted another child, but he still wanted my mother to give him satisfaction. How he thought he could have the latter without the former, I have no idea. When I was born he wanted to have me drowned, especially since I was so undersized and sickly, having been born almost a full month early. But my mother pleaded with him until he relented." A haunted look crossed Joseph's face, but he continued on. "I spent the first few years of my life secretly wondering if it wouldn't have been more merciful for him to have drowned me after all. I lived in terror and misery, spending most of my time trying to hide from my father. But Lucas had taken on the task of finding me wherever I was, and bringing me forward on various bogus charges. I begged him to stop, and he agreed to not turn me in, if I did everything he told me to do. After just two weeks as his slave, I tried to run away from home at every opportunity I got. But wherever I went, the guards always brought me back.

At the time, there were no laws set in place to protect children like me. Lord Haldor changed all of that. For the first time in my life, I knew what it was like to feel safe and happy. I was loved by more than just my mother, who could only see me when my father was at the capital, as per his orders. Once Lord Haldor lifted the terror from my life, I felt what it was like to be free for the first time. The magic helped me get over my condition and build up natural defenses against disease, and in just a few months, I was as healthy as any young boy." Joseph looked at me, his eyes both happy and sad. "Lord Haldor was a much better father than I had ever dreamed it was possible to have. Most people saw him as this overly stern old man, but not me. I know what each of his little frowns meant, and I was the only person who had the ability to make him smile. I'll miss him."

"Me too." I agreed, thinking of all Lord Haldor had done for me, and also for my family.

\*\*\*

I was very confused when the king summoned me to talk to him. It was three days after Lord Haldor's funeral, and I was in the middle of a lesson from Joseph on advanced tactics when the messenger came. Joseph walked me as far as the drawbridge of the castle, and then he told me to go on alone. I gave him a look, and he smiled at me.

"Don't worry about it Peter, the king just wants to meet you and talk to you about your memories of his great Uncle." He assured me.

The king was in his study, with a scribe sitting at a table behind him.

"Welcome Peter, please take a seat."

A servant rushed forward and pulled my chair out for me, pushing me in towards the table once I was seated. I watched the servant pour me a cup of cool milk and set a plate of sweets in front of me.

Seeing I was confused and nervous, the king explained what he wanted.

"Peter, I am making a collection of memories from the people who were most prominent in my uncle's life. I would like you to tell me your story of Lord Haldor's influences on you."

"Your majesty, Lord Haldor has had an influence on pretty much everything I've done for a very long time. My story would be as long as a book if I were to try to tell it to you." I explained hesitantly.

The king looked at me with his piercing grey eyes. He didn't seem at all concerned at that fact. "Then tell me about your whole life if it helps. You have learned the art of storytelling I'm sure?"

"Yes your majesty, I know the art. But I'm not very good at it sir." I said weakly.

"That is ok, you are only thirteen, and you don't have to be good at it." King Stephen II waved his hand back at the scribe. "I want you to tell me your story without worrying how it will sound. I will make a note at the beginning of your tale that reminds people that you are just a boy; no one will look down on you. Besides, this is for my families' personal collection; only the royal family will have direct access to what you tell me. Please, tell me how my great uncle's life has influenced your life. Don't worry about ranger secrets, the royal family have access to them all anyways."

I sat back, wondering where to begin. I decided to start with the day I met Lord Haldor, and go from there. "Your majesty, every young boy dreams of being a squire…"

# Would you like to see your manuscript become a book?

If you are interested in becoming a PublishAmerica author, please submit your manuscript for possible publication to us at:

acquisitions@publishamerica.com

You may also mail in your manuscript to:

**PublishAmerica**
**PO Box 151**
**Frederick, MD 21705**

# www.publishamerica.com